THE WEB

Also by Megan Chance

THE WEB

THE FIANNA TRILOGY
BOOK TWO

MEGAN CHANCE

SKYSCAPE

SKYSCAPE

Published by Skyscape, New York

www.apub.com

Amazon, the Amazon logo, and Skyscape are trademarks of Amazon.com, Inc., or its affiliates.

ISBN-13 (hardcover): 9781477827093
ISBN-10: (hardcover): 1477827099
ISBN-13: (paperback): 9781477827086
ISBN-10: (paperback): 1477827080

Cover illustration by Don Sipley
Cover design by Regina Flath

Library of Congress Control Number: 2014912060

Printed in the United States of America

For Maggie and Cleo

She left the web, she left the loom,
She made three paces thro' the room,
She saw the water-lily bloom,
She saw the helmet and the plume,
She look'd down to Camelot.
Out flew the web and floated wide;
The mirror crack'd from side to side;
"The curse is come upon me," cried
The Lady of Shalott.

"The Lady of Shalott"
—Alfred, Lord Tennyson

✆ Cast of Characters ✆

———— THE KNOX FAMILY ————

Grainne Alys Knox [GRAW-nya]—*Grace*

Aidan Knox—*Grace's brother, and the Fianna's stormcaster*

Maeve Knox—*Grace's mother*

Brigid Knox—*Grace's grandmother*

———— THE DEVLIN FAMILY ————

Patrick Devlin

Lucy Devlin—*Patrick's sister*

Sarah Devlin—*Patrick's mother*

———— THE FIANNA (FINN'S WARRIORS) ————

Diarmid Ua Duibhne [DEER-mid O'DIV-na]—*Derry O'Shea*

Finn MacCumhail [FINN MacCOOL]—*Finn MacCool,
the leader of the Fianna*

Oscar

Ossian [USH-een]—*Oscar's father*

Keenan

Goll

Conan

Cannel Flannery—*Seer*

—————— THE FENIAN BROTHERHOOD [FEE-NIAN] ——————

Rory Nolan

Simon MacRonan—*Seer*

Jonathan Olwen

—————— THE FOMORI ——————

Daire Donn [DAW-re DON]

Lot

Tethra

Bres

Miogach [MYEE-gok]

Balor

—————— THE DUN RATS (A BROOKLYN GANG) ——————

Hugh Bannon—*their leader*

Miles

Bridget

Little Joe—*Bridget's younger son*

Colin—*Bridget's older son*

Molly—*Bridget's older daughter*

Sara—*Bridget's younger daughter*

—————— IN LEGEND ——————

Tuatha de Dannan [TOO-a-ha dae DONN-an]—*the old, revered gods of Ireland, the people of the goddess Danu*

Aengus Og [ENGUS OG]—*Irish god of love, Diarmid's foster father*

Manannan [MANanuan]—*Irish god of the sea, Diarmid's former tutor*

The Morrigan—*Irish goddess of war; her three aspects:*

Macha [MOK-ah], Nemain [NOW-nm], and Badb [BIBE]

Danu—*Irish mother goddess*

Domnu—*Mother goddess of the Fomori*

Cuchulain [COO-coo-lane]—*Irish hero*

Etain [AY-teen]—*Oscar's wife in ancient times*

Neasa [NESSA]—*the Fianna's Druid priestess*

Cormac—*ancient High King of Ireland*

Grainne [GRAW-nya]—*Cormac's daughter,
promised in marriage to Finn, eloped with Diarmid*

King of Lochlann—*Miogach's father*

Glasny [GLASH-neh]—*Neasa's protector*

Cliodna [KLEE-uh-na]—*Irish goddess of beauty who was taken from
her mortal lover by a great wave sent by Manannan, which brought
her back to the Otherworld (Cliodna's Wave)*

Boar of Ben Bulben—*Diarmid's half brother, who was shape-changed
into a boar and killed Diarmid on the plain of Ben Bulben*

——— OTHER PEOPLE ———

Rose Fitzgerald—*Grace's best friend*

Lewis Corley—*fortune-teller and mystic*

Billy—*leader of the gang Billy's Boys*

Justin—*newsboy and messenger for the Fianna*

——— THE SIDHE [SHEE] ———

Deirdre

Battle Annie—*queen of the river pirates*

—————— OTHER WORDS ——————

ball seirce [ball searce]—*the lovespot bestowed on Diarmid*

cainte [KINE-tay]—*one who speaks/sees, Druid poet*

dord fiann [dord FEEN]—*Finn's hunting horn*

Dubros—*an ancient woods in Ireland where the legendary Diarmid and Grainne find refuge*

geis [GISE]—*a prohibition or taboo that compels the person to obey*

mo chroi [muh CREE]—*my heart, an endearment*

ogham—*ancient form of Irish writing*

Samhain [SOW-in]—*ancient Celtic festival, October 31*

Slieve Lougher [Sleeve Lawker]—*location in ancient Ireland*

veleda—*ancient Druid priestess*

ONE

New York City
July 9, 1874
Grace

You must find the archdruid. He can help you."

I stared down at my grandmother. She was still as death, pale and barely breathing, in a coma that had begun the night she'd said those words to me more than two weeks ago.

Since then, I'd thought of them nearly every moment. *"There is a key . . . The sea is the knife . . ."* I'd twisted those phrases over and over in my mind, trying to undo the puzzle of them, but I was no closer to understanding what they meant.

"Please, Grandma," I whispered. "Please. Wake up."

There was nothing to tell me she heard. No one could reach her. Not even me. And I had more need than anyone.

That night of the summer solstice, my whole world had changed. It had started when Patrick Devlin—now my fiancé—told me that he and the Fenian Brotherhood had called the ancient Irish warrior-heroes, the Fianna, from their undying sleep to help Ireland win self-rule from Britain. But the

Fianna had not appeared, and so they'd called the Fomori—the Celtic gods of chaos, and the enemies of the Fianna. But in fact, the first spell had worked: the Fianna were here, and the old prophecies were in play. Prophecies that had at their center a priestess called a *veleda*, who now had to choose between the Fianna and the Fomori, and sacrifice her life and power to her choice during a ritual on Samhain—October 31, only a few short months away.

And I was that *veleda*.

Or so Patrick said. But my grandmother had spoken of curses and archdruids and asking the *sidhe* for help, the most confusing thing of all. I'd heard tales of the fairies my whole life. Grandma had always said the *sidhe* were cruel and tricky and that I should avoid them. And now suddenly . . . *"The sidhe will help you."* I had never thought they were real. But I'd also thought the Fianna and the Fomori only legends, and here they were, in New York City.

"Grandma, please," I begged again—for the hundredth pointless time. "Please. Tell me more about the *veleda*. Tell me what I must do."

"The *veleda*?"

I looked over my shoulder to see my mother frowning in the doorway. I hadn't wanted to trouble her with any of this.

"It's nothing, Mama. An old story Grandma told me."

"The *veleda* is nothing but Irish superstition." Mama stepped up beside me. Her elegant fingers gripped my shoulder, stronger than I would have suspected. "What did she tell you?"

That terrible night, I'd seen things I couldn't explain, and I knew my mother had too. But she'd denied everything. I didn't want to distress her, which I was certain to do if I reminded her that my brother had been shooting purple lightning from his fingers. The habit of not worrying my mother was hard to break. Since my father's death two years ago, we'd lost nearly everything. She was so frail that I'd kept the worst of our financial troubles from her. My marriage to Patrick was supposed to help us. And yet . . . what did it matter now? I was supposed to *die*.

How did one say, *Well, Mama, it seems I might be this* veleda *you say doesn't exist, and I have to die on Samhain?*

I decided to blurt it out. "Grandma said *I* was the *veleda*."

Mama's sigh was pained. "Don't tell me you believe her? And I suppose she told you that you have to sacrifice yourself for some foolish choice. And that you must die."

I stared at her.

"I've heard the stories, too, Grace. When the Fianna are called from their undying sleep, the *veleda* must decide if their fight is worthy, and then she must sacrifice her life to her choice. But this is the nineteenth century. There's a reason most Irish are living in the slums. Superstition and nonsense keeps them backward."

"Patrick believes it," I said.

"Patrick's father was no better than your grandmother. Collecting all those . . . those relics. They're from days long gone, Grace."

"Some of them still have the old magic, Mama. My old hunting horn, the one"—*Aidan lost in a bet,* I started to say, but then bit back my brother's name—"that was lost. Remember it? Patrick says it was the *dord fiann*—"

"The horn meant to call the Fianna?" My mother's voice rose. "Ancient warriors? Really? And where are those august heroes now?"

In a tenement near Mulberry Street, pretending to be a gang. But I didn't say it. I didn't want to think of it. Not of the tenement, nor the Fianna warrior who'd been sent to find me: Derry O'Shea, who was not really Derry O'Shea, but Diarmid Ua Duibhne, possessor of the legendary lovespot, which compelled any girl who saw it to love him. The lovespot I knew he'd used on me.

I hadn't seen him since that night. But I hadn't stopped dreaming of him. Every night, and each dream as troubling as the last. Patrick's words circled in my head: *"He means to seduce you into choosing them, and then once you do, he'll kill you."*

You're compelled. Bespelled. This desire isn't real. Everything you felt for him was a lie.

Mama's voice brought me back to the moment. "Grace, this is all nonsense. What makes you think you could possibly be a Druid priestess?"

And that was the crux of it. Because I didn't have any power. I'd seen the Fianna glow, and I'd been burned by a Druid spell-casting stick, but that was all. And Aidan . . . My brother was a drunk, a gambler who'd lost whatever the bill collectors hadn't taken from us. But that night, he'd been glowing with power, calling up thunderstorms and opening the clouds to release a drenching downpour.

Impossible. It was impossible.

"Aidan will know," Grandma had said. I burned to ask him questions. I wondered if he might understand the things she'd said. If he could tell me what I suspected: that everyone was wrong and I was not the *veleda*. But Aidan had disappeared that night.

"I don't know what power I'm supposed to have," I said to Mama. "But Grandma said there was an archdruid who could help me. She told me to find him."

Mama snorted. "An archdruid? Well, there haven't been Druids for . . . for what? A thousand years? More than that? I don't know why a clever girl like you would believe such things. Your grandmother is mad. It's time we admitted it. She's been living in a world of fairies and legends, but it's not real."

I wanted to believe I was just a normal seventeen-year-old girl who was marrying a boy who loved me and whom I thought I could love, and that Derry was only a ruthless gang boy I could easily forget. I wanted to ignore the fact that the story of the *veleda* explained everything that had confused me over the last months.

But I couldn't. There *was* magic in New York City. I'd seen it. I couldn't dismiss everything, and because I couldn't, I had to admit at least that I *might* be the *veleda*.

Which meant I had to find the archdruid. I needed whatever help Grandma thought he could offer. Maybe he would tell me that it was all a mistake. But if not, then perhaps he could help me find some other spell, some other ritual. Some way that I didn't have to die on October 31.

Until I could find him, though, I could not just continue as if nothing had happened.

Mama took my chin between her fingers, forcing me to look at her. "You listen to me, Grainne Alys Knox. You are no *veleda*. You are not going to die on Samhain. You have a long life ahead of you. One full of love and blessed with children. A happy life."

"I hope so," I said.

"There is no doubt. In fact, perhaps we should set a wedding date."

"I thought you wanted to wait until my debut."

"Yes, I did. But we may have to abandon those plans."

"Why?"

"I received the summons this morning. The doctor . . . he's suing for the house."

I took a deep breath. We hadn't been able to pay the doctor who had treated my grandmother, and he'd threatened a lawsuit. Not just a threat now. "I see."

"It's the real world we must worry about," Mama said with a bitter smile. "Though it would be nice to think there were fairies to save us, I'm afraid we're on our own. You must speak to Patrick about a date. And now I suppose you'd best return to him. You've been here over an hour and Patrick's men are getting restless. You know he doesn't like you to be away from him for long."

"I know." Guards attended me every time I left Patrick's house, where I was staying. To keep me safe, he'd said. From the Fianna.

From Derry.

I rose, glancing back at my grandmother. "You'll let me know if she wakes?"

"Of course. But Grace, I don't expect her to. You must get used to the idea that she's not long for this world."

That was another thing I could not bear to think about.

When I looked at my mother, she was blinking away tears. I hugged her. "I should be here with you."

"Patrick needs you more. And your safety is all I care about. Now go on—you're very busy these days. Patrick told me of the dinner tonight. How wonderful that he's introducing you to his friends."

Tonight was more important than Mama knew. Tonight I would formally meet the Fomori, though I'd already met the beautiful Lot the night they had arrived, and I'd seen the others from a distance. They looked nothing like the monsters described in the stories. Patrick said that history was written by the victors, and the Fianna had reason to make the Fomori seem as vicious as possible. He also said that the Fomori had promised to find a spell to save me, and I wanted to trust them. Perhaps none of it mattered anyway. Perhaps I wasn't the *veleda*.

If I wished hard enough, perhaps I could make it true.

TWO

That night
Grace

I dressed carefully in my best gown of dove-gray silk, a dress Patrick had already seen too often. He knew how poor we were, so the only thing it hurt was my pride, but it hurt that quite a bit. There was no help for it. I couldn't snap my fingers and conjure another dress—and as long as I was thinking about powers I didn't have, I might as well add that one to the list.

When I was ready, I went to the parlor. I was early, and I'd hoped for a few moments alone to settle my nerves. But Lucy, Patrick's sister, was already there. She stood at the French doors looking out over her mother's rose garden, and I saw her yearning. I knew who she was yearning for. I turned to go, not wanting to hear it all again.

"Grace," she said, stopping me. Lucy's pink silk gown set off her fair coloring to perfection, but there were dark circles beneath her blue eyes that hinted at sleepless nights. "You were out today. Did you see him?"

Him. Derry.

I tried to be charitable. Who understood Lucy's feelings better than I? Derry had used the lovespot on her to get close to Patrick and the Fenian Brotherhood, and her love for him hadn't faded in the weeks since he'd abandoned her. He'd manipulated her as easily and as well as he'd manipulated me.

How long did it take for such a spell to fade? More than three weeks? I was afraid of how Lucy's longing lingered. I hated thinking I was the same. I'd always thought myself cleverer than Lucy, and yet here I was, *dreaming* of him. And not just innocent dreams, either, but ones that had me waking in the middle of the night, longing for a kiss that burned.

"I know he'll come for me," Lucy declared. "I think my mother's hiding his messages."

"He's sent no messages, Lucy," I said, as kindly as I could. She didn't know the truth of him, of course, but still, she was being ridiculous. "He hasn't written. He's left you."

"No he hasn't! Oh, how could you understand? You've never been in love like this. You don't know how it feels to be separated—"

"Lucy, he's a gang boy. He's killed people. He's dangerous."

"Who told you that? Patrick?" Lucy's eyes flashed. "He doesn't want me to marry a stableboy, that's all. Those are just lies he's made up."

"Who's been making up lies?" Patrick asked as he entered the room.

Lucy only glared at her brother and marched into the garden.

Patrick sighed. "Him again?"

"Always." I went to Patrick. It should have been easy to forget Derry. Patrick was so handsome, with his almost-blond hair and his gray-green eyes. And just now those eyes were so full of love for me that I let myself get lost in them.

He grabbed my hands. When he kissed me, I felt a shiver of pleasure, along with a sense of safety, of possibility.

He drew away. "Are you ready for tonight?"

"I'm nervous," I admitted.

"Afraid they might eat you alive?"

"Well, I've reason, don't you think? What of Balor's terrible eye, which could kill a man with a single look?"

"Covered with an eye patch. And I haven't seen him kill a man with it yet."

"What about the gnashing teeth in Lot's breast?"

"I haven't seen that either. Though I confess I've only seen her fully gowned."

"Thank goodness for that."

"Jealous?" His eyes glowed. "I rather like that."

I felt myself redden. "Why shouldn't I be? You've spent a great deal of time with her. And she's very beautiful."

"I've eyes for only one beautiful girl." He brushed his fingers down my cheek. "Should I kiss you again and show you?"

I raised my face, he pulled me closer, and his kiss was less tender this time, more possessive, leaving me breathless when he drew away. "What I wouldn't do to have you alone somewhere. Just the two of us. And soon."

"So impatient. You and my mother both. She asked me today to set a wedding date."

Patrick frowned. I knew what he was thinking. What was the point in a wedding I might not be alive to take part in? "I would like nothing more. But—"

"I understand," I told him quickly, not wanting to hear the words.

"You know what—let's do it! Let's set a date."

"But Patrick—"

"That's how certain I am that we'll find a way to save you, Grace. You'll still be here after October thirty-first. I believe it."

"Perhaps I'm not the *veleda*. Mama said I'm not."

"She did?"

"She overheard me talking to my grandmother. And she's heard the stories all her life too. But she says it's all superstition."

"It's not just me and the Fomori who believe it. The Fianna do too."

"Their Seer is a sideshow fortune-teller. What can he possibly know? What real reason do we have to think I'm the *veleda*? It's Aidan who has power, not me."

Patrick glanced out the French doors to where Lucy meandered among the roses. "You're certain that before that night you never had a hint of what Aidan could do?"

"I told you. The only thing I remember is that he said he saw Derry glowing."

"The same way you did."

"Yes. But I'm not shooting lightning from my fingertips."

"I don't like it," Patrick said, not for the first time. "I've men searching everywhere, and no one's seen a trace of Aidan. I've had them in every gambling hell and every saloon—"

"You'd best try the opium dens too."

"I have. There's no sign of him. No one's seen him in weeks."

"Patrick, I'm afraid something terrible's happened to him."

Patrick cupped my chin. His thumb brushed my lips, sending an ache through me, one I was glad to feel. I hoped it meant the other feeling was fading. "Nothing's happened to him, Grace."

"You can't promise that."

"But I can promise that I'll do whatever I can to help him. To help your whole family. You must know I'd do anything for you."

"Yes, but—"

"I heard about the doctor's suit, by the way. You should have said something."

It was a relief to change the subject, even to this. "I only found out today."

"I don't want you to worry. I've already talked to my lawyer."

I was both happy and troubled. My family expected so much of Patrick, and it made me feel guilty too; he was so kind and yet I could not stop thinking of a boy who'd branded me with a kiss, who haunted my dreams. I hated Derry for that. I hated that he was in the way of something real.

I would not be controlled by some spell. Not when true love was staring me in the face. I twisted my hands in Patrick's hair, bringing him down to kiss. I heard his little gasp, and then he was kissing me back, and I waited for the shiver to take me over, to become something more—

"It's not fair! You get to kiss her whenever you want, and I can't even *see* Derry!"

I sprang away, but Patrick wouldn't let me go far. He took my arm as he turned to his sister, who stood in the doorway glaring at both of us.

"My *fiancée*," he said coldly. "Not some inappropriate immigrant gang boy."

"So it's only the Irish in Ireland you care about?"

"He stole from me, Lucy. And when I dismissed him, he left without complaint. He used you."

"He loved me, and you frightened him away! But he'll come back for me. I know he will."

The knock on the front door silenced her. "They're here." Patrick looked at his sister. "None of this nonsense in front of them, Lucy. You'll only look the fool."

"Oh never fear, I'll behave for your precious Fenians. All hail Ireland!" She flounced away.

I was suddenly nervous again. Patrick squeezed my arm reassuringly and winked, and I felt immediately better. It was hard to imagine that Balor of the terrible eye or Miogach,

Lochlann's son, could do any damage in a parlor in the middle of Manhattan. Once more, the whole thing felt so unreal.

And when they came into the parlor, I was more convinced. The Fomori were elegantly dressed. Tethra, the Fomorian god of the sea, had cut his long, twisted locks into a more fashionable style, though his mustache was still huge and curling over his full lips. Balor was the tallest man I'd ever seen, and while his face was craggy and intimidating—his eye patch only adding to the effect—he looked more like a rugged explorer who'd just returned from Africa or the North Pole than a deadly god. Bres, their leader, the supposedly cruel Irish king, was fair and handsome. Daire Donn, who called himself the King of the World, was simply one of the warmest and most charming men I'd ever met. Lot was stunning in a blue gown that made her eyes look even more purple.

The only one who gave me pause was Miogach. He was thin, with dark hair and a sharp gray gaze, and I had to remind myself of what my grandmother had always said, that Miogach's hatred of the Fianna was well-founded. Still, his voice raised gooseflesh on my arms when he said, "So this is the *veleda*."

But when we went to the dining room and took our seats, Miogach sat beside me. He gave me a mischievous smile that was so at odds with what I thought I knew of him that I was taken aback.

"What is it?" he asked.

"Nothing. You surprised me, that's all. The stories—"

"What stories? Has Finn been telling tales of me? Has he made me a monster before I have the chance to defend myself?" His grin broadened. "You know, we were friends once. Finn was like a father. Diarmid taught me to play chess. Keenan was my sparring partner. We shared many a good time. But now I suppose they've told you that I betrayed them."

"They never told me that," I said. "But the old stories say it."

"I see. And who wrote those?" he asked. "You shouldn't believe everything you hear. 'Tis true we were at odds, but . . . perhaps sometime I'll tell you my side of the story."

"I'd like that," I said, and it was true. I *did* want to know his version.

"I must confess you're not as I expected either. You remind me of someone I used to know."

"Neasa?" I asked. Finn and Derry had both told me I resembled the Druid priestess who was my ancestor.

"You know of her?"

"I've been told I'm like her. Though I was also told she had great power, and I'm afraid that part managed to elude me." I flicked my fingers at him. "Not even a spark from these fingertips."

"What? No hope of setting your enemies afire? How tragic."

I laughed. "I suppose I'll have to settle for glaring them to death."

He laughed with me, and for a moment I forgot that this was the same Miogach who'd betrayed Finn and imprisoned him. I was caught by his friendliness. *The same way Finn once was.*

The thought made me pause just as Daire Donn said, "'Twas a terrible thing you had to witness the other night, Miss Knox. A bad fight. Those gangs must be attended to. Now that Balor and Miogach have taken jobs with the police, we can begin to rid the city of them."

He glanced at Lucy and Mrs. Devlin, who had no idea who his companions really were, and I heard the message beneath his words: they were looking for the Fianna, and they were determined to keep me safe.

Miogach sobered, and the talk at the table quieted. Bres's chiseled jaw tightened. His voice was commanding as he said, "We plan to start by pursuing the most dangerous. Those who spend their days riling up the others."

"I wish they understood that rabble-rousing only makes things worse," said Patrick's mother. "I know the city's cut off aid for the poor and times are hard, but why can't they get jobs like decent men?"

"Jobs are hard to come by now, Mama," Patrick said.

"Our hope is that we can convince some gangs to make peace. Then the others would follow," said Bres.

"To do that, we must first roust out those who have their minds set on war." Balor's one eye lit as if he relished the idea.

"Well, I must admit it's reassuring to see *someone* determined to mend things," Mrs. Devlin said. "The city's so dangerous lately. And to know the gangs were so far north, in poor Grace's very backyard! Why, it's quite alarming."

"Oh yes, indeed." Lot took a portion of fish from the hovering servant with a smooth poise that I envied. "But I believe we'll have reason for celebration quite soon, Mrs. Devlin."

"Oh?"

Bres explained, "The worst of the gangs will be in police custody before the end of next week, I promise you. Finn's Warriors—who began the fracas in your yard, Miss Knox. I hope that sets your mind at ease."

Finn's Warriors. The Fianna's gang name.

I glanced at Patrick, who shook his head in warning. So there was a plan in place to arrest them. They could not come after me if they were in jail. *He* could not come after me. I wondered why Patrick had said nothing of it earlier. My appetite withered.

"Really?" I tried to keep my tone light. "I didn't know."

"There was no reason for you to know," Patrick said with a smile. "I told you we were doing everything we could to ensure your safety."

"*Her* safety?" Lucy paused with her fork in midair. "Finn's Warriors—is that Derry's gang?"

"They've been rampaging and killing for months now," Bres said. "We'll have them behind bars quickly. And hanged quickly as well."

Lucy paled. "If you'll excuse me . . . I'm feeling ill." She left the room in a rush.

Mrs. Devlin said, "Oh dear. I should see to her. Please continue; enjoy your dinner."

When they were both gone, Patrick said, "I must apologize for my sister. The lovespot has affected her badly."

"'Tis a pity to see such a pretty lass so sad," Miogach said. "But soon she'll be herself again."

I asked, "Is that how it works? I've never heard what happened to girls when he was done with them. Does the spell just . . . go away?"

Too late, I heard the intensity in my voice. I couldn't look at Patrick.

Miogach said, "Why, Miss Knox, 'tis like all love. In absence, it fades."

"'Twould depend on how much in love she was," Daire Donn added as he sipped his wine. His brown eyes were dark with compassion. "Was she under his spell for days or weeks? Months or years?"

"A few months only," Patrick said, and I felt his gaze on me. "Perhaps less."

I made myself meet his eyes. I thought I saw suspicion there—or was it only concern? In my guilt, I couldn't tell the difference. "I feel sorry for Lucy. It wasn't her fault," I said.

"No, but she's always been a fool when it comes to love. He was obviously not for her."

Lot said, "Ah, but Diarmid has his charms." She smiled as if in memory, and I felt a hot surge of jealousy. "I always felt the *ball seirce* was unnecessary. What he could do with touch alone . . ."

It's only a spell. You don't really feel this way.

"You sound as if you had dealings with him," said Patrick.

Bres and Tethra laughed.

Lot's smile was thin. "Only observation, good sir. Only that."

"Not that she didn't wish otherwise a time or two," said Daire Donn with a grin.

I do not care. I chose Patrick.

"It won't help him much behind bars," Bres chuckled. "Once the Fianna are put away, we can concentrate on finding a Druid who can help us. Unfortunately, it cannot be just *any* Druid. We need an archdruid, which may be hard to find. They are not just of the highest Druid rank, they also hold the most knowledge and power. If anyone knows how to circumvent a Druid spell, 'twill be an archdruid."

"Aye," Lot agreed. "The *sidhe* are beginning to gather. Every day we've seen more of them about. They'll help us."

An echo of my grandmother's words. "You mean . . . there *are* fairies here? How could they help?"

"They're drawn to Druid power," she said. "They'll be drawn to you as well, my dear. You should be very careful."

"She'll have guards around her every moment," Patrick assured us.

"But . . . you're saying they could lead us to the archdruid?"

"Not *you*, Grace," said Patrick. "The rest of us. You won't be near them."

"They are very dangerous, to you especially," warned Daire Donn. "But never fear, Miss Knox, we are committed to finding him."

"And to finding the spell to save you," Patrick said softly.

Bres nodded. "You are our main concern, milady. Trust me when I say we will do all we can to save you. We are united in this, are we not?"

The others made noises of agreement. They all looked sincere.

Miogach's gray eyes were so warm it was difficult to remember that I'd ever found them sharp. "'Tis our most ardent task, Miss Knox. I promise we will not fail."

I had expected monsters, and instead I'd found something so different that I didn't know what to believe.

But the old stories would not leave my head. *The same stories Patrick knows.* He would not be easily fooled. Patrick truly loved me, and he would not put his faith in them if he had even a moment of doubt. They would protect me whether I was the *veleda* or not. I had to trust that the choice I'd made that terrible night was the right one.

T his way." Diarmid dodged the stick before he twisted it from young Will's hands and brought the end around, slamming it into Will's back, sending the boy sprawling.

Will gasped, "How'd you do that?"

Diarmid helped the boy to his feet. "That was hardly a blow. If you do it right, you can break a man's back. Or your own, if you do it wrong."

"Show me again," Will demanded.

Diarmid obliged. All around them were the sounds of fighting as he and the other Fianna put their fledgling militia through their paces. The tenement yard was hazy with the dust they raised, and full nearly to bursting—since the city had stopped giving relief to the poor, more and more were joining their ranks every day. They were all hungry and angry. Finn promised riots and protests. He promised they would have what they deserved.

But it wasn't really bread and work he was promising. The Fianna needed an army to fight the Fomori. If the gang boys joining their cause thought they were fighting the government, so much the better. Who knew if, in the end, the two things wouldn't be one and the same? Some of the most important men in the city belonged to the Fenian Brotherhood. In the short time the Fomori had been in the city, they had taken jobs in the police force and in city government. They'd already infiltrated the rich and powerful.

But the Fianna had the poor, of which there were plenty. And the poor had nothing to lose.

Diarmid drilled Will one more time, and then stepped to the half barrel sitting by the stoop. Diarmid sluiced water over his head, letting it run down his bare back and chest, washing away sweat and dust. He welcomed the exertion, because as long as he was training, he couldn't think of her brown eyes flashing at him through a drenching rain. Or her words—*I hate you!*—or how she'd chosen Patrick Devlin. Or of the heartbreak that dogged him, or the way he'd endangered them all.

But now the thoughts overwhelmed him again, as they did every moment he was still. That night a month ago when they'd retreated, Finn had been furious, and his rage hadn't lessened in the days since. *"You had a hundred chances to show her the* ball seirce. *Instead you let the* veleda *fall into the hands of the Fomori. What choice do you think she'll make now?"*

The gods knew how often Diarmid had berated himself. He had no excuse except that he'd hoped Grace might be the girl he was waiting for, the one who could ease his loneliness, who loved him for himself and not because she was compelled. He had wanted more than anything to see true love in her eyes, and to corrupt her hatred into some obscene parody . . . it seemed the worst sort of betrayal. A lie he couldn't live with.

But he couldn't tell Finn that. Because she wasn't just a girl he wanted, she was the *veleda*. Without her, they would fail. Without her, the Irish in this city were doomed. And he'd let her fall into the hands of the enemy. He deserved Finn's anger. Diarmid had let himself forget the most important thing of all: he was under a *geis* to kill her during the ritual on Samhain—and there was no getting around it.

Just then, Finn rounded the corner. Their leader had been gone all day, and he looked stormy now. Finn gestured impatiently for the Fianna to follow. Practice was over.

They fell into line behind him: white-blond Ossian and his son, Oscar, Diarmid's best friend; dark-haired Keenan; skinny Goll with his newsboy's cap; bald Conan, wearing that stinking fleece no matter that the day was brutally hot. The stairs were dark as pitch, reeking more than usual—who knew why—and hot as an oven, and the tenement room they shared was no better, even with its single window open to let in whatever breeze reached the top floor.

Cannel, their Druid Seer, was napping on a mattress that Ossian had scrounged from somewhere, while Aidan, Grace's brother, sat listlessly at the table, sending purple sparks back and forth between his fingers. The already scarred and blood-stained table was now blackened with burns too.

Aidan glanced up, his penetrating gaze going directly to Diarmid, as it often did. Diarmid ignored him with difficulty. He was aware of Grace's brother every moment. Aidan was a reminder of Diarmid's failures—not just losing Grace, but also his failure to see the power in Aidan when he'd first had the chance. This was another cause for Finn's anger; for some reason, the Knoxes—both sister and brother—left Diarmid blind. And the way he'd been feeling lately made him wish he'd never met either of them.

They gathered around the table. The smell of Conan's filthy fleece filled the room—Diarmid wanted to throw the thing out the window. Goll kicked Cannel lightly in the ribs so the man grunted and came fully awake. "What is it? What's going on?" the Seer asked.

"A meeting." Finn leaned into the table, bracing his hands on the top. He'd tied his golden-red hair back in a queue, but loose strands clung to his face. His pale eyes burned. "Our spies tell us that Patrick Devlin and the Fomori are looking for an archdruid."

"An archdruid?" Oscar echoed. "What for?"

"The *veleda*," Cannel said, running a hand through his thinning red hair. "She truly must not know the incantation for the ritual. You said she seemed not to remember it." He looked at Diarmid, who looked at Aidan.

The sparks arcing between Aidan's fingers extinguished. "It's been a long time, hasn't it? Things get lost."

"The spell might have been buried in songs or stories. You remember nothing like that? Nothing passed down?" Finn asked.

"Everything was passed down. Every story you can imagine. But no spells, and if there was anything in a song, I never heard it. But Grace has strange dreams, you know. Maybe there's something in them." Aidan nodded at Diarmid. "He might know."

Diarmid was taken aback. "*I* might?"

"She talks to you, doesn't she? You know about her dreams."

"She said they were of battles and lightning. Ravens. That's all I know."

Finn's mouth tightened. "The incantation must be in her mind somewhere. Buried deep maybe, but there. We have to find a way to discover how much she truly knows. And to get her out of Fomori hands. She's already been there too long."

Even a day was too long with one of the Fomori, charming and persuasive as they could be, evil hidden beneath beauty and guile. Diarmid had never expected to look upon any of them again. He couldn't forget the shock of seeing them in the alley that night, enemies from battles fought so long ago they were like dreams. The Fomori had changed too. The poisonous, one-eyed Balor was still a giant, but no longer the size of a small building. Except for the blue lightning blazing from his fingertips and the long tangles of hair flying about his head, the sea god Tethra looked like any other man. Only Bres, Miogach, and Daire Donn had looked just as they always had, but they were men descended from the Fomori, not gods or monsters themselves. And Lot . . . so beautiful she took one's breath, bringing to mind the last time Diarmid had seen her, when he'd refused her advances and she'd graced him with the sight of those gnashing teeth in her breast.

Diarmid shook away the image. Grace would be helpless against their allure. Unless she remembered the stories and believed them, which she might not do, given that Patrick was her fiancé, and Patrick believed the Fomori were reasonable.

"Devlin's got her guarded," Oscar said. "Fomori warriors everywhere. It won't be easy to get to her."

"I'm thinking we'll need persuasion." Finn stared at Diarmid.

Diarmid shook his head. "Not me. You heard her. She hates me. And Patrick knows what I look like. Send Oscar."

Oscar said, "Aye, I'll find a way. I'll bring her back, and Derry can work his magic then. Perhaps Aidan could—"

"No." Aidan's blue eyes were stony.

Finn said, "No? If you don't mean to help, why did you join us, stormcaster?"

Diarmid recognized the deadly tone that had cowed greater men than Aidan Knox. But Grace's brother seemed unaffected. "If you want her, you won't do something as stupid as send Oscar when we all know it should be Diarmid who goes."

In exasperation, Diarmid said, "By the gods, I've already—"

"It needs to be you," Aidan stated. "She'll be worried enough over my disappearance that she'll elude Patrick's guards if I ask her to. But it's not me who will convince her to do anything. That has to be you."

Everything Diarmid disliked about Aidan was in those words. "It doesn't trouble you at all that she worries about you, does it? Or that your mother does the same."

"It's none of your concern."

"I've seen the misery you put them through. It's because of you that she has to marry Patrick—"

"I'm trying to *help* you."

"But 'tis her you should be helping. She's your sister, and you know what I have to do—"

"Things may not be exactly as you imagine them," Aidan said.

Finn broke in. "The two of you are in charge of it then. Get it done quickly. In the meantime, we'll start looking for this archdruid. The Fomori clearly think it necessary. And we should be prepared for the fact that the *veleda* knows nothing."

That was it, over and decided. Oscar came up to Diarmid with a mug of ale. "She's the *veleda*, Derry. That's all that matters. That's what you have to remember."

"I know," Diarmid said.

Oscar's green eyes shone in the half-light of evening. "I'll tell you what—let's go out. We'll go to the Bowery, get a couple of lasses. We'll find one who'll make you forget your mooning."

It sounded good, actually. Some soft and sweet-smelling lass to bury his hurt in. To forget one kiss in other kisses. Diarmid was halfway to agreeing when he saw Aidan. Grace's brother had his knees drawn up, hands dangling between as he again sent sparks jumping from one finger to another.

Aidan made Diarmid uncomfortable, and he wasn't sure why. It had always been so, from the first time they'd met. There was *something* about Grace's brother that left Diarmid uneasy, but what?

For one brief moment, their gazes met, and Diarmid felt a connection, a thread spun between them, that startled him into looking away. He had too many troubles; he had no wish to make Aidan another.

But he knew then that no other lass would be easing his pain tonight. He couldn't leave and he couldn't pretend, and he couldn't bear Aidan knowing how he was betraying Grace.

Betraying her. Now that was something to laugh at, wasn't it? She wanted nothing to do with him. How could he possibly betray her?

But he felt it would. He couldn't explain why and he didn't try. "Not tonight, brother," he said to Oscar. "Not tonight."

Diarmid woke deep in the night, sweating. Burning. The straw he slept on scratched his suddenly too-sensitive skin. Besides Ossian's snores, all was quiet. He rose as soundlessly as he could, stepping over Oscar and Keenan to get to the window, which was open—always open—and pulled himself out. His foot no sooner touched the rail of the fire escape than he realized someone else was already there. He knew who it was even before he saw him.

"Couldn't sleep either?" Aidan whispered.

Diarmid hesitated. It was too late to go back inside without insulting Aidan, and besides, Aidan looked as if he expected Diarmid to do just that. So Diarmid gestured toward the metal grating, and Aidan moved to make room for him to sit.

"I miss the drink," Aidan said. "Keeps me up at night. Never thought I'd be so thirsty, and Finn won't let me near the ale."

"He wants you stronger," Diarmid said.

"He wants the impossible."

"Sometimes, aye."

The brick was rough against Diarmid's bare back. The night air pulsed against his skin. He felt restless and haunted. He longed to be alone.

Aidan said, "There's . . . something about you. I wish I understood what it was."

"What d'you mean?"

"I don't know—that's the problem. Grace needs you, that's all I know. I don't even know *how* I know it, if that makes sense. And what makes it worse is that I'm damn certain I don't want you within twenty feet of her."

"I can't blame you for that."

"I don't mean because of the *geis*. I see the way you look at her. And I saw the way you kissed Lucy Devlin too."

"Oh."

"Yes. Oh." Aidan's gaze bore into him. "I'm helping you because something tells me I need to, and I don't know why. I mean . . . you're supposed to kill her, yet . . . I don't understand any of this. Not the damn stormcasting or these strange dreams I have . . . or you. But I promise: if you hurt her, Diarmid Ua Duibhne, I will burn you into oblivion."

Diarmid laughed. It was all so absurd he couldn't help himself. And he was surprised when Aidan joined in. The moment was quick, over nearly as it started. Their laughter died, the sound lingering oddly in the air.

Aidan said, "I know you don't think much of me. But I love my sister. More than . . . well, more than anything else, I think."

That surprised Diarmid too. And it was a relief. He'd seen for himself Grace's affection for her brother. Maybe it wasn't so one-sided after all.

"Protect her," Aidan said. "That's all I'm asking of you. Just . . . protect her."

Diarmid opened his mouth to respond when he heard a sound below. He wasn't sure what it was—a footstep, perhaps, or a cough—but he froze. He saw a shadow on the street, a huge, moving shadow that coalesced into people—into men. Rushing footsteps, a torch.

Diarmid jerked to his feet, pulling Aidan with him. "It's a raid!" He plunged through the window, shouting, "Get up! Get up! It's a raid!"

The others woke instantly, grabbing weapons that were never far from their beds. He heard the shouting outside, and Aidan saying, "What raid? Who?"

"We'll have need of you, stormcaster," Finn said, grabbing a dagger. He yelled, "Get out, however you can! We won't be caught in this room like rats in a cage!"

Diarmid jerked his shirt over his head, and seized his daggers—shoving one into his belt and one in his boot—and then he was following the others back out the window, sending the fire escape ladder screeching and clanging into the midst of the gang who'd now entered the yard. Not just any gang either, but Fomori warriors, most of them deformed in some way—lame or one-armed, or one-eyed, just as they had been in the old days. The gods of chaos attracted those society dismissed, and that hadn't changed in the modern world. Fianna streamed from the tenement door into the yard and found themselves surrounded.

Oscar threw himself off the ladder and into their attackers. The moment Diarmid set foot on the ground, he was trapped, but still he sliced and danced and moved. Though the attackers—fifty or more, it seemed—were all maimed in some way, they were quick and lethal.

Diarmid stabbed one, then twisted and lunged, neatly gutting another. His hands were slick with blood. He heard Finn yell, "Now, stormcaster!" and then the crack of thunder and lightning. Purple light filled the sky. He glanced up once to see Aidan on the fire escape, arms raised, his dark hair standing on end, limned by the blaze so he looked as if he were glowing, and then the fight overwhelmed Diarmid again. He stumbled over bodies; his boots slipped on blood.

Then he saw someone bending to the cesspool by the privies with a torch.

The pool erupted, flames skittering across its surface, water on fire—something he'd never before seen. Flames leaped to consume the rickety privies. And then he saw more torches, men setting them to the splintering wood of window frames and stairs. Smoke rose in dark and poisonous clouds, obscuring Aidan.

The building caught within moments. Windows flashed with flame, the brick outer walls containing it at first as the inner timbers, doorways, sills, and plaster walls caught. The fire whooshed upstairs, rushing into empty spaces. People spilled out of the smoke, sliding down their fire escapes, screaming. There was only chaos and smoke and heat until Aidan opened the clouds to bring a drenching rain.

But the rain didn't quench the fire, which devoured the cheap wood and plaster as if they were nothing. Diarmid heard Finn yell, "Aidan! Get out!" and glimpsed Aidan coming down the ladder, lightning electrifying the metal as he came, which seemed not to faze him at all. After that, Diarmid saw nothing but fists and knives. He heard nothing but thunder and screaming.

And then Finn grabbed his arm. "Take the stormcaster and get out of here."

"But I—"

"Do it," Finn snapped. "The two of you get the *veleda*. Take her to the Dun Rats. D'you understand me? Take her there and keep her until I send for you. We can't wait any longer to secure her. Until I know we can keep her safe, you'll stay there."

"I can't leave you to fight alone. You need me."

"We need her more. And Diarmid—use the *ball seirce*."

The night was alight with the flaming pyre of the tenement. Diarmid saw Cannel huddling in the shadows with frightened women, crying children.

"Go." Finn pushed him. "Now."

Diarmid didn't like to leave any of them, not in the middle of the fight. But Finn bellowed, "Do as I say, curse you! Go!" And so Diarmid was off, running toward Aidan, while behind him it sounded like the end of the world.

FOUR

July 20
Grace

I woke, panicked, from a dream of fire. Flames raging and purple lightning glowing eerily through black smoke. Children crying and women screaming and the screech of ravens. It was a moment before I realized there was no smoke. No fire. No screaming. I was in my room at Patrick's house.

I closed my eyes and fell into another dream, where my brother called, *Come,* and *Hurry.* I ran toward him but no matter how fast I ran, he only got farther and farther away, and then darkness slammed between us. I wasn't alone in the darkness—someone else was there, too, watching and waiting. Not Aidan, but a familiar presence, and then it too disappeared.

And in its place came Derry, looming over me, his face pale and his hair falling forward to hide the lovespot, and I could only think, *Touch me. Kiss me.*

The dream lingered after I woke. Except for the fire, I'd had some version of it nearly every night. I hadn't seen Derry for weeks; why wouldn't the spell just fade? And dreaming about Aidan only made me worry. Where could he be?

I'd slept late. When I went downstairs I found the others already gone, Patrick to the store—Devlin Hatters and Tailors—and Mrs. Devlin and Lucy to make calls. Which meant I was left to my own devices for the day. Not that there was anywhere I could go. There were Fomori guards at every door, watching my every move.

I ate a quick breakfast and then went back to my room. My window didn't look out onto anything interesting, only the house next door and the narrow, shaded yard between. It made me feel closed in, trapped. I grabbed the book on my nightstand—one of Patrick's, Irish poetry of revolution and bloodshed—and settled down to read. But I couldn't concentrate. I kept hearing my grandmother: *"Aidan will know. There is a key . . . The sea is the knife . . . You must find the archdruid. He can help you."* I knew Patrick and the others were doing all they could to find the archdruid, but still I felt I should be doing *something.*

It's only a story, Grace. There is no veleda.

I jumped at a knock on my door. The maid called, "Miss Knox, you have a visitor."

"A visitor?" I felt a leap of hope, and then dismay when I realized whom I'd been hoping for. *It's just a spell.*

"Miss Fitzgerald, ma'am."

I hadn't seen my best friend, Rose, since I'd come to stay with Patrick. She'd been out of town with her parents, who traveled constantly. I hurried down the stairs to the parlor. "You're back!"

"Two days ago. I tell you, I'm beginning to loathe Boston. I told Papa I didn't care if I ever set foot there again. It's so awfully straitlaced. I could hardly move without Grandmama reminding me about some rule or another." Rose's red hair was flawlessly curled in ringlets beneath a tiny hat festooned with purple and blue flowers. She looked demure and sweet, but I knew better. Rose was neither. "I went to your house and your mother said you were staying here—I can't believe it! Why, what will people say?"

I hugged her and grinned. "It's all very proper. Mrs. Devlin and Lucy make certain Patrick and I are rarely alone."

"And you're engaged? Really and truly?"

"Mama told you! I wanted to tell you myself."

"Well, how can you blame her? She's so pleased."

"All her dreams come true," I said.

"Yours, too, I hope."

"Of course."

"Because I've wondered, you know, about Derry—"

"Derry's gone. Patrick dismissed him and it was all quite terrible. It's why I'm here. Patrick was afraid Derry would . . . trouble me."

Rose frowned. "Trouble you? Why would he? Oh, Grace, don't tell me you haven't put him aside."

"Of course I have! And keep your voice down."

"You didn't tell Patrick that Derry kissed you?"

"I'm not a fool."

"Good." She didn't seem convinced. "Lucy must be beside herself that he's gone."

"That would be an understatement. I hope you've time to stay for tea."

"Actually, I've come for another reason." She reached into her pocket, pulling out a piece of paper. "I've promised to give it to you when you're alone."

As I looked at the paper, I went cold. A folded advertisement much like the one I'd received before, when Derry had written to ask me to meet him in Battery Park. "Who is this from? Why do you have it?"

"Just open it, Grace."

I did, nervously, but the moment I saw the writing, my nervousness turned to sheer relief. This wasn't from Derry. It was from Aidan.

Grace,

I've sent this with Rose and asked her to keep it secret, because I don't want Mama or the Devlins to know where I am, at least for now. But I need to see you. Please meet me today. I'll be at Fulton Market at three o'clock on the ferry side. Don't tell anyone where you're going or that you're meeting me. Please. I'll explain everything but you must keep this secret.

A

"He's all right," I said, unable to hide my joy. "Oh thank God. He's all right."

"I don't know about that," Rose said. "He hardly looked himself, Grace, and he frightened me half to death lurking in my garden. He seemed odd. I think you're right to worry about him. What does he want?"

"Nothing. Just to tell me he's fine."

Rose rolled her eyes. "He most assuredly is *not* fine. I just told you that. He's scheming, isn't he? And he's told you not to say anything—even to me? That's not fair. He trusted me to bring you the note."

I was not good at keeping things from Rose, and we had always shared secrets. And most importantly, she had a carriage waiting out front, which I needed. "Oh, very well. I suppose it's all right, and I don't know how he expects me to meet him without your help."

"He wants you to meet him?"

"You can't tell a soul, Rose."

"No, no, I won't. Where?"

"Fulton Market at three."

Rose had never disappointed me, and she didn't now. She glanced at the clock on the mantel. "There's not much time then. We'll take my carriage."

"The guard—"

"Yes, I meant to ask you about that."

"Patrick says the city's dangerous, what with the labor strikes and poor riots. He's asked me to go nowhere without a chaperone."

"You have one. Me."

"Somehow I doubt that's what Patrick meant."

Rose's smile was wry. "He didn't say *not Rose*, did he?"

"No, but—"

"Then you're not disobeying him. You're not going unchaperoned, so he can't be angry if he finds out. Besides, I am *very* good at sneaking out."

I laughed. "Which is why I'm sure he would have said *not Rose* if he'd thought about it."

Rose tilted her head like a bird. "What we need is some distraction. If we could just get you to the carriage unseen . . ."

"How do you propose we do that?"

"A little flirtation, perhaps."

"Flirtation?"

"You should have seen the way the guard looked at me when I came up to the door." Her eyes twinkled. "I'll draw his attention, and you sneak out and get into the carriage. No one will ever know you're gone."

I still had my doubts, but I could think of nothing better. We went to the door, and Rose said gaily to me as she walked out, "I'll visit you again later in the week!" Truly, she'd missed her calling. She'd been made for the stage.

The front door closed. I waited, hovering, keeping my eye out for any curious maids. I heard Rose talking on the other side, the guard's rough-voiced replies. The guard laughed and moved away from the door, and I saw their shadows through the rippled glass of the little window, moving down the stairs, out of sight.

Carefully, I cracked open the door. I heard her voice around the corner, saying, "No, no, that flower there—look closer, the pink one! Oh, I have *such* a fondness for flowers."

Rose and the guard were bent over Mrs. Devlin's pinks, their backs to me. I hurried down the stairs, past the cast-iron railing and the yew border. I went to the far side of the carriage and climbed in. Then I huddled in the corner, restraining the urge to look out the window, my heart racing.

After a few moments, Rose stepped inside, waving to my guard, a flat-nosed man who was watching her longingly as he limped up the walk after her. The legends were true when it came to the Fomori warriors—they were all deformed in some way.

Was everything else true as well?

Rose said, "Perhaps you'll be on duty next Wednesday, Gerard? Oh, I do hope so," before she called to her driver, "Fulton Market, Sam."

"I cannot believe that worked," I said.

Rose giggled. "Well, you've always doubted my charms. But I'll confess I really don't like him. He has a squashed nose."

"I appreciate your sacrifice."

Before long we were at the market. I thought of how worried Patrick would be if he returned early to find me gone, but I expected to be back in time. My brother was the most important thing. Patrick would understand.

It was late in the day for shoppers; the merchants were packing away their wares in ice and wicker baskets, though the oyster saloons and restaurants that ran down both sides of the street were doing a booming business. Fulton Fish Market oysters were famous the world over.

The driver opened the door, and Rose and I stepped out into the strong smells of fish and the river, oil and smoke from the ferry station behind. Rose wrinkled her nose as she lifted her skirts to avoid a puddle of blood and fish parts. "Ugh. I'd like to kill Aidan. Why not a nice decent park?"

We rounded the corner to the Brooklyn ferry station, and I searched anxiously for my brother.

He was nowhere. No one even looked like him, tall and lanky, with curling dark hair and skin pale from drink and too many nights in gambling hells. The clock above the ferry station read three o'clock exactly. "Where *is* he?" I murmured.

"Oh! There!"

I looked to where Rose pointed, and saw Aidan emerge from behind one of the iron pillars supporting the market roof. My brother—looking not as I'd last seen him, with his hair flying eerily around his face and his eyes a shimmering, hot blue—but disheveled, needing a haircut and wearing no hat, his face streaked with dirt, his coat wrinkled and stained. No different than usual, despite Rose's warning that he was not himself.

I ran to him, throwing myself into his arms so he stumbled. He hugged me, laughing lightly in my ear. "That's quite a greeting, Gracie. Miss me much?"

"I've been so worried! I didn't know—my, you smell of smoke."

"I got caught in a bit of a fire last night."

I stepped back. "Where was there a fire? Where have you been?"

He glanced away, and suddenly I didn't want to hear some flippant remark about saloons or hard floors or sleeping in the ashes of a hearth somewhere.

"Never mind. I'm just so glad to see you. We've all been beside ourselves." I lowered my voice, though there was no one around to hear. "I have so many questions, Aidan. About . . . what you did that night."

Aidan squirmed. "Listen, Grace, this is important. Just know . . . when you think I've betrayed you, please know that I haven't. I never would—ah, Rose. Couldn't resist tagging along, could you?"

Rose stepped up. "I couldn't let Grace come all this way alone. Really, Aidan, you should have picked somewhere easier to meet. Like . . . I don't know . . . Borneo."

I wished I hadn't brought Rose after all. I wanted answers, and I knew my brother would reveal nothing while she was here, just as I wouldn't.

As if he knew what I was thinking, Aidan said, "We've a great deal to talk about, but I don't want to do it here."

"Where then? I'm staying with Patrick now. You could come there. He has men searching everywhere for you. He'll be so relieved to know you're all right."

"Not there. I thought . . . Come for a ferry ride with me. Can you? Just a ride to Brooklyn and back. We'll be alone. We can talk. You needn't wait for her, Rose. I'll see she gets to Patrick in one piece."

Rose warned, "You wouldn't be back before supper, Grace."

Which meant I wouldn't be back before Patrick. I knew Patrick would be angry that I'd ignored his orders, but I needed answers so desperately. And Aidan was no danger to me. "Why the ferry? We could walk somewhere quiet——"

"I was just thinking about all those steamer trips we took upriver on the Fourth of July. D'you remember? It'll be like old times." Aidan smiled that charming smile I loved.

It was sweet and sentimental, and it decided me. "Yes. Like old times. Let's do it."

Aidan said, "Come on. Let's buy the tickets."

"I hope you don't get into too much trouble for this," Rose said to me, giving my brother a dark look.

Together we walked through the large open doors of the station. The ferry was loading, wagons thudding over the ramp, people getting on. Aidan bought our tickets and said to me, "Go on and board. I'll take Rose back to her carriage."

"I'll go with you——"

"It's loading now, and you can't run in a corset and skirts. Get on and I'll run back."

"Please don't miss it, Aidan."

"I won't. I'll meet you in the front salon."

He handed me my ticket, and I boarded the ferry. The boat was crowded with people returning home from offices and markets. I went to the railing overlooking the wharf to watch Aidan run back.

But he wasn't running back. He was standing on the street, talking to Rose.

I shouted, "Aidan! Hurry!"

Just then the ferry whistle blew, the signal for depar-
ture, piercingly loud. He turned to look, and Rose did too. I
heard the huge churning side-wheel creak and thud. I felt the
lurch as the boat began to move away from the dock. I saw
the expression on my brother's face—not regret or panic, but
an *I'm-doing-this-for-your-own-good* look. He mouthed, "I'm
sorry."

And then, from behind me:

"Hello, lass."

The voice that had haunted my every dream.

FIVE

That afternoon
Grace

Now I understood my brother's words: *"When you think
I've betrayed you, please know that I haven't."* Oh, but he
had. He *had*. Damn him.

I whirled to face Derry—*Diarmid*, I reminded myself.

He was beautiful, as always. As if he'd stepped from my
dream. Dark hair nearly hiding his deep blue eyes. *Hiding the
lovespot.* He smiled so that the long dimple creased his cheek.

"'Tis good to see you, Grace," he said.

In his deep voice, my name sounded like a caress. *No. No.
It's all a lie. He'll seduce you and then he'll kill you. He has to.* I
rushed past him, shoving out of the way some man who said,
"Hey, miss!" Where I meant to go I didn't know. Just away.
Away from him, from that smile and the way I felt and every-
thing I knew about him.

Derry caught my arm, and his touch sang through me. I
stumbled.

"Leave me alone!" I said desperately. "I chose *Patrick*, or don't you remember? I'm *engaged*."

"I just want—"

"I know what you want!" *To seduce me. To kill me.* "But I'm done with you. I told you that."

"Just let me talk to you."

"We've already talked. I don't care what else you have to say." I wrenched away. "If I'd known this was what Aidan meant to do—"

"He's joined with us. He believes in us."

I stopped short. "Aidan's *joined* with you?"

"Aye. Not with the Fomori. With *us*." He glanced around. "Come with me away from the crowd—"

"I don't want to go anywhere with you."

"Grace, please." He wrapped his fingers around my wrist. Again that singing touch. I nodded slowly, and he led me to a wooden bench outside the salon. There was a little boy sitting there, but at one look from Derry, he fled.

Derry pulled me onto the bench beside him. I yanked my arm from his hold, rubbing my wrists as if I could rub away the feel of him. He watched me with a contemplative look that reminded me of the last time I'd seen him, standing in the halo of a streetlamp. He was the most dangerous thing I knew. The next time I saw Aidan, I would kill him for this.

"Well, I'm here, thanks to another of your tricks," I said. "So go ahead—tell me why you felt the need to trick me again."

He didn't answer. I heard the *thump-splash-thump* of the side-wheel, people talking as they walked along the deck, someone playing a violin in the salon. Derry clasped his hands between his knees and looked at the ground, his hair shielding his face, his shirt gaping open at the collar to reveal his throat, the start of his collarbone.

I tore my gaze away. "Well?"

"I'm sorry," he said. "But you wouldn't have come if I'd just asked."

"How would you know, given that you've never tried anything so honest?"

"Would you have?"

"No."

"You see?" His mouth quirked in a small smile. "If I could predict the future as well as I can predict you, I'd be a rich man."

"Keep boasting. The gods love that sort of thing. Maybe they'll reward you by turning you into a goat."

He laughed—it was warm and real. "I've missed that sharp tongue of yours."

I tried to hide how much I liked his words, and his laughter. I tried not to think that I'd missed him too. "Tell me why I should trust you now, after what you've done?"

His good humor died abruptly. "You think Patrick hasn't done his share of lying? He needs you to choose the Fomori. Perhaps your whole *engagement*—"

"Patrick loves me."

"Does he?"

I started to rise. "I'm not going to listen to this."

He reached for me. When I lurched away, he drew his hand back. "Please, Grace—please. I'm sorry. Sit down. I just . . . I just want you to hear our side, that's all."

The door to the salon opened; the thready violin music grew louder for a moment before the door closed again. I looked at the receding city. We had the journey to Brooklyn before us, and then there would be the long ride back. I would not be able to escape him on this boat, unless I was willing to throw myself over the side. But the water was cold; I wasn't a good swimmer and escape by drowning seemed a bit extreme, so I sat again. "Very well. You've got until this boat returns to the city. But before you start with all your 'the Fomori are evil' stories, I want to tell you I've met them. They're not the monsters you say they are. They seem charming and sincere."

"You said Finn was charming too. You said all of the Fianna were. All of them but me. Yet you were afraid of Finn that night, and now you've seen us in a fight. Do you still think we're charming?"

"I think you're ruthless."

He inclined his head in acknowledgment. "So don't you think the Fomori could be just as ruthless? They've been our enemies a long time, Grace; why do you think we hate them so? You know the stories already. They're hiding their true natures so you choose them."

"Patrick knows those stories, too, and he believes they're exaggerations."

"He's blinded by his own ambition."

"He wants only to help Ireland—"

"And instead he'll condemn it to evil."

"I don't believe that," I said. "Patrick's no idiot, and neither am I. I couldn't see evil in them, and I *tried*. I'll admit Balor is intimidating, and I don't really like Lot, but she's not *wicked*—"

He laughed. "Refuse her sometime."

"Refuse her? You mean . . . what did you refuse her?"

He was quiet.

"Dear God, is there no one who doesn't want you?"

"You," he said.

But he had to know that wasn't true. He'd made certain of it. Another lie. "They said they wanted to help me. They want to find a way so that I don't have to die."

"So you don't have to die?" he repeated.

"If I'm the *veleda*, I have to die. Isn't that so?"

Now he seemed wary. "That's the prophecy."

And I have to be the one to kill you. I waited for him to say it, to tell me the truth. When he didn't, I said angrily, "They think there might be another spell. Another ritual."

"There won't be another spell."

"Why not? They're looking for an archdruid. They think he might know." And then I realized what I'd just said. Derry—*Diarmid*—was my enemy. The Fianna needed the ritual, too, didn't they? I surely didn't know it. They needed this archdruid as much as Patrick and I did. "Now I suppose you'll run to Finn and tell him all about the archdruid."

"He already knows. We're searching for him ourselves."

"But not to save my life."

"I never thought of it," he admitted. "Nor did any of the others."

"How surprising. The truth at last."

"I think they're lying to you about wanting to find another spell. I think they just want the ritual and the incantation. Unless . . . maybe you know it already? The *veleda* is supposed to."

"I don't."

"Nothing in the stories you heard? Or maybe your dreams? 'Twould be like a song, I'm guessing. Music."

My dreams. Wars and screaming and lightning. Darkness crashing down. My brother's voice: *Come. Hurry.* The sun shone blindingly on the deck, the water beyond sparkled, and the side-wheel beat a steady, soothing rhythm, but all I could see was darkness, shadow, and pain. Derry leaning to touch me, and my yearning—

"Not in my dreams."

"Then it must be the ritual they're looking for."

"How cynical you are. You're so certain there couldn't be another spell."

"I know this magic, Grace. 'Tisn't . . . kind. It always asks blood for blood. It's tangled in . . . in a man's desires and it means for suffering to be the cost. Once Patrick called us, he put the magic in play. There's no other way. The Fomori know it, too, and they're lying to you. They'll tell you what you want to hear to make you choose them."

"And you wouldn't."

He shrugged. "I'm just telling you there's another side. Maybe it's not something you want to know, but you have to. You owe the world that."

"The world." I laughed harshly. "You realize how ridiculous that sounds, don't you?"

"Aye. But 'tis nothing less. If the Fomori win, they'll destroy or enslave every Irish man, woman, and child. They won't rest until they rule the world."

"I don't think they want to, Derry. And even if they did, the Fenian Brotherhood won't let them. This isn't the same world. This is America, not Ireland—"

"But America's full of Irish, isn't it?" he countered. "I'm guessing more than half of Ireland is on these shores now. The Fomori see a new world they can corrupt and despoil. Why take only Ireland when they can have America too? They're already on the police force. The Fenians are putting them in power all through the city government. What happens when they decide not to listen to Patrick and his friends anymore? D'you think anyone will be able to get rid of them?"

"Things have changed. Patrick says—"

"Patrick never fought them. I did."

"In a world of horses and spears. We have a government now, a democracy—"

"You can't control them. No one can."

"And what would the Fianna do instead? You might have been beloved once, but you weren't when you died, were you? You were selfish and arrogant and demanding."

"What if I told you we learned our lesson?"

I thought of Finn rubbing my hair between his fingers, Derry knifing a gang boy without thought or question, the battle behind my house while lightning flashed overhead. Bloodlust and excitement in the air, and my sense that they loved it more than anything.

I thought of how Derry had kissed me, and how I'd kissed him back. How he'd used the lovespot on both Lucy and me. For the Fianna. It was why he did everything: for them. *He means to seduce you and to kill you.*

"I don't think you've changed. Any of you."

His expression hardened. "Then what makes you think the Fomori have?"

He was right. It was stupid to think otherwise. But I'd been at supper with them. They were offering to help me live, and in spite of the stories and my confusion and my fears that I shouldn't trust them, I wanted to.

"Perhaps what I think about them doesn't matter."

"What d'you mean?"

"What if you're all wrong about me? What if I'm not the *veleda*?"

He frowned. "But you are."

"How can you be certain? I've no power at all. Aidan has all of it. And I don't know anything. My mother says it's all superstitious nonsense and everything Grandma said . . . well, none of it makes sense. She *did* tell me to find the archdruid, but—"

"Did she say how to find him?"

The sidhe will help.

I started to say it and then I saw how intently he was watching me, and I remembered who he was, what he wanted from me. *Be smart, Grace.* I'd already told him too much, but I'd forgotten how easily we could talk to each other. That was a lie, too, wasn't it? Just because his hair covered the *ball seirce* didn't mean I should forget it was there.

"Unfortunately not," I lied. "She's mad, Derry. None of it means anything." We were drawing closer to Brooklyn. I saw the rise of the monolith they were building for the bridge tower, a great, dark shadow on the far shore, and I felt a sudden, sinking despair. "I don't know what's true anymore. I don't know anything, and I want nothing to do with any of this. I wish I was far away from here."

"So do I," he said. I saw a yearning in his eyes that reminded me sharply of my dream, along with a pain that confused me. What did he mean—that he wished *I* was far away, or that *he* was?

I looked out toward the paddle wheel, hearing its *thwap* and the muted violin music in the salon, along with laughter and talk—people who had nothing more to worry about than going home after a hard day's work. I wished I were one of them. I wished I were on an innocent boat trip with my brother.

"When did Aidan join you?" I asked.

"The morning Patrick discovered who I was."

"I see." I wondered if Aidan knew about the *geis* as well. I couldn't believe he would have put me in Derry's hands if he did. *"When you think I've betrayed you, please know that I haven't."*

"He's trying to help us, Grace. He's on our side. He wants you to be as well."

"Well, I've done what he wanted. I've met with you and I've listened. So now you and I can go our separate ways. Will you promise me you'll do that? When we get back to the city, will you please just leave me alone?"

He looked away uncomfortably. "There's one other thing."

"One other thing?"

"We're not going back to the city."

"What?"

"I'm not letting you go back to the Fomori." His voice was heavy with apology—and determination.

"You're kidnapping me."

"I'm protecting you."

"You can't do this. You have to take me back. Patrick's waiting. I'll . . . I'll run. I'll scream."

"It won't change anything, Grace. I'll drag you with me if I have to. D'you really think anyone on this boat can stop me?"

I glanced around at the businessmen and factory girls. I'd seen him fight; I knew what he was capable of. Someone might try to help me, but they'd get hurt. Someone might even die. "Derry, please. Take me back. What can you hope to gain? If you don't return me to Patrick, I'll . . . hate you. It won't help, not if you want me to choose—"

"The way I see it, you won't choose us now. And you hate me already. You see? Some things I don't forget."

The misery in his eyes filled me with a nameless fear—no, it wasn't nameless. I knew exactly what it was. "What do you mean to do? Take me to the Fianna?"

"'Tis too dangerous. Your fiancé's men raided the tenement the other night. Burned it to the ground."

"Patrick?"

"He didn't light the match, but he gave the order. You see how noble he and your Fomori friends are? They nearly roasted everyone who lived there, just to get to us."

"I don't believe that. He never said anything to me about it."

"I'm thinking there are a lot of things he hasn't said to you."

Bres had said that before the week was out, the Fianna would be arrested—but nothing about burning the tenement. The people I'd seen there, huddled on their fire escapes, cheering the fight between Finn's Warriors and the Black Hands. Mothers and children and working men . . .

How could Patrick have allowed something so horrible? I thought of my brother, smelling like smoke. "Was Aidan with you?"

"Aye. We haven't another place yet, and we can't protect you well enough on the street. So until we can keep you safe, you and I will be staying in Brooklyn."

"You and I," I repeated. My mouth went dry. People were moving forward as the ferry drew closer to the dock, the salon emptying. All around us was bustle and talk, but all I could hear were his words.

"There's a gang there loyal to Finn's Warriors. They'll shelter us for a time."

"Derry . . . you can't. I can't. I'm engaged. Do you know what people will say? What they'll think?"

He laughed. "None of that matters now, Grace. How can it matter?"

That was true enough. How could it matter? I was going to die . . .

No. I wouldn't think that. Either I wasn't the *veleda* or the archdruid could help me. I had to believe I could find him, that I had a future.

"Then Patrick. What Patrick will think—"

"I confess I don't much care about that. If it makes him miserable, so much the better." The venom in Derry's voice startled me. "My job is to keep you safe. You'll pardon me if I think I can do a better job of it than Patrick Devlin."

"He'll come after us. Rose will tell him where I am. She knows I got on the ferry. She knows where we're going—"

"Aidan will take care of that."

"How?"

"'Tis his job to convince her to say nothing."

I knew my brother's charm. I knew how reasonable he could make everything seem, even as he was destroying everything around him. *Just as the legends said of the Fomori. Though the Fianna were no different, were they?* Rose would do as Aidan asked. He would make it seem as if she were helping me by keeping quiet. I burst out, "Damn you! I hate all of you! Patrick will be so worried. And my mother—she's already upset not knowing where Aidan is. If both of us go missing . . . Derry, *please*. I can't do that to her. She's so frail—"

"I'm sorry for that," he said, but I saw that he would not change his mind.

The ferry thudded into the slip of the Brooklyn dock.

We stood alone on the aft deck. A crowd had gathered at the bow to disembark. I had to get back to Patrick, to my family. The fire at the tenement must have been an accident. Patrick would explain if I could only get back. If I could only escape . . .

But Derry was too fast and too strong. I would never get through all those people before he caught me. My skirts and my corset would hamper me, and the attempt would only raise his guard and I would never get another chance. But later, when we were off the ferry, when we were alone and he wasn't expecting it . . .

"Very well. I'll go with you."

He held out his hand. "I promise you won't regret it."

But I already did. Both my mind and my heart screamed, *Run!*

Patience, I told myself. *Wait for the right moment.*

I prayed it would come soon.

SIX

That evening
Patrick

Patrick arrived home to find Lucy sitting wearily in the parlor and his mother embroidering. Grace was nowhere to be seen. His mother said, "She's in her room, dear. She'll no doubt be down soon. Now go dress, please. You've the stink of the store about you."

The stink of hatmaking, glue and chemicals. He went upstairs, pausing as he passed Grace's room. He'd thought about her all day—he couldn't *stop* thinking about her. He wanted to reassure himself that she was all right—though why wouldn't she be? He had guards posted everywhere. No member of the Fianna would get close to her.

But he worried, and he felt guilty. All of this was his fault. It had been his idea to call the Fianna. He hadn't known then that Grace was part of the prophecy, nor that the *veleda* had to die. He'd wanted to be a hero, to save Ireland, and all he'd managed to do was endanger the girl he loved and her family.

He worried over Aidan nearly as much as he worried over Grace. It was as if Aidan Knox had dropped from the face of the earth that night in their backyard, when he'd been corralling lightning, his hair standing on end. *Stormcaster*, the Fomori had called him, as if a young man shooting sparks from his fingertips was not unusual.

Whatever the power and wherever it had come from, Patrick had been struck with the sense that Aidan was in trouble and needed help. But finding him—that was the problem.

When Patrick went downstairs again, Grace still wasn't there. His mother called for supper and told the maid to get Grace.

Mattie returned in moments. "She's not in her room, ma'am. No one's seen her."

"Since when?" Patrick asked.

"Not since this morning, sir."

His mother said, "She was still asleep when we left to go calling this morning."

"You didn't see her when you returned?" Patrick asked Lucy.

"The door to her room was closed. I thought she might be napping. Or reading poetry or something."

Impatiently, Patrick told Mattie to ask the rest of the staff if anyone had seen Grace.

"I'm certain she's about, dear," his mother said. "She's probably only gone for a walk."

He didn't bother to explain what his mother already knew—Grace couldn't have gone for a walk without a guard.

Instead, he went to the parlor doors, calling to the Fomori warrior standing in the garden, "Have you seen Miss Knox?"

"Not since I came on an hour ago, sir."

The shift change. Each of the guards said the same thing: they'd been on shift only a short time, none of them had seen her. No one had. Not a single servant.

"Except possibly the upstairs maid, Lila," said the butler, John. "But she's off for the night."

Patrick's worry grew. "There were no visitors to the house? You answered the door for no one?"

John's discomfort seemed to increase. "I'm afraid I don't know, sir. I had a bout of dyspepsia and had to lie down for a bit. Lila was supposed to answer the door."

Patrick's worry turned to fear. He went outside, through the gate, and into the park that every house on Madison Square bordered. It was nearly deserted now. He strode the length of it, even as he told himself that Grace wouldn't be here. The guard would have stopped her. She wouldn't have left the house without telling someone.

Where the hell is she?

He sent one guard to the confectionary on the corner and another to her mother's house. There was no sign of her at either place. By twilight, Patrick was panicking. All of his precautions, and something had slipped past him. The Fianna. Diarmid. The lovespot. It took only a moment of persuasion. *Only a moment.*

The Fomori had to be told. They would know what to do. When he returned to the house, the maid gave him a letter that had just arrived from Rory Nolan, his friend in the Fenian Brotherhood. Patrick tore it open, his heart pounding, hoping to read that they already knew of Grace's disappearance, that they'd found her. Instead, it was only a summons, requesting his presence immediately.

He called for the carriage and told his mother and Lucy he was going to the police station. The short journey to the three-story brick clubhouse of the Fenian Brotherhood seemed to take an eternity.

When Patrick arrived, the others were already there. The moment he crossed the threshold, he blurted, "Grace is missing! No one's seen her since this morning. We've searched the grounds—nothing. Your guards let her slip through their fingers."

Lot's purple gaze darkened. "Our guards? They would not be so careless."

"Then you tell me how she could be gone. Did she just evaporate? Or is there someone you know who can make a girl disappear into thin air?"

"Let's not be hasty," Rory said soothingly. "Had she any visitors?"

"None that we know of, though the maid who was on duty earlier today is gone for the night. I've sent someone to fetch her. I want the guards questioned. Each one of them."

"It will be done," said Bres, jerking his chin at Balor, who stood near the door. The hulking beast of a man nodded and left the room, accepting Bres's command so easily it was hard to remember that he was a god himself, and one who had slain scores of men with his poisonous eye.

"If the Fianna have her, it's already too late," Lot said.

Patrick sank into a chair. "I thought your warriors were infallible. You said they would never let one of the Fianna within a hundred yards of her."

"Perhaps it wasn't one of the Fianna who snuck in, but Miss Knox who snuck out," Rory suggested.

Simon MacRonan, their Seer, a man with generations of Druid blood in his veins, said, "Are you certain she didn't go for a walk, perhaps, or shopping? Young girls are so easily bored—"

"She couldn't have walked past the guards, could she?" Patrick glared again at Lot. "Or at least, she *shouldn't* have been able to, and she would never have gone willingly with the Fianna."

"Have you forgotten the *ball seirce?*" Lot asked.

"No," Patrick said, and then hopelessly, "No."

"Clearly, it is more imperative than ever that we find the Fianna," said Bres. "The raid last night was a failure. We'd hoped to trap them in their rooms, but they got away. They won't be back, unfortunately. The tenement was burned to the ground."

"Burned?" Patrick echoed in horror. "Who gave the order to burn it? There were innocent people there."

"It was beyond unfortunate," Jonathan Olwen said angrily. He was Patrick's closest friend in the Brotherhood. They'd been in Ireland together, and had returned together, too, after the failed rebellion. "It was unconscionable. I've been saying so all evening."

Bres looked apologetic now. "I'm afraid our men got a bit overzealous. Thankfully, no one was harmed."

"I fail to see how we're going to win any converts if we're burning them out of their homes," Patrick said. "Or how we'll lure any informants. Your men were careless."

"They won't be again," said Bres grimly.

"Just how trustworthy are your men? They see nothing when Grace disappears, and they've burned a building filled with innocents. What have we gained? Have we any idea where the Fianna are now?" Patrick demanded.

"None." Miogach turned from the window where he'd been listening. He sighed. "We've been winning some gangs to our side, but there are many more who see Finn's Warriors as heroes. 'Tis no different than in Ireland. How they win such blind devotion is a mystery. I've never understood it."

"They have a rough charm that appeals to the downtrodden. 'Twas always so," Lot purred.

Bres scowled. "You'd think they wouldn't be so difficult to find—seven lads with a reputation for ruthlessness—but those who know their whereabouts are fiercely loyal. We'll either have to capture hoodlums who will talk or wait until the next riot."

Miogach turned to Daire Donn. "Perhaps there's better news in the hunt for the archdruid?"

Daire Donn shook his head. He alone of the Fomori men hadn't cut his thick hair. *"A small vanity,"* he'd explained sheepishly. He'd tied it into a queue, but at his motion, strands escaped to fall over his shoulder. "I'm afraid not. The archdruid is as elusive as the Fianna. The *sidhe* we've questioned seem confused. They're drawn here by magic, but they don't know where it comes from. However, they've only just begun to mass in the city. They'll find him, and when they do, we'll find him as well."

"Grace's grandmother seemed certain that an archdruid was the answer," Patrick told them. "She knows more of the old stories than anyone I've ever met—or *knew* them, anyway, when she was lucid. She told Grace to search out the *sidhe*."

Miogach said dourly, "Aye, the *sidhe* will help her. Right over a cliff. If they leave her alive that long."

"She had no plan to search on her own, did she?" Lot asked.

Her fear surprised Patrick. "I don't think so. She seemed content to leave the search to us."

"Thank Domnu for that. Mere mortals have no chance with them at all. They're drawn to Druidic power. A *veleda* would be irresistible to them. If they were to discover her . . . I doubt she would survive them."

"But if they're so dangerous, why would Grace's grandmother tell her to search them out?"

"Whatever her reasons, they're mistaken."

"Have there been any signs that she might wake from her coma?" Bres asked.

"No," Patrick said. "I've hired a nurse to help care for her, but there's little hope."

"You've taken care to investigate this nurse thoroughly? The Fianna will infiltrate us any way they can."

"Yes. She's no spy."

Bres rubbed his chin in thought. "Perhaps 'twould be wise to take the *veleda*'s grandmother into our care before the Fianna decide she has something they want."

"I could bring her into my home, I suppose," Patrick suggested.

"I will put Balor in charge of securing a new nurse. I'm certain you were vigilant, but one cannot be too careful."

"And as long as you have the grandmother, perhaps 'twould be a good idea for Mrs. Knox to be your guest as well," Lot said.

"Why?" Patrick asked.

"A girl never truly leaves her mother. If Grace escapes, she'll go to her first."

"You must do it, Devlin," Simon urged. "We can protect them better if they're all in one place."

Patrick remembered Diarmid Ua Duibhne in his study, saying, *"You've started a war, Patrick. Perhaps you didn't mean to, but you did. And in wars, people die. Especially innocents."*

He looked around the table, at the men he'd worked with over the years to secure Ireland's freedom, and the Fomori who had so eagerly blended their cause with his, and his fear began to ease. He'd done the right thing in asking for their help. They would find Grace and bring her back. They would find the archdruid and save Grace's life.

This was a war they could win.

• • •

Patrick woke with the clang of swords ringing in his ears, the smell of hemp smoke in his nose, and a sense of disaster in his heart. He struggled from the visions the smoke had helped him to find and blinked at the shadows in the darkness. Someone had let the fire die. He reached for his sword; it wasn't beside his pallet, and he wasn't lying on furs but on thin blankets on top of something elevated. Something was wrong. He opened his mouth to call for Aidan—he needed him. The *veleda* was in great danger. Aidan would have the answers. Aidan would know—

The images from his dream melted away. Patrick realized he was safe in his own house, and this was a bed, not a pallet, and the only swords he had were ancient and locked away in a safe. How did he even know what burning hemp smelled like?

But his fear and unease didn't abate. Nor did the words ringing in his mind:

You need Aidan. Find him.

SEVEN

Earlier that day
Grace

Derry grabbed my hand as people began to disembark the ferry. Very deliberately, he wove his fingers through mine.

"I said I would go with you," I told him, trying to ignore the heat of his touch. "You can let go of me."

A half smile. "Just until we get off the boat."

"You don't trust me."

"I'm sure the feeling's mutual."

The station was crowded, but Derry kept a tight hold on me as we pushed our way through the masses. Once we were outside, he didn't release my hand; he dragged me after him into the chaos of the Brooklyn Bridge construction, stone and mortar and timbers so big I wondered what trees they could have come from. The streets beyond were full of people, wagons, and horses; slinking half-feral dogs; weary peddlers hawking what hadn't sold at market; women bartering and men stumbling into saloons. We passed warehouses and the navy shipyard, with its giant hulls looming like buildings.

I tried to memorize our path—I would need to know it when I made my escape—but Derry never traveled in any one direction for long, and I realized he was intentionally creating a maze. Well, how hard could it be to find my way to the ferry? All I had to do was ask someone.

"We're almost there," he told me as the neighborhood changed. Warehouses and dockyards gave way to rickety buildings, tenements. It was a little better than the area where he lived—the yards weren't quite so festering and the privies were still standing upright. There were men drinking and women bickering with their husbands and yelling at playing children. Derry cut a wide swath around three huge rooting pigs, muttering about them beneath his breath. I was so lost that we could have been in New Jersey, for all I knew.

He came to a stop at a four-story brick building stacked next to three others just like it. A group of ragged children played baseball in a tiny square of dirt that passed for a yard. Privies bordered a cesspool. A man sat motionlessly in the doorway.

"There's something you need to do," Derry told me.

"What is it now?"

"I don't know any of the Dun Rats well enough to trust them. Finn's made an alliance with them, but 'tis Keenan they've talked to, not me. They'll do what Finn asks, but 'twould be better if they thought I had a personal reason for wanting to protect you."

"A personal reason?"

"I need you to pretend to . . . be my lass." His hand tightened on mine. "'Tis for your own safety."

I won't be here long. "Fine."

He was obviously relieved. He pulled me with him to the door. The man there shifted, staring up at us blearily.

"Who're you?" he asked.

"None of your business, old man," Derry said, stepping past him.

The man caught Derry's ankle. The bleariness disappeared from the man's eyes and his whole face hardened. "I said, who're you?"

Derry glanced at me before he said, "Derry O'Shea, of Finn's Warriors. I'm looking for Hugh Bannon."

"Derry O'Shea?" The man quickly released him. "Hugh's on the third floor."

"Much obliged." Derry dragged me into the dark tunnel of the stairs, just as black and pitiless as the ones in his own tenement—*now burned to the ground by Patrick*—with the same mix of smells: cooking and sweat and sewage and mud, though at least here it didn't smell like rotting dead things.

I whispered, "So they've heard of you even in Brooklyn."

"I've a reputation," he whispered back.

I didn't have to wonder what it was. The way that man had released his hold, the mix of respect and alarm in his eyes . . . it only reminded me again how dangerous Derry was, how careful I had to be.

When we reached the flat, he rapped on the doorjamb, calling, "Hugh Bannon?"

"Who wants to know?"

"Derry O'Shea."

"Come in!"

We stepped inside. The flat was small, a main room and one on either side. A window in the main room looked out onto a brick wall, and everything inside was gray: gray floors and walls; tattered gray blankets against every wall and in every corner; and gray boys ranging in age from six years old to mid-twenties. Three girls were equally gray, their dresses and skin smudged with dirt and soot. One of them was at the potbellied stove, where she stirred something in a great enamel pot, her dirty blond hair straggling into her face. She turned when we entered, and the smell of cabbage wafted toward us. My stomach rumbled. I hadn't eaten since breakfast, which seemed a hundred years ago.

"I'm Hugh." One of the boys detached himself from the others. That he was their leader was clear by the way they watched him, alert to his every move. He looked to be Derry's age, eighteen or so, with a face so bony you could imagine what his skull must look like. His hair was brown and shaggy. He wore a brown scarf about his throat—they all did. A dun-colored scarf. The Dun Rats.

"Finn sent me," Derry said. "We're looking for sanctuary for a few days. Not long. Just until things blow over."

"Troubles with the law, eh?" The boy grinned and winked at his followers. "Got riots over there today?"

"Not yet. But one's coming in a few days."

I was startled, though I shouldn't have been. I knew of the dissatisfaction in the city and the growing gang violence, but to hear Derry admit his involvement so casually—well, I'd already known he was dangerous, hadn't I?

Escape. Just as soon as you can.

"We welcome the fight, right, boys?" Hugh asked the others.

"Right!" they chorused.

"There'll be fighting enough in the days to come," Derry assured him. "And we'll be able to use you. In fact, we'll have need of you. We'll do some training while I'm here."

The boys cheered. Hugh looked at me. "So who's this one?"

Derry pulled me close, and when I tensed, his hold tightened in warning. "The cause of the trouble, I'm afraid. A new gang in town took a liking to her and won't take no for an answer."

Hugh laughed. "I think we can help you out. Ain't no room here, but Bridget's got a panny downstairs where she can put you up."

"We're grateful for whatever anyone can spare," Derry said.

"Miles," Hugh said, "take our guests downstairs, will ya? And tell Bridge that I said to keep them."

Another boy melted from the wall. He was about my age, and he had coloring like mine: dark hair, pale skin, and brown eyes so dark they looked black. His trousers had a hole in the knee, and the sleeves of his coat showed the bones of his wrists, which jutted out sharply.

"This way," he said, gesturing for us to follow him to the stairs. He took us down one flight, pushing open a door as he said, "Got some guests for you, Bridget. Hugh says to keep 'em."

The flat was much like the one upstairs, though there were fewer people inside—only two skinny boys and two waiflike little girls. In the middle of the room was a table, and a tall, gaunt woman sitting at it, darning what looked like much-repaired socks. Her dark hair straggled loose from the bun on top of her head. In spite of her thinness, her face was so round it made me think of a lollipop on a stick.

"I'm Derry, ma'am. And this is Grace. We were sent by Finn."

Her expression had been stern and wary, but now she burst into a smile. "Finn, eh? Well, well."

Derry smiled back at her, and she flushed with pleasure. It only irritated me more. Was there no one he couldn't charm?

He said, "There was a little trouble. Best for the two of us to get out of the city for a bit."

"Riots?"

"Not today. But a raid last night. Burned our panny to the ground."

"I'm sorry to hear it." She said to Miles, "Tell Hugh I'll hold onto them. They're pretty enough to keep. And polite too."

Derry said, "Thank you, ma'am. We won't forget it."

Her smile turned calculating. "No, and neither will I. When you go back you'll tell Finn how accommodating I was?"

"He'll hear nothing but praise from me."

She pointed with her darning needle to another room at the back. "You'll be sharing with my boarders. Most of 'em ain't here yet. I got nearly every inch rented out but for the alcove. The two of you can have that. I usually charge three cents for it, but it's empty just now so you can have it for free."

Derry reached into his pocket. "I don't want to put you out—"

"No member of Finn's Warriors pays for anything in this place. Miles, show 'em there, will ya?"

My dismay grew when Miles led us into the second room. It was windowless and dark and small, with piles of rags and makeshift pallets lying everywhere, along with guttered, unlit candles melting into the floor. Miles took us to a shallow alcove built into the wall—I wasn't certain for what purpose. "Here you are."

I threw a panicked look at Derry, who ignored me and said to Miles, "Thank you, lad."

"'Tis a pleasure, Derry. I heard o' you, you know. We all have. You need anythin', you just tell one of the kids to fetch me."

"I'll do that."

Miles nodded eagerly and left. When he was gone, I jerked my hand from Derry's. "This isn't what I imagined."

"'Tis the best I can do," he said.

My plan to escape tonight evaporated. I was surrounded by people, all of whom would be watching us. And it had taken us too long to get here; it was no longer day, but evening. This part of town was perilous—for a girl alone, so close to nightfall, it could be deadly. I remembered too well my encounter with the gang boys near Derry's tenement, how they'd cornered me in an alley, and how frightened I'd been until Derry arrived to save me, how close I'd come to disaster. I also had no real idea where I was. I had to spend the night here. With him. In this tiny alcove, which was perhaps five feet wide by three deep—barely enough room for one person.

"I can't do this," I said.

Derry's laugh was short. "You'd be surprised what you can do, I think. And you've no other choice. I can't have you escaping. In case that's what you were planning."

"I don't want to be here," I said softly.

"Believe me, I know. I'll see if I can't get us something to eat." He left me staring at that alcove, at the pile of filthy blankets. I was trapped, at least for the night. I leaned against the wall, crossed my arms, and cursed Aidan.

Tonight, escape was impossible. But there was tomorrow. Once I was out of here, I would hunt Aidan down and tell him just what I thought of his betrayal.

I heard Derry in the other room talking to Bridget, his deep voice, her answering laughter. What light there was faded until I stood in complete darkness. I heard the clang of a pot, more laughter, a child whining, and Derry's quiet response.

Then he came back into the room. He had a lit candle. I didn't see he was holding something else until he nudged it at me.

"Here," he said. "Cabbage soup. I didn't want to ask where she got the cabbage, but it tastes all right."

I took the mug, bringing it to my mouth and taking a tentative sip. It was good, salty and flavorful.

There was movement at the doorway, some of the borders returning from a long day's work. One or two of the men had candles; none of them did more than look cursorily at us as they took up their spots on the floor. Derry moved to block me from their view.

"I won't let anyone near," he reassured me.

But I wasn't worried about them. I glanced again at the small space, the wretched pile of thin and ratty blankets. I thought of what sleeping here with him would be like.

"I don't want any more," I said, handing him the mug. "You can finish it if you like."

He set it aside and dripped wax to hold the candle in place on the floor. Then he began to unbutton his shirt.

"What are you doing?" I asked.

"Getting ready for bed."

"You're *undressing.*"

"Not completely." He gestured to his trousers. "I'll leave these on, unless you'd rather I don't. But I'm not wearing any-thing underneath."

"I don't want you to take anything off."

"'Tis too hot to sweat all night in a shirt," he pointed out. "You should take off your gown, and that thing you wear with all the hooks and ties. You won't sleep in that."

"You must be mad."

"'Tis nothing I haven't seen before."

"I'm sure it isn't. That's not the point."

"I've seen you in your shift, remember."

"Yes, I remember, unfortunately. But if you think I'm going to lie here with you *undressed*—"

"I won't touch you. I promise. Not unless you want me to . . ." He sounded hopeful.

"It's the *last* thing I want," I hissed.

He shrugged off his shirt. The candle lit his skin with a golden glow. He was tightly muscled. His trousers hung low, revealing his hipbones. I thought, *How could I have forgotten this?* at the same time I knew I'd never seen him without a shirt. But the sight was so . . . familiar, as was the yearning that swept over me. My dreams returned with force.

I realized I was staring at him, that he was watching me stare, and I went so hot I was certain he could see the red of my cheeks even in the near darkness.

Tomorrow you'll escape.

He said, "I'm going to turn away and block the doorway so no one can see. You're going to take off your gown and that contraption so you can at least sleep. You must be hot and uncomfortable already."

I hated that he saw it. My corset was jabbing into my ribs; the room was sweltering with the many bodies and no window. And I needed to be clear-eyed for tomorrow.

"You promise you won't touch me? And you won't look?"

He nodded and turned, and I undressed as quickly as I could—which wasn't very—not taking my eyes from him, from the shadowed muscles in his back and the gold of his skin. When I wore only my chemise, I knelt, gathering one of the blankets to me for protection, as stinking as it was.

"All right," I said hoarsely. "I'm finished."

He turned around again, barely glancing at me as he lay down, stretching as well as he could in the cramped space. "'Tis going to be a long night for both of us." He put his arm over his eyes. "Good night, lass."

It was only one night, I told myself. *One night.*

Tomorrow, I would be far away.

EIGHT

July 21
Diarmid

Diarmid woke sore and stiff, with warmth and softness radiating into his side. He opened his eyes to see that Grace had pressed up against him at some point in the night, and now she was spooned as if she belonged there. Her skin was pale above the neckline of the thin shift, her shoulder bare where the sleeve had slipped.

Keep your distance, he told himself. *You've made promises.*

Ones he'd already broken, of course. How long did he have before Finn decided it was safe enough for them to return? One day? Two? And if she wasn't mad in love with him by then, Finn would see it as a breach of loyalty, that once again, Diarmid had chosen a girl over the Fianna.

The only difference was that this time it was more than simply a blow to Finn's pride. This time, their very lives were at stake.

Diarmid felt beneath his hair for the raised scar of the *ball seirce*. Twice already, he'd meant to use it on her—once on the ferry, once here—but both times, he hadn't. In the weeks since he'd seen her, the weeks since she'd screamed *I hate you!*, he'd forgotten how strongly she affected him. He even liked her sharp tongue—she said exactly what she thought, which was different from most of the girls he'd known, and a relief. It made it easy to talk to her. Easy to laugh with her. But most of all, his loneliness disappeared when he was with her, as if it were an empty place named *Missing Grace* that needed only her presence to fill it.

He was a fool. She wanted nothing to do with him—she'd made it obvious from the start. So why did he feel as if the world somehow demanded they be together? It felt . . . fated.

Diarmid laughed softly to himself. That was the biggest delusion of all, wasn't it? What was fated was the *geis*. He had to kill her to save them all. That was what the world demanded—that he make the sacrifice required of him. He could not forget that. He wondered if she knew about his part in the prophecy, if Patrick had told her.

It didn't matter. He was Fianna, and he'd made vows to his brothers, to Ireland. He had to convince her to choose the Fianna—whatever it took.

He felt her startle awake with a quick gasp. Then she went still. She eased away, leaving him cold where she'd been.

He whispered, "Nightmares again?"

"I think I'd like just once to wake without dreams and headaches."

"'Tis the power in you waking."

Now she rolled to face him, pulling her blanket with her as she moved for safe cover. If she was wary, so much the better. Everything would be easier. But then she met his gaze, and it was like a blow, stunning and right to his gut, and he knew he was in trouble. What this girl did to him . . . there were no words.

"I'm dreaming of Aidan. Over and over again. I'm running toward him and then darkness comes between us and he disappears."

"Your brother's been a mystery to you a long time, I'm thinking," he managed to say. "'Tis only that."

"Perhaps."

She looked disappointed, as if he hadn't given her the answer she wanted.

She said, "I want you to tell me something, and I want you to be honest—if that's even possible. Is it?"

He tried not to let that hurt. "I don't know. Try me."

"Is divination ever wrong?"

"Wrong? I don't know if that's the way to put it."

"You know what I mean."

"Aye. All I can say is that nothing's set. Everything depends on what a man does or what he chooses. So what's foretold one day only means that as things stand, this is what will happen. But when things change, what's fated can change as well. Why do you ask?"

"What made the Fianna decide I was the *veleda*?"

He remembered yesterday, her doubts. "The way you saw us glowing, the way Patrick's ogham stick burned when you touched it—such things burn only those with Druid blood. And Cannel divined—" Diarmid broke off, realizing what she was really asking. "Grace, choices don't change what something *is*. Your family—Neasa and her daughter and every girl child on down—the *veleda* is your destiny. 'Tis the prophecy and the promise. It has to be you."

"Even though I have no power."

"'Twas your blood on the horn that called us. You do have power."

"Can you tell me that my power is anything like Neasa's? Aidan's maybe, but not mine."

Diarmid recalled the Druid priestess he'd known, the confidence shining from her, the power one felt the moment Neasa entered the room. "Yours feels different," he admitted.

"How?"

"It feels . . . muted." He tried to find the words—how to separate her power as a *veleda* from the other power she had over him. That *something* he'd never been able to define. "It's there, but it feels unfinished." Though that wasn't quite right either. "I always knew something was different about you, but 'twas hard to know what it was. And then, the night I kissed you, I felt your power in a way I hadn't before."

She was quiet. He wondered if she was remembering that kiss the way he was, that fierce, overwhelming fire that left him shaken and *wanting*.

She said, "Do all the Fianna feel it?"

"I don't know. I never asked them." And he wouldn't. The way Finn had looked at Grace . . . Diarmid had known Finn was seeing Neasa, who'd shared his bed, and he didn't want to know what Finn had been thinking beyond that. He had no wish to compete with his charismatic and ruthless captain. There was too much of the past between them. Better not to think of how he'd betrayed Finn by running off with his betrothed, or how Finn could have saved Diarmid but had let him die. It was long ago and far away. What mattered now was his fear of what Finn would do if he failed to win Grace.

"You said my power feels unfinished," Grace said. "Do you think that means it's not enough for the ritual? Or perhaps . . . not the right power?"

He heard the hope in her voice and said reluctantly, "I think it just means you're untrained."

"But what if it doesn't mean that? What if it means I'm not the *veleda*? What if Cannel's divination was wrong? What if you're all wrong? Wouldn't I feel power if I had it?"

"Maybe you do feel it and you've just learned to bury it. Your world doesn't welcome women with power, does it? 'Tis different from my time—then it was celebrated. Most women of power didn't even marry. At fourteen they could choose— they were welcome to seek learning among the Druids, so why should they bind themselves to a husband if they didn't care to? But now . . . 'tis what the world wants of you, isn't it? To be a wife like every other woman. I think you've only learned to be what the world wants." The regret he felt at that was hard to express.

"What *I* want too," she insisted. She sat up, twisting, reaching for her corset and her gown and her petticoats, which she'd been using for a pillow. "Would you turn away please? I want to get dressed."

"I'll see if there's anything to be had for breakfast." Diarmid pushed aside the filthy blanket and rose, stepping from the alcove. Most of the boarders from last night were gone, some still sleeping, one or two snoring, and in the dim light he had to pick his way through the spaces as if they were stepping stones.

Bridget was already up, sewing. There was a pile of folded white cotton beside her, and he knew she was doing finish work for one of the ready-made factories, putting hems on pantaloons for seven cents a pair. Her two boys—Little Joe and Colin, he'd learned—were sitting at the table, eating mush with the older girl, Molly. The younger, Sara, sat sucking her thumb in the corner. When Diarmid smiled at her, she ducked her head.

Bridget took in his half-naked state. "If you ain't a sight for sore eyes this morning. There's some mush if you like."

He'd come out to get breakfast, but the mush looked gray and smelled unappetizing, and it occurred to him now that it was all Bridget had. He didn't want to deprive them. He could go out and buy a couple of apples, perhaps bring some back for the children as well. "Thanks, but I'll go and get us something."

"There'll be a peddler selling rolls. They're at least a day old, but your lass will know which are best."

"She won't be going," Diarmid said. "I'll call Miles down to watch over her."

Bridget glanced up in surprise. "You thinkin' to keep her locked up till Finn says it's safe to come home? This is Brooklyn, lad. Whatever gangs're after you won't be coming here."

"She's a bit of a prize," he said wryly.

Bridget laughed. "I'll bet. But she won't thank you to keep her cooped up on such a pretty day."

"I've promised to train the Rats—"

"You have all day for that. Take her somewhere." Her expression was wistful. "When you're young, it seems you got forever, but then, just like that"—she snapped her fingers—"it's gone, and you're left wishin' you'd spent more time makin' her smile. What does she like to do? Beyond look at you, I mean?"

Diarmid restrained a sarcastic comment. "I don't know. I'll ask her."

He started back to the other room. Little Joe said, "You like to play ball, Derry?" in a plaintive voice that made Diarmid look over his shoulder and answer, "Perhaps this afternoon, lad."

Little Joe rewarded him with a smile that warmed him. When he returned to Grace, she was fastening the last of the buttons on her bodice. Then she ran her fingers through her hair in an attempt to tame it, her dark curls twisting and tangling. The sight, so innocently beguiling, reminded him of another girl, brushing her golden hair that shimmered in the sun. Grainne had not been the least bit guileless, though, and every single thing she'd done had been to tempt him. Another foolish relationship that had cost him, and he would do well to remember it.

He said, "There's nothing here to eat. I'll go out and——"

"I'll go with you."

"No. I'll call Miles down. 'Tis best if you stay."

"I see. So I'm a prisoner."

"'Tis for your own safety."

"Do you plan just to keep me in this room until Finn tells you to bring me to him?"

Uncomfortably, he said, "I suppose so."

"And what am I to do? Stare into space?"

"Well, Bridget thinks you'd be happy to stare at me, and I guess I wouldn't mind it. I'll even keep my shirt off for you. You seemed to like it well enough last night."

He regretted his tease when he saw how pink she went.

"I'm sorry. I forgot you don't like flirting."

"If you mean to keep me here, at least find something for me to do. A book or . . . a book would be good."

"You really think to find a book in this place?"

"Perhaps there's a bookstore nearby? Or some kind of shop? We needn't go far."

"I don't know. Probably there is, but——"

"We're in Brooklyn, Derry. Who would have followed us here? You said Aidan would make certain Rose said nothing."

That was true, but . . . "I'm supposed to be training the Dun Rats."

"Training them? For what?"

"For war."

She said quietly, "Then perhaps you should try to please the one who has to choose a side in it."

That soft acceptance made him feel guiltier than any harsh word she had said to him. Grace had not asked for this. She was in this miserable place because he'd dragged her away from decent food and a soft bed and everything she loved. If a walk to a shop and a book would help make it better, it was the least he could do. "All right. But you'll need to stay close. And if I say we have to come back, we come back. No arguments."

"No arguments," she agreed.

"I mean it, Grace."

"I'll be like a burr in your side."

He winced. "Perhaps something less irritating."

She smiled sweetly. "Shall we go?"

He put on his shirt and they went into the next room. When he asked Bridget about the closest shop that might have books, she looked at him suspiciously.

"Books? What d'you want those for?"

"Grace reads," he explained.

Bridget looked vaguely impressed. "Two blocks up, away from the river. On your left."

He nodded, leading Grace out. Without thinking, he grabbed her hand to help her down the pitch-black stairs. She started when he wrapped his fingers around hers, and the moment they reached the bottom, she pulled away, looking up and shielding her eyes from the bright overcast sky. "How muggy it is. It feels like a storm's coming in."

He thought of Tethra's blue lightning, unsettling thunder, and ravens screeching, and couldn't help shuddering.

She noticed. "I didn't like it much either."

"Tethra's storms are bad enough, but Neasa—now, she had a *talent*. She could bring thunder to make the whole earth move. Purple lightning, just like Aidan's. She'd call it up when we rode into battle. 'Twas meant to scare our enemies."

"So it's true then."

"What's true?"

"My dreams," she said, not looking at him. "Thunder and lightning. Ravens. You with a spear."

"You dream of me?"

"Not just you," she said quickly. "The dreams feel very . . . real. Was that how it used to be? That terrible?"

"Aye. Always terrible, especially when the Druids were involved. Or when the goddess, the Morrigan, deigned to 'help.' I always thought her ravens were as willing to tear out my eyes as my enemy's. And the thunder and lightning— sometimes you couldn't even think."

"I suppose you got used to it."

"Never."

"And this battle, the one between you and the Fomori . . . will it be like that?"

He shrugged. "They're all different, Grace. And they're all the same. I wouldn't have thought storms would be part of it, but now there's your brother and Tethra. And Finn and the others are training up gangs in Manhattan to fight just as

I'll train the Rats while we're here. There won't be spears and swords, though."

"Just clubs and knives," she said.

"Aye. And there'll be death. You'd best get used to it."

"Like that gang fight you had with the Black Hands. That boy you killed."

He remembered how angry and frightened she'd been then. The way the Black Hands had surprised the Fianna when he'd brought her to meet Finn. The night they'd discovered she was the *veleda*. The blood on his hand that had ended up on her cheek when he'd kissed her, his battle lust still raging.

He didn't know what to say, and so he began to walk, relieved when she fell into step beside him. The streets were a little better here than at home, but there were still broken sewer pipes leaking into puddles and piles of garbage overflowing the ash cans. Women leaned wearily over stoops to talk to their neighbors; children dodged wagons, horses, and cartmen; and peddlers hawked bruised apples, swill milk, and day-old bread. Diarmid stopped to buy apples and some stale rolls, stuffed some into his pockets for Bridget's children, and gave one of each to Grace.

She said, "You're certain there will be a battle?"

"Aye." He took a bite of an apple. It tasted dry and sour. Still he made himself chew and swallow and take another bite before he said, "And it won't be a pretty one. The Fomori are fearsome. We've lost some of our best men to them."

"I know they were that way once. The things the tales say—"

"True tales."

"Perhaps. But I don't see it now. Or . . . I don't think I do. Balor with a poisonous eye that slays anyone he looks upon? It seems impossible in this world. Daire Donn is a flirt, and Miogach made me laugh—"

"Miogach." He couldn't hide his scorn. The Fomori had persuaded her as easily as he'd feared. It was no surprise. Lot's beauty captivated. Daire Donn's smile and confidence made you want to like him. Bres was so beguiling he'd seduced the whole of Ireland before anyone began to notice that the land was ruined and he wasn't the benevolent ruler they thought him.

"Miogach has strange eyes," Grace went on. "At first I didn't know if I liked him, but he's been the most reassuring of all when it comes to the archdruid. And the hope that there's another spell."

"He's also the biggest liar. Finn treated him with nothing but kindness. I taught him sword fighting and chess, Keenan trained with him every day. He was to join us, but he betrayed us instead and killed Finn's son. I don't like any of the Fomori, but Miogach . . . I'd be happy to meet him in battle again, hopefully skewered on the end of my red spear."

"He admitted that you were at odds."

"*At odds.* Ha! That's one way to put it."

"Perhaps he has reason to hate the Fianna, Derry. My grandmother said Finn was too arrogant to believe that he wasn't beloved by everyone. How could Miogach love any of you? You killed his father and his brother."

"Is that what people think? That we deserved his betrayal?"

"It's the way my grandmother tells the story, but I don't think anyone else does. She knows things no one else seems to know. Or she did anyway." She took a bite of the apple and made a face, but she didn't spit it out.

Diarmid said quietly, "The world changes, and the gods change with it. Monsters don't always look like monsters."

Grace finished the apple in a few bites and threw the core into the street, where it was set upon by dogs. She tore off a piece of her roll. "Are Grandma's stories about the Fianna true also? The ones where you would fight for whoever paid the most money? Or that you demanded tributes and women until the people grew tired of you and the king decided to fight you himself? His own elite guards?"

Diarmid stiffened. "'Tis the reason for the *veleda*. You know the prophecy as well as I do."

"I suppose kidnapping isn't so different from those things."

"You don't want to choose the Fomori, Grace."

"They say the same about you," she challenged.

"And they're wrong. I've seen what they can do. But you'd rather trust Patrick, who believes that history is wrong even though he hasn't lived it."

"I don't need Patrick to tell me what to think. I can see the truth for myself."

They'd reached the secondhand shop that Bridget had told them about, and Grace's gaze leaped beyond him to the dirty windows, where *Murphy's Treasure Chest* was painted in peeling white.

The shop was small and crowded. Tables throughout were loaded with pots and pans, stacks of dishes, and piles of cups, spoons, and forks. Racks to one side sagged with clothing. Beneath were piles of shoes. Above, bedraggled hats perched one atop the other. A bearded man sat behind glass cases that held fans and hairpins and all manner of cheap jewelry.

The man glanced up as they entered the shop. "C'n I help you folks?"

"We're looking for books," Grace said.

The owner jerked his head toward the rear of the shop. "What I got is back there. Ain't many."

Diarmid followed Grace to a table that held perhaps ten books, all worn, most with split bindings and frayed covers. He leaned back against a table of crockery and watched her leaf eagerly through them. For the first time since he'd kidnapped her, she looked relaxed and happy, and he was surprised at how good it made him feel, to give her the books she loved.

"You don't need to hover," she said. "I'm fine. Why don't you go look at . . . at knives or something."

"I don't need another knife."

"Then why don't you read this?" She threw a book at him. He caught it easily, but he didn't open it.

"I can't." He threw it back. She missed, and the book fell to the floor.

"You can't—" She frowned. "But you said you read that book of Patrick's. The one with 'Lament for Banba.'"

The poem was in a book he'd stolen from her so that Cannel could divine if Patrick was the one who'd called them. "Cannel read us the poem. I remembered it, that's all."

"You can't read?"

"Not this language. But I can read ogham. Of us all, I'm the one with the most learning. Taught by Manannan's Druids." He said it with pride, hoping to impress her.

"Manannan," she said. "The god of the sea."

"Aye."

"It's disconcerting, you know, having legends suddenly come alive."

"I imagine so," he said dryly.

"Were they legends even then? Were there stories written about them?"

"Nothing written down," he told her.

She looked stricken. "But then, what was there to read? How did anyone know the legends? What about poetry?"

"Not many could read but for the Druids, and not even all of them. There was no need of it, not with so many bards traveling about. There was at least one every night, no matter where you were. Everyone gathered around the fire, drinking ale and listening to tales and songs . . . 'twas the best time of day." He had a vision of her sitting beside him in the hall, nestled in furs, rapt as the bards sang and joked. For a moment, it was as real as a memory. "I wish I could show you. You would have loved it."

She smiled as if she shared the vision, and the moment was companionable and sweet, until her expression tightened;

her eyes hardened. He wondered what had changed, what she was thinking.

"Go look at knives," she said.

"I think 'tis better if I stay close."

"I'm perfectly safe and you're right here if I need you."

He didn't move.

She said, "Please. Just give me a minute. Please, Diarmid."

It was his name that did it. She hadn't said it before, only *Derry*, and the way she said it, that acknowledgment of who he really was—everything he was, as if she'd never called him anything else—sank into him. He found himself doing as she asked. What could it hurt? He would be between her and the door; nothing could get to her without going through him.

The knives were cheap and dull and useless. He hefted one or two anyway. Then he saw a movement at the window, and he glanced up to see a boy, tall and thin and pale, with brown hair and black, fathomless eyes, pressing his hands against the glass. There was something troubling about him, something not quite right—

Diarmid heard a door behind him creak open and slam closed.

He twisted around. Grace was gone.

NINE

The next moment
Diarmid

Diarmid dropped the knife in his hand. It clattered to the floor as he sprinted to the back of the shop.

The owner called out, "Hey, wait a minute!"

Diarmid pushed through racks of clothes that hid a door he hadn't seen. Stupid! More than stupid. He jerked it open, plunging into a dim back alley, pausing only long enough to see which direction she had gone—and there she was, lifting her skirts as she ran full-out, her dark hair flying behind her.

Even without her skirts and corset, she would have been no match for him, and he reached her in seconds. He grabbed her arm, spinning her to a stop. "By the gods, what do you think—"

They materialized from around a corner. Four of them—three boys and a beautiful girl, their eyes glittering and cunning. It was only then that Diarmid realized there were more behind him—the boy from the shop window, along with three others—and before he knew it, he and Grace were surrounded.

Grace squinted in a way that was familiar. "They're glowing *silver.*"

And he knew. *The children of the* sidhe. Diarmid could barely breathe. There was nothing more dangerous to a *veleda.* He'd seen Druids drained by the *sidhe*, left mindless, soulless. He cursed himself for not thinking of it—a *veleda* and archdruid together in the same city, and Aidan too . . . of course the *sidhe* would be swarming. He should have locked Grace in that tenement room. He should have known.

A fair boy glided forward. "We mean you no harm, friend Diarmid."

Grace swayed as if they pulled her. Diarmid pushed her behind him, keeping a tight hold. "Perhaps that's true."

"Nor her either." The boy looked at the beautiful girl with eyes the color of cornflowers. "Do we, Deirdre?"

"Of course not," she said.

The boy reached out. "We merely want to touch—"

Diarmid slapped his hand away. Grace lurched as if suddenly released from a tether. "You'll have to go through me first."

The boy frowned. "We only want to gift her."

"I know your gifts. She wants nothing from you."

"Why not let her tell us that?" said Deirdre. "She has her own voice, does she not? She does not belong to you."

"My task is to protect her."

"Is it?" The fairy's eyes widened in obvious disbelief. They all laughed. The sound was like music, enchanting. "Perhaps she would be safer with us."

Grace said, "You're fairies, aren't you? The children of the *sidhe*?"

"Quiet," Diarmid said to her. He looked back at the girl. "I've never harmed one of you, though I've had reason. We've been friends in the past. Let us go now."

Deirdre ignored him. She said to Grace, "Your people call us fairies sometimes. We're happy to serve you. What would you ask of us?"

"Nothing," Diarmid said. "Ask nothing, Grace."

The fairy stepped up to him. She pressed her hand to his chest. The touch shuddered through him. Fairies were beautiful and seductive and quick to offer either pleasure or cruelty, depending on whatever they felt at the moment.

"You are very beautiful, Diarmid," the fairy said. "But perhaps you would be better as a stag."

Grace said, "You'll turn him into nothing of the kind."

"Grace, don't," he said sharply.

Deirdre looked at Grace. "Is that your command?"

"Does it have to be a command for you to do as I ask?"

The fairy cocked her head as if considering. "As a favor—"

"No. No favors. Tell her, Grace," Diarmid demanded.

Deirdre's eyes narrowed. "I would hear it from her." But she lifted her hand from his chest.

Grace wrenched free of his hold and stepped from behind him. "No favors. But I'm looking for someone. I need an archdruid. Can you tell me . . . do you know of one?"

"Aye, we know of one," Deirdre said.

"Where is he? Where might I find him?"

"In County Kildare. Near the Hill of Allen."

The fey boy from the shop window laughed. "Oh, 'tis a long time since he's been gone, my love, remember? When we were there last, only stones remained."

"Two hundred years ago, I think," said another.

"No, three!"

"Four!"

They all began to laugh. Diarmid felt Grace's tension; it matched his own. He whispered to her, "They don't know anything. Let's go."

Grace didn't budge. She said to Deirdre, "Not in Ireland. There's one here. I know there is."

Deirdre reached out. Diarmid moved, ready to bat her away, but she stopped, her fingers only inches from Grace, who was swaying again, staring at Deirdre's hand.

"Don't let her touch you," he said.

"'Tis what I require," Deirdre said, her voice hard as diamonds. "Whatever I know is hers to discover. For a price."

The price was Grace's power, he knew. "Grace," he warned.

She didn't look at him. She was staring at that hand, mesmerized.

"Grace," he said again, louder. When her gaze came to him, he held it. "She can hurt you. Listen to what she's saying. She's not saying she knows anything at all. Don't be fooled."

Deirdre laughed—clear and rushing as a river over stones. She gestured to her fellows. "Enough of this game!" And they were gone, vanishing into corners and alleyways as if they'd never been. Not even footprints remained in the dust.

Diarmid grabbed Grace's hand and ran, dragging her after him. The apples he'd bought for the children tumbled from his pockets, rolling away. He couldn't risk retrieving them. When he finally slowed before the tenement door, he was surprised to see that none of the *sidhe* had followed.

Grace was gasping, her hand pressed to her stomach as she tried to grab a breath. He let go of her and she wavered; he reached for her. But he'd no sooner touched her than she managed to draw a breath and pushed him away. "It's only . . . the corset."

He took her arm again. "Come. 'Tis safer inside."

She wrenched away. "I want to go *home*."

"You can't. And now you see part of the reason why."

"I want to find the archdruid."

"You don't know what you're doing. You can't go around asking the *sidhe* for favors, Grace. You can't. Do you know what they would have done if you'd agreed?"

"What?"

"They would have sucked your power dry and left you a madwoman. Or an owl or a doe or something else equally unpleasant. You were lucky I was there."

"How are those things worse than what my future holds now? At least the fairies will help me—"

"Help you? Weren't you listening? They'll drain you to nothing. They'll leave you mad if they don't kill you."

"But they must know where the archdruid is. My grandmother said they'd help me."

"Your grandmother said *what?*"

"She told me to find the archdruid, and she said the *sidhe* would help me."

"Your grandmother's mad. You said it yourself. That she suggested you hunt out the *sidhe* only proves it."

"Some of what she told me was true. Maybe this is one of those things."

It was true that if an archdruid was about, the *sidhe* would know it. But to ask for their help . . . it was foolishness. Beyond risky. Still . . . Diarmid saw Grace's determination and he knew she wasn't listening. She would try to find the *sidhe* again if he let her.

Use the lovespot and then if you tell her to stay, she'll stay. Keep her safe. Do as Finn wants.

"I know what the *sidhe* want," she said desperately. "I heard them. They sang to me, and it was so . . . so beautiful. I wanted to let them touch me. They frighten me, but I need that archdruid. I don't want to die, Derry. I'm only seventeen, and I want . . . so much. My only hope is to find him. The *sidhe* can help. I know they can."

Diarmid's throat tightened. "Then at least let me talk to them."

"How will you be any more safe? She threatened to turn you into a deer."

"I know how to deal with them. Deirdre's threat was an idle one. There are those in Ireland who'd be enraged if they harmed me, and I don't think she'd risk their ire. I'm a favored child."

"Yes, so I heard," Grace said, and he wondered what that meant. She sighed. "Let me go, Derry. You told me once that you thought I could do anything. Prove to me you mean it. Tell me it matters to you that I live. Show me you really do care."

Her words reminded him of another time when she'd told him the things she'd wanted: *"Can you change the world?"*

He wondered if there *was* another spell, one that would keep her alive and remove the *geis*. Was there a future he hadn't been able to see because he was mired in prophecy and fate? But fate was ever-changing; he'd said it to her only this morning. When a man's will was free, nothing was set in stone.

Can you change the world?

Could he?

Use the lovespot. Keep her safe.

Let her go.

In the end, he could do neither. Neither make her his against her will nor let her run headlong into danger—not just the *sidhe*, but the Fomori too. He felt bound, the world demanding his compliance. He wanted to give in to his desire. He wanted her to love him because she wanted to, not because

THE WEB

of any spell. He wanted her to share whatever future he had. His and no one else's.

Because of that, he found himself clinging to the hope she'd offered. What if an archdruid *did* know a way to save her? If so, showing her the lovespot now would ruin any chance at real love they might have.

You are a fool. The gods knew he wasn't even sure he *had* a chance with her. She was engaged to someone else she claimed to love. He was just asking to be hurt. And there would be a price to pay for this too. Finn would never forgive him if it turned out badly.

What could a few more days matter? In the end, if he had to use the lovespot, he would. For his brothers. For Ireland.

"I can't let you go, Grace. You must know that."

She let out a disappointed sigh.

"But I'll help you," he went on. "If you promise not to try to escape me again, I'll promise to help you find this arch-druid. But I need to trust that you'll stay."

He saw her reluctance and her doubt, but also . . . consideration. She was measuring him, and he knew he would come up short.

But she nodded. "All right. I'll stay. In exchange for your help."

He couldn't keep from smiling. Her smile in return was small and tentative, but he would take what he could get.

"Good," he said. "Good."

She turned to go through the doorway, giving him her hand so he could lead her as he always did through the darkness, and again he felt the soul-deep thrill that came every time they touched. But today it only frightened him. He knew the truth of himself then: Diarmid Ua Duibhne, undone by a woman again, choosing one over the Fianna again. He felt out of control, drawn by something he couldn't name. And he had the sickening feeling that he had made the wrong decision, that he was only delaying the inevitable, that somewhere, the gods were laughing at him.

July 22
Grace

I was lying to him. I didn't intend to stay, though I felt guilty
when he seemed so relieved by it—especially because there
was something in his voice that told me it really mattered to
him, that he *wanted* me to stay, and I liked that more than I
wished.

The lovespot. He was manipulating me, just as he had
Lucy, but it was hard to remember that when he looked at me,
or when he touched me. What had Lot said? *"The things he
could do with touch alone . . ."*

I had to escape. My mother would be worried, my grandmother, Patrick. Even as Derry had said he would help me, I
didn't believe him. He'd said nothing of the *geis* and it made
me suspicious that he was only telling me what I wanted to
hear. His promises were meaningless; he would say anything
to persuade me to choose the Fianna. Patrick was the one who
loved me, who wanted to save me.

The burning of the tenement still troubled me, though. So many innocent people. I knew the Brotherhood and the Fomori wanted the Fianna, but I would have thought Patrick incapable of such a terrible act. He couldn't have had anything to do with it, which meant the Fomori had made the decision. The thought only fed my confusion. Now, away from them and their allure, the stories I'd known all my life regained their power. Derry's certainty that they were monsters only added to my fears, but there was also my grandmother telling me that every story had two sides. And there was Patrick and his belief in them, and my hope that they might find another spell when the Fianna weren't even pretending to look.

I felt tossed to and fro; I didn't know what to think about anything, and my dreams that night only confused me more. There were no battles, but I dreamed of being on a ship in the middle of the ocean, the deck shifting beneath my feet. Someone was watching me, waiting, someone I couldn't see. Then there was Aidan, disappearing as I ran to him, just as before, but this time he said, *The key—we need the key*, before the darkness came between us. And then . . . the sound of waves lapping against a beach, and Derry, and it was as if I'd waited a lifetime for him. The urge to touch him made me dizzy.

When I woke the next morning, it was all I could do to resist the desire to reach out as I watched him put on his shirt, his muscles flexing beneath smooth skin.

It's all a lie. Fight it.

I lowered my gaze, but not before he caught me watching. For once he didn't tease. "I'm going to train the Dun Rats today. But later we'll talk about what we'll do next."

I nodded.

He gave me a searching look. "In case you're thinking about breaking your promise, I'm reminding you the *sidhe* are out there. They'll drain you before you have a chance to ask them anything if I'm not there to protect you."

It was what I'd meant to do—run off to find the *sidhe*—but when he said that, I remembered how tempting I'd found their song: *Let me touch you. Touch you . . . touch you.* I'd felt snared like a fish in a net, dragged toward them against my will. Now I knew why my grandmother had warned me to be careful.

He went on, "They'll be looking for you, too, now that they know you're here. And there will be more of them. They won't be so easy to escape next time, and if you think to talk them out of hurting you, well . . . you won't succeed. You wouldn't make it as far as the ferry, even if you knew the way. And I don't want to be taking a corpse back to your mother."

I'd thought he believed me when I'd promised to stay. It flustered me to realize I hadn't fooled him.

He finished buttoning his shirt. "I'll call down Miles to keep you company. We'll be training in the yard—between the door and the street. If you want to, come watch."

Between the door and the street. I heard the warning there too. I wouldn't get past him. I couldn't run, not with him and

Miles keeping guard, and even if I tried . . . well, I knew he was right about the *sidhe*.

If nothing else, Derry had kept me safe yesterday. He had to keep me alive until Samhain, didn't he? If I was the *veleda*, the Fianna needed me.

And if I was not . . .

But it was harder than ever to keep hoping that, because I'd felt something besides temptation during the *sidhe*'s song. A strange itch in my blood. What it was, I didn't know. Magic? Power? Could it be that I had some after all?

The thought chilled me. I tried to forget it as I dressed and went out to where Bridget was sewing. Miles was already there, sitting at the table, playing solitaire with a well-worn pack of cards.

He smiled at me. "Mornin', Gracie. Care to play a game or two?"

"You should be training with the others."

"I c'n hear 'em well enough."

So could I. Their voices rose from the yard below, the sound of *thud*s and laughter, Derry's voice above the others: "Not that way. Dodge like this so I can't get you in the knees. Twist around—aye, that's it!"

Someone shouted, "Show me that again!" and Derry shouted back, "No distractions this time, Hugh. A glance at a pretty lass will only get you a knife in the back.

Bridget jerked her head toward the window. "The girls're out there watching."

I abandoned whatever remaining hope I had for escape today and went to the window, bracing my hands on the sill and leaning out, hoping for a cool breeze. It was only late morning, and already the sun beat down on the fire escape, reflecting brightly off the girls' dark heads. Molly had wedged herself between the flimsy railings of the narrow platform, leaning out over the cesspool two stories below so she could see. Sara sat in the corner, sucking on her hair and looking bored. She spat the hair from her mouth long enough to say, "Come out, Gracie."

I stepped out, peeking through the wide grate at my feet to see how very far down it was. It reminded me of the last time I'd sat on a fire escape. The Fianna's tenement and the Black Hands and watching Derry kill that boy. And then the kiss that had sent me running to Patrick in the hopes that he would remove Derry from my life for good.

That had worked well, hadn't it?

Molly said, "You c'n see Derry if you lean out."

"Why don't you just tell me if he does something amazing?"

"'E already has," she said admiringly. "'E took down Hugh with one hand. An' Hugh's *strong*."

I sat, and Sara pressed into my side. She ran her dirty fingers over the sage-green twill of my dress. "I want a dress like this one."

Molly said, "Ha! That's a fine lady's dress, Sara. It ain't for the likes of us."

I said, "You never know. Maybe you'll have one like it someday."

"I'd like to be rich. Riding 'round in carriages all day." Molly made a little, mocking bow. "'Ello there, sir, ain't it fine weather we're havin'?"

I laughed.

Molly gave me a serious look. "Well, ain't that how it is? Don't you have fine things to eat too? Ice cream and strawberries that ain't rotten?"

I thought of how often I'd been at the confectioner's down the street from Patrick's house. Sugared violets crunching against my teeth. "Yes, I suppose."

"I don't guess I'll ever know what they taste like."

"You might, Molly. Things change."

"I guess I might meet a rich man someday. 'Cause Derry met a rich lady."

I didn't want to contradict her, because I wanted to give her hope that she might escape this hard life. I'd seen too much of it already. The streets were full of beggars and men looking desperate and afraid. Little girls swept the streets for the odd penny, or sold themselves, and boys picked pockets or cleaned chimneys. The cabbage Bridget cooked into stew was half-rotten, whatever hadn't sold at market, or stolen from the garbage piles behind restaurants or groceries.

Bridget sat inside all day long, sewing tiny, careful stitches on pantaloons—she'd refused my offer of help last night because she had to pay for mistakes. I'd seen such pantaloons a hundred times in the store my father had owned before it was taken with everything else after his death. He'd bought them in bulk and sold them for good profit at Knox's Clothing

Emporium, and I had never—not once—thought to wonder who had made such careful stitches or what they were paid for their hard work.

These people were hungering for the battle Finn had promised them. I thought of the rebellion Patrick was planning in Ireland to overthrow British rule. He'd told me of the desperation there, the terrible conditions of the poor, and now I wondered if he'd ever seen the poverty in his own city. Patrick wanted what was right, and I admired him for that. But was the fight for Ireland really the battle he should be waging?

Sara said, "Tell a story, Gracie."

Molly turned, her brown eyes lighting. "You must know a lot of 'em, don't you? 'Cause you can read. Mama said so. She said you was out buyin' *books* yesterday."

Books. The shop. The scene Derry had laid for me, so real I'd felt I was in it with him. Sitting beside a fire, wrapped in his arms, a bard singing. "Yes. I didn't find one I liked, though."

"But you don' need a book to tell us a story, do ya?"

"I want a story 'bout princesses," Sara said.

"And fierce battles," Molly put in.

I knew many like that. A whole lifetime worth of tales. Just beyond, I heard the boys shouting and Derry's laugh, a laugh I somehow knew as well as my own, though I'd only heard it a few times. In Battery Park. In my dreams.

I found myself saying, "Once upon a time, there was a princess. Her name was Grainne, and she was the daughter of the High King of Ireland . . ."

By the time I'd recounted all of Diarmid's glorious feats—conquering the sea champions and their armies and the hounds of Slieve Lougher and the giant of Dubros—it was falling into afternoon. The little girls were as entranced by the story as I had always been, and when I reached the part where Diarmid was gored by the boar and Finn let him die, Molly said, "But he didn't really die, did he? Tell the rest—'bout how there was some magic that brought him back."

I thought of the *dord fiann*. "The legend says that one day someone will blow Finn's hunting horn, and the Fianna will return to help Ireland at her time of greatest need."

Molly frowned. "Why just Ireland? Why couldn't they come back and help anyone they wanted?"

"Because they're Ireland's heroes." I stretched my legs, realizing I no longer heard the shouts and cries of the boys. Training must be over. I got to my feet, picking up Sara, who snuggled into me with a yawn.

Molly said, "But they're *Irish* heroes, ain't they? Not just *Ireland's*." She climbed back through the window.

I followed her, ducking beneath the sash, trying to maneuver myself and my skirts and a sleepy Sara.

"Here. Give her to me."

Derry stood just inside the window, and I felt the same little rush I always felt when I saw him. I wondered just how long he'd been standing there. He plucked Sara from my arms, then offered his hand to me. I shook my head and climbed in myself—the last thing I wanted right now was for him to touch me.

"That was a good story you told, lass," Bridget said from the table. She barely looked up from her sewing. "Made the time pass a mite faster. Thank you."

"Why did Grainne marry Finn after Diarmid died?" Molly asked.

I glanced at Derry. He was carefully putting Sara on the bench. I quickly looked away again, but I felt the way he listened, and I tried to pretend the story I'd been telling had been about some stranger, not the boy who stood before me. "She might have had no choice, but I believe she loved Diarmid until she died. It's romantic, don't you think?"

Derry snorted.

"You don't think the story romantic?" I asked, as casually as I could.

"I don't know the story," he said bluntly. "Not the one you told anyway."

Molly said, "But everyone knows 'bout Diarmid and Grainne."

"I know the names, that's all." He strode past me, into the other room, without a glance or another word.

I looked at Bridget, who shrugged and turned again to her sewing. "He stood there and listened. Him and Miles both, until he sent the lad away. Molly, go on out and see if you can't find another cabbage."

The little girl nodded and flew out the door as I stood there uncertainly. I should have told another story. About the hero Cuchulain, perhaps, or the Children of Lir, but that tale was so sad, and . . . well, why shouldn't I have told my favorite of them? He'd been outside. It had never occurred to me that he might hear. It wasn't my fault he'd decided to listen.

Bridget said, "Let the lad stew. Somethin's got to him, but 'tis best just to ignore 'em when they're like this. Come on over, child, and talk to me awhile."

Miles was gone. Derry was in the other room. I could tell Bridget I was going for a walk and just slip out. It was a tempting thought, but I knew I'd no sooner be down those stairs than Derry would be after me. And then he would probably chain me to the wall—if I managed to elude the *sidhe*.

The fairies had changed everything, and I needed to be smart, so I sat at the table and talked idly with Bridget and told myself I didn't care about whatever was bothering Derry. Why should I, when he was keeping me against my will?

By the time Molly came back with half a browning cabbage, the day was gone and the men who rented Bridget's floor space began to return, straggling in a few at a time, most haggard and dirty. It was only then that Derry came into the room again. He said hardly a word. He sat at the end of the table, concentrating on spinning a dagger between his fingers.

When Molly served up cups of the cabbage, I took my own, but Derry pushed his away. "Give my share to Joe."

The tension between us felt taut as a wire. My stomach was in knots as I ate my soup, and even though everyone in the room was talking, and the children were running around like wild things, Derry's silence was so heavy I felt suffocated by it.

Bridget suggested, "Why don't the two of you get out for a spell? Take a walk while it's cool. You been crowded with kids long enough. A couple in love should be alone once in a while."

I bit my tongue to keep from making a snide comment.

Derry's head jerked up. "A walk?"

"Aye. You could go out by the river."

He glanced at me and I recognized the watchful, waiting expression from my dream. I remembered waking with the need to touch him. And even though I told myself again that it was only the spell compelling me, I was afraid. It would be a bad idea to be alone with him tonight.

I rose. It was dusk outside, a breeze easing in through the open window for the first time all day. "I think I'll go lie down."

"A headache?" Derry asked.

"Just tired. Good night, Bridget."

I prayed he wouldn't follow, at least not right away. I stepped through the men arranging themselves on the floor. Some read newspapers by candlelight, others were smoking, no one sleeping yet. I felt their glances as I went to the darkened alcove and sat to take off my boots. I rolled down my stockings, feeling trapped and desperate again. Time was passing. One more day slipping away.

He blocked what light came from the candles beyond. I looked up. Derry stood before me, his hands braced on either side of the alcove.

"Are you all right?" he asked me.

"No," I said bitterly. "I want to go home. Or I want to find the archdruid. You promised to help me and today was just . . . just wasted. I only have until Samhain, Derry, or have you forgotten?"

"No." He squatted down. "I've been thinking of the best way to go about it."

"Deirdre said she would tell me whatever she knew."

"Which means nothing. She might not know anything. And she wanted something in return."

"But what if she does know something?"

"She doesn't. 'Tis a trick. They're good at that, you know."

"I can't just ignore the possibility. I want to search her out again."

"It's too risky—"

"You *promised* to help me. This is the only way."

"I'll go alone. I'll talk to them and—"

I grabbed his arm. "No. I'm going too. I need to hear for myself."

"You don't even trust me to tell you what they say?"

"This is my *life* we're talking about. I think it matters more to me than to you."

He went quiet. Then, very softly, he said, "What if I told you it did matter to me? That I want nothing more than to save you?"

The misery I saw in his eyes startled me more than his words—and then that misery changed to something else. I felt his desire as if he'd plunged me into it. His gaze fell to my mouth; I knew he wanted to kiss me. *Touch him. Kiss him.* My dream wrapped around me, ghosts of images and feelings. My own longing was so fierce it was all I could do to resist it.

You don't feel this way. Remember the geis. *He has to kill you.* I realized I was still holding his arm.

The lovespell was so strong. To fight it took everything, but I did it. I released him and scooted back. My heart pounded. "Turn around," I ordered. "I want to get undressed."

He paused, and then he rose, turning his back to me. My hands trembled as I fumbled with the buttons on my bodice, and then the lacings of my corset. It seemed to take forever, long enough that he said, "D'you need help?" in this voice that told me just how much he wished I would say yes.

"No," I said—too sharply. When I was down to my chemise, I grabbed the blanket to cover me and said, "All right. I'm done."

He bent to take off his boots, then unbuttoned his shirt, and I averted my gaze. I heard the fabric drop to the floor beside me, and then he grabbed it up, balling it to serve as a pillow. I heard the rustle of the blanket and his breathing. I turned onto my side, my back to him, closing my eyes to fall into my usual, uneasy sleep.

But I wasn't surprised when he said, "That story you told today . . ."

"I'm sorry I chose that one. I didn't know you were listening."

"Molly said everyone knew it."

"Everyone does. It's a favorite."

"Why? Why is it a story anyone tells?"

"Because it's beautiful. The things you did for love—" I suddenly realized what I was saying. The things *he*'d done for love. For *her.* The beautiful Grainne had been alive, and though I'd known the story was about him, I hadn't thought of her. No wonder he had been upset today. I'd been telling the story of a girl he'd loved, who was gone. Two thousand years or more gone.

He had *loved* her.

I was struck with a jealousy that robbed me of my voice. It took me a moment to remind myself that I had no business feeling it. "I'm sorry. I didn't mean to remind you of her. It must be terrible, and very painful, and—"

"It wasn't like you said." His voice was rough. "It's a pretty story, but it's just that. A story."

I was turning to face him before I knew it. He was just a deeper shadow within the darkness. He was very close— we were less than an inch apart, even with him shoved up against the wall. "What do you mean, it wasn't like that? You mean . . . it's not true?"

"True enough, in parts. But not the best of it."

"The best of it?"

"The love story. She was bespelled. She laid a *geis* on me so I was compelled as well."

"I know you didn't love her at first, but surely you grew to?"

"I don't know what it was." He seemed to be searching for a way to explain. "I felt . . . it wasn't real. She would have married Finn if not for the *ball seirce.*"

"But she was beautiful."

He sighed. I felt the warmth of his breath. "Aye, she was beautiful. What has that to do with it?"

"Surely you felt—you must have wanted her. But you resisted her—"

He laughed derisively.

I went hot, but I could not stop now. I wanted to know. "You *did* resist her, didn't you? Out of loyalty to Finn, and to protect her. That part of the tale was true?"

"It seems strange that people know that. That it matters to anyone. Whose business is it?"

"Not everyone's heard that part of it. Patrick never had. But it was how my grandmother told it. And I always thought it was romantic, but if it didn't happen that way—"

"It did happen that way. Though 'twas nothing romantic about it. I felt responsible for her. I hoped the *ball seirce* would wear off quickly—sometimes it does—and then there was the chance that she would change her mind and lift the *geis* so I could take her back. To marry Finn . . . any other lass would have thought it an honor. I wanted to make it easy for him to forgive her."

It was so different from my imaginings that I wasn't certain I wanted to hear the rest. But there was a part of me that wanted it to be different, that thought *he didn't love her* and was happy for it. *You're as bespelled as she was.*

I said, "That was . . . considerate."

"I have my moments. And I wanted forgiveness, too, don't forget. But Grainne didn't see it that way."

"She didn't?"

"Her love for me wasn't real, but it felt real to her. She was a princess. She was used to having what she wanted—a little like Lucy."

I didn't want to think of Lucy, of him kissing her, or of what we had in common. "And what Grainne wanted was you."

"She knew I meant to resist her and she spent every moment working against me. She wanted to make sure Finn wouldn't forgive either of us. And she succeeded."

"Oh. So you're saying . . . she seduced you."

"One day she was bathing her feet in the river, and she said, 'Oh, look how the water splashes up my skirt. It's braver than you, isn't it, Diarmid? Who would've ever thought water would be braver than a Fianna warrior?' Things like that. All the time. I won't deny I wanted her. She was beautiful, as you say. And we were together. Bound. My fate was tied up with hers, wasn't it?"

I won't deny I wanted her. "I see. It wasn't as romantic as it sounded."

"Like your white knight, Patrick. Nothing's ever as it seems. You can keep thinking of it as a romance if you like, if it makes you think better of me."

"Derry, I—"

I heard his movement, and the next thing I knew, his hand was at my cheek. I felt his touch in the deepest part of me, a flare of light, as if something were breaking open, the same way I'd felt when he'd kissed me. He moved closer—the inch between us disappeared. And then he stopped as if he were waiting for me to push his hand away.

I was supposed to resist him. There was Patrick. My family. My life.

But I did nothing. The yearning for his touch paralyzed me. He traced my cheekbone, the line of my jaw, and with each touch a light seemed to grow and pulse inside of me. I had no breath and no will. It wasn't until his thumb brushed my lips and lingered, pressing like a kiss, that I came to myself, that I remembered who he was and that I was letting him do these things. I grabbed his hand. "Don't. Please don't."

"Grace—"

"I want to ask you something."

I could feel his surprise in the darkness. "All right."

"Aidan told me not to go with you. Once he knew your name, he told me not to go. He said it was like the legend, but—"

"Like the legend?"

"You and Grainne. Because that's my name too."

He started. I was still holding onto his hand, and he drew it away. "What?"

"My given name is Grainne. My father chose it, but my mother—everyone—has always called me Grace. She says it sounds more American."

He backed up so hard he thudded against the wall.

I tried to laugh. "Funny, isn't it? Aidan thought so. Well, not funny, exactly. But that's when he told me not to run off with you. He was so afraid I would, but he's the one who put me in your hands. He told me I would think he had betrayed me, but that he hadn't, that he never would. So I don't understand. What's between you and my brother?"

"I barely know him." His voice was a whisper.

"But you were the one who made him leave the gambling hell the night that Patrick learned the truth about who you were. You took him to Patrick's stables to keep him safe. I thought it was Patrick, but Aidan said it was you. Why? Did you know he was a stormcaster then? Is that why you did it?"

"No. I didn't know. I should have seen it—all the signs were there—but I didn't."

"Then I don't understand. Why?"

I was tense, waiting, wanting his answer and dreading it in the same moment.

Finally, he said in a voice so low I had to strain to hear it, "Because you love him. I did it for you."

"But I'd slapped you. I'd told you I wanted you to leave me alone."

He let out his breath. "I knew I wouldn't. I couldn't."

"Because I might be the *veleda*," I said.

"Aye, that, and . . ."

"And what?"

I felt him weighing what he might say, and suddenly I didn't want to hear it. I was terrified to know. I rolled so my back was to him again. "Never mind. It's not important."

I closed my eyes, willing him away. The memory of his touch lingered on my skin. *Fight it! You're no better than Lucy.* But the spell he'd cast wound more tightly than ever.

I had to find a way to escape him, whatever it took. I could not wait another day. "I want to find the *sidhe*. Tomorrow."

I expected him to argue, but instead, he agreed. "Tomorrow."

It was a long time until I slept.

ELEVEN

The same day
Patrick

S he's disappeared," Patrick told Jules LaPlante, the reporter from the *New York Times*. "We fear gangs are involved."

"A kidnapping, you mean?" LaPlante's pencil paused.

"Mr. Devlin's success makes him a target," put in Daire Donn, who stood at the window of Patrick's study. "These ruffians scarcely think of what Mr. Devlin and the Fenian Brotherhood have done for the Irish. Finn's Warriors are the worst of them."

LaPlante said, "Yes, well, there are too many hungry. Too many without work. The Warriors have become heroes to them."

Patrick turned on him angrily. "And so it's all right to kidnap innocent young girls to make their point? My *fiancée*, for God's sake. Am I just to sit here and excuse them?"

"Absolutely not, Mr. Devlin," LaPlante said.

"I'm offering a reward for any information."

"How much?"

Daire Donn looked over his shoulder and said mildly, "Perhaps we should wait for a ransom note, my friend. You don't want to pay more than necessary. And these gangs think so small. Why offer five hundred when they'll ask for only two?"

Patrick jerked his hand through his hair in frustration. "I don't care. I'll pay anything. Anything at all."

LaPlante asked, "Could the girl have just run off? A new fiancé, a wedding . . . Perhaps it's merely a spate of nerves."

"No," Patrick said firmly.

Daire Donn smiled, though his brown eyes were hard. "Just put in the paper what we tell you, eh? She's missing, Finn's Warriors are involved, and there's a reward for any information."

LaPlante nodded. The *Times* was a friend of the Brotherhood; Patrick knew he would write whatever they told him to. He hoped it would help. Grace had seemingly disappeared into thin air. He had the entire police force at his disposal, and they'd discovered nothing. The guards here that day had seen and heard nothing. The maid had not returned from her day off and no one could find her.

Daire Donn showed LaPlante to the door, and Patrick sank into a chair. He was sleeping badly, dreaming of smoky rooms and danger whenever he did, and the words *Find Aidan* had taken up residence in his head.

"Patrick."

Grace's mother. She and Grace's grandmother had moved into his house only that morning. "What did you tell the reporter?" she asked.

"I've put out a reward. It's the most I can do until we know more." She looked so worried that he added, "I'm certain she's all right." He did believe that was true. If the Fianna had Grace, they would keep her physically safe until Samhain. It was Diarmid and the lovespot he was worried about.

"Are you comfortable?" he asked Mrs. Knox. "Is everything to your liking?"

She smiled at him wanly. "Yes, very much so. And I'm grateful for your protection, though I'm still not certain we have need of it."

"If Finn's Warriors are involved, you do. They were the ones in your yard that night. If they're fearless enough to come to that part of town . . . I feel better that you're here." He'd also set a constant guard at the Knox house, in case Grace showed up there.

He'd done what he could, but he felt helpless, and he hated it. *Come back, Grace,* he found himself praying every other moment. *Come back to me.*

Mrs. Knox said, "Patrick, there's something I must ask you—"

A flurry of footsteps interrupted her question.

Bres was at the study door, a harried butler bustling behind him, along with Daire Donn.

"Sir," the butler said, red-faced, "I'm so sorry, but—"

"It's all right, John," Patrick said, seeing Bres's urgency. "I'm sorry, Mrs. Knox. Could we talk later?"

"Of course," she said. "Yes, of course."

Bres waited until she left before he said, "The maid's been found. Apparently, she disliked the guards. She had a run-in with one of them and decided 'twas better not to return."

Servants left without notice all the time; it was one of his mother's most frequent complaints. They'd lost three maids in the last year, all of them over the most trivial things. The demand for a good maid in the city was high; it was easy for them to find a job more to their liking. It had never mattered to Patrick before now. "What did she say about Grace?"

"There *was* a visitor that day. A Miss Rose Fitzgerald."

"Rose." Patrick let out a sigh of relief.

"This girl is—?"

"Grace's best friend. I should have thought of her, but I haven't seen her in weeks. I'd thought she was out of town." Patrick was striding to the study door as he spoke, Bres and Daire Donn following.

He didn't bother with the carriage. Rose's house was only blocks away. When they reached it, Patrick showed his card to the maid who answered the door. "Might we call upon Miss Fitzgerald?"

The maid took them to the parlor, which was large and crowded both with furniture and with knickknacks from the Fitzgeralds' travels: strange shells and feathers, a coconut and two exotic stuffed birds, fans and maps, magnifying glasses and on one table a stereoscope next to a box of cards. Daire

Donn studied the stereoscope curiously before he turned to rifle through the cards.

Only a few moments passed, but it seemed like forever before Rose arrived. She came into the room with such a cheerful, welcoming smile that Patrick realized she didn't know anything.

"Why, hello, Patrick," she said. She glanced at the others.

Patrick introduced them. "We've come to ask you about Grace. You know she's disappeared."

Rose's smile died. She looked suddenly uncertain. "Disappeared? No, I had no idea."

"Two days ago. We thought you might know where she is."

Rose looked at him wide-eyed. "Why would I know that?"

Now Patrick realized with a sinking heart that she was lying. Which meant Rose thought she was protecting Grace. Which meant . . . he didn't want to think about what it meant.

"The maid said you'd paid a visit to Miss Knox the day she disappeared," said Bres in such a friendly, confiding tone that Patrick saw Rose struggle with the urge to tell. It explained better than words how the king had entranced an entire country.

But Rose was also fiercely loyal to Grace. Patrick might have appreciated it another time; now he only felt desperate when she said, "Oh. Yes, I did. We had a very nice chat."

"And then?" Bres asked.

"Then I went home."

"You don't seem worried, lass," Daire Donn noted. "Your best friend has disappeared, and you ask not a single question?"

Patrick said, "She's in danger, Rose. Whatever you saw, whatever you know, you must tell us. Please."

"I don't know anything," she insisted.

"Come, lass," Daire Donn urged. "As you can see, her fiancé is imagining the worst. Why make him worry?"

She wavered. "But Aidan said—"

"Aidan?" Patrick echoed.

"He made me promise not to tell. He promised she would be fine."

"Where is she? What happened?" Patrick demanded.

Rose took a deep breath. "I didn't know she hadn't come back. Aidan said she would be all right, and he's her brother, so I believe him. But I'll admit, that *he's* involved worries me."

"Aidan?"

She shook her head. "Derry."

Patrick's heart sank deeper.

Daire Donn gave Patrick an understanding look before he said to Rose, "Tell us what happened, lass."

"I . . . I brought her a note that day. From Aidan. He asked us to meet him at Fulton Market. She'd been so worried about him, you know. She wanted to go and so I . . . I went with her."

"How did you get past the guards?"

"Oh, that was easy. The one at the front door was very sweet."

And a liar too. The guard had said nothing about Rose when they'd questioned him. Patrick glanced at Bres, whose expression had hardened. A king, yes, but not a friendly one now. One who looked fearsome, and Patrick was glad not to be on his bad side.

"I see," Bres said.

"It wasn't his fault," Rose said. "Really. You shouldn't blame him."

"What happened then?" Patrick asked.

"We met Aidan at the market. He wanted Grace to go on the ferry with him so they could talk, but he had to walk me back to my carriage, and he missed the boat. And then I saw Derry with her on the deck. Aidan said it was all right—he said he and Derry were friends, and he would wait for the ferry to return and bring her home. He said Derry needed to talk to her and that was all. You know Aidan, Patrick. He can be so . . . so . . . Well, he made me promise not to say anything. I didn't want Grace to get into trouble, but I didn't know she was gone. Truly I didn't."

Patrick hardly heard her. "Fulton Market, you said. They were on the Brooklyn ferry?"

She nodded.

"Then, we know where they are, don't we?" Bres said with satisfaction.

"Aidan wouldn't put her in danger, Patrick," Rose said ardently. "He's her brother—"

"Where is he now?"

"I don't know. I haven't seen him since."

"How did he find you?"

"He waited in my yard until I appeared. He nearly frightened me to death."

"And he gave you no idea of where he'd been? Of what he'd been doing?" Patrick asked.

"No," Rose said with a sigh.

"I need you to think very hard. We need to find Aidan as well. I think he may be in trouble."

"Aidan *is* trouble." Rose scowled. "But he said nothing of where he'd been. He looked like he'd been sleeping in a hearth somewhere. He smelled of smoke."

Slowly, it came together. Aidan calling Diarmid a friend. Aidan smelling of smoke. The fire in the tenement that had roused the Fianna.

Aidan had joined them.

It was not good news. Grace's brother, whom she loved, was on the other side. Aidan had helped the Fianna kidnap her. And now Grace had been two days with Diarmid Ua Duibhne. Two days with the lovespot.

Daire Donn put a hand on Patrick's shoulder. It didn't soothe him.

Bres said, "Thank you, Miss Fitzgerald. You've been most useful."

Patrick said, "If you hear anything more from Aidan, Rose—anything at all, you *must* contact me. He needs help. I can help him. Tell him that, if you see him, would you? Tell him I can help him."

She nodded, looking frightened. "Yes, I will."

"And if you think of anything that might help us find him, or Grace . . ."

"I'll let you know that too. I'm so sorry, Patrick. But . . . Aidan is her brother. What was I to do?"

He strode to the door without answering, without even saying good-bye, hearing the other two make apologies behind him. When they were outside, Daire Donn said, "We know where they are, Patrick. 'Tis only a matter of time before we find them."

"Time." Patrick spat the word. "We don't have time. There's the lovespot, or don't you remember?"

Bres sighed. "Aye. You'd best accustom yourself to it. 'Twill already be done."

"However, it's only been a short time. The lovespell will wear off quickly if we get her soon enough," Daire Donn assured him.

Patrick said hoarsely, "Send every man we have out to look for her. We'll put up 'Wanted' posters everywhere. I want her back."

"And we shall have her back," Bres said.

But Patrick's fear was beyond comfort.

TWELVE

July 23
Grace

I dreamed again of the ship, its sails fat with wind and the deck rolling beneath my feet, and that *presence* hovering as if it waited for something. Then narrow streets, the *sidhe* coming out of hiding as I passed, forming a gauntlet I must run to reach Aidan, who was shouting, *"The key. We need the key!"* before he faded into darkness.

I woke in the middle of the night, breathing hard as if I'd been running.

"Sssh," Derry murmured, not really awake. He pulled me back against his chest. At his touch, my terror eased, the last vestiges of the nightmare disappeared. I closed my eyes and went back to sleep. This time I dreamed of the two of us sitting on a beach beneath a leafy maple, and I leaned back against his chest while his laughter rumbled.

When I woke again, I found myself tangled with him. His arms were around me, and his hand was in my hair, as it had been in my dream, and it felt as if I was exactly where I was meant to be.

But then I remembered everything, and I was afraid of how much I liked being in his arms.

What he'd said last night about wanting to save my life was a lie.

Carefully, I disentangled his hand from my hair, waiting for him to wake, but he slept so deeply it was as if he'd been spelled. He looked relaxed and peaceful in a way I'd never seen.

I rose and dressed. I expected him to wake at any moment, but he didn't, not even when I left the alcove and tiptoed out of the room, through the few boarders still sleeping. In the other room, faint dawn light crept through the open window. The air was already warm; it would be another hot day. Bridget was sewing at the table, which held bread and a jug of milk with a faint bluish cast. Swill milk, Derry had told me, along with a caution not to drink it, because you never knew what was in it: chalk or river water or something worse. But I had a choice to drink or not, unlike Bridget's children, who had nothing else.

Bridget looked past me.

"He's still sleeping," I told her, sitting down at the table. Bridget pushed the bread toward me. I shook my head. "Thank you, but I'm not hungry."

"There's enough," she said.

But I knew there wasn't, and what I'd told her was true. My dreams still haunted me. I wanted Derry to wake up. I wanted him to stay asleep. I tried not to think of the way I'd let him touch me last night, or the yearning that seemed to have lodged inside me.

How did one fight such a thing? What had Miogach said? *Like all love, it fades with absence.* But Derry wasn't absent, and I was afraid it was growing worse. No, I *knew* it was growing worse.

Today must be the day I escaped. I glanced at the door, tempted again just to walk out. But he'd promised to help me, and I was afraid to confront the *sidhe* on my own. I would take his help, and once we'd learned what we could, I would run.

I heard a commotion from the bedroom, and I looked over my shoulder to see Derry racing out, barefoot and shirtless, panicked.

He saw me and slid to a stop before he crashed into the table. "You're here," he breathed.

Bridget *tsk*ed. "You keep too tight a grip, lad, and you'll push her clean away."

He ignored her. "How did you get out without waking me?"

"You were sound asleep."

"I never sleep like that."

"Well, don't look at me as if it's my fault. It's not as if *I* cast a spell on *you.*"

"She didn't go anywhere," Bridget said. "But I'm beginning to think she should be runnin'."

I smiled sweetly at him. "I'm waiting for you to take me on that walk you promised."

"Walk?" he asked blankly.

"You remember." I gave him a pointed look. "You said we could search for wild things. Deer. Owls. Things like that."

Bridget laughed. "The only wild things you'll find around here are boys."

I saw that Derry understood, though, and he didn't look happy about it. "I'll get my things."

He disappeared into the other room, reappearing moments later with his shirt and boots in his hands. The muscles in his arms and his back flexed as he dressed, and I looked to the window instead.

"Do you think it's too early?" I asked.

"Perhaps not early enough. They like dawn and twilight—the change of worlds, the edges. But maybe we'll be lucky." He said the last drily.

"Aye, you might see a rat or two," Bridget said. "Or a hog."

Derry grimaced.

"A hog? You goin' lookin' for hogs? C'n I come?" Molly asked.

Derry smiled at her. "Not today, lass. Some other time."

"But you said you'd play ball with us today."

"And so I will." He tousled her hair. "Be good for your mama and we'll play when I get back."

"We'd best get started," I said.

He took my hand to lead me down the stairs, and as always, I felt him like the pull of gravity. I thought of the press of his thumb against my lips.

Stop.

When we got to the bottom of the stairs, he warned, "They might not tell you anything, especially if they know how badly you want it."

"Then I won't tell them how badly I want it."

"They'll sense it. Even I can feel it."

"I'll just have to take the risk. I could have gone without you, you know. You were sleeping like the dead this morning. I could have sneaked out—"

"Aye. I don't understand it. Anyone could have come in and slit my throat, or yours. Are you sure you didn't bewitch me?"

"I don't even know how to do such a thing. And why would I, anyway?"

"To escape."

"I actually *want* you to come with me today, as hard as that is to believe. The fairies frighten me, truthfully. You know what they're like and if nothing else, you'll try to keep me alive, for now. Until we know . . . what can be done. So where do we start? Where would they be, do you think?"

"Wherever you are," Diarmid said grimly. "They're watching already. If we stand here long enough, they'll start gathering. But I'd rather they not know where we're staying."

I shuddered. "What a lovely thought. Just what I want, fairies serenading me outside the window."

"Better than me singing," Derry noted. "Though my song won't turn you into a madwoman—or at least, I don't think it will. Truthfully, it might be a close thing."

I laughed.

He looked surprised, and then pleased, and his smile brought heat creeping into my cheeks and I thought of my dream again, and his touch.

Quickly, I said, "So where do we go?"

"The river's a good start. The edge of things, as I said."

"Which direction is the river?"

He paused as if debating how much to tell me. "This way."

He stayed very close, though he never tried to take my arm or touch me. I felt his wariness as he led me away from the tenement, putting himself between me and any alleyway or darkened alcove. But I sensed we weren't going directly there. He turned down one street after another, confusing the route, and while I was annoyed at his lack of trust, I also admired his cleverness.

"I can't run from you," I told him. "You're too fast. So there's no sense trying to hide the way back to the ferry."

He slid me a glance. "I'm fast, but you're canny. And stubborn. You'd run right into danger if I let you. Think of it this way: I'm saving you from yourself."

"How noble of you."

"I'd call it selfish instead. If you go running off, I'll be facing Finn's punishment, instead of joining the fight the way I want."

"I've never met anyone who loves a battle as you do."

"We're warriors. But no one loves battle—not after they've been in a real one." He looked up at the sky. "It's hard to remember that I used to think it exciting. When I was small, I'd hear that thunder and the clash of swords and horses galloping, and wish I was in the thick of it. The Fianna rode through the village sometimes and . . . well, there wasn't a lad that didn't want to be one of them. But when you're in the middle of it, with those ravens screaming and men coming at you with death in their eyes . . . the life of a farmer starts looking good."

"A farmer? You? Somehow that's hard to picture."

"Is it? I'm guessing I wouldn't have any talent for it. The closest I ever got to growing anything was spitting out an apple seed." He looked at his hands, turning them over, holding one out to me, palm up. "Look at that. Calluses still, even though I haven't thrown a spear in . . . two thousand years or more." He laughed. "Two thousand years. 'Tis impossible to think it."

"It's difficult for me to imagine as well, that it's true and you're . . . who you are. Or that there really was an Aengus Og who fostered you and a Manannan who taught you. That they were really gods."

"It didn't seem so odd then. They were gods, but not as you imagine them, I think. You couldn't trust any of them, really, but Aengus loved me, and I him."

I was so fascinated by the things he said that the world seemed to dissolve around me as we walked. The way he spoke of gods and monsters that existed in some far place and time—not just as legends, but as perplexing, real people that he'd *known*—made me forget how incredible it was.

"Aengus wasn't happy when I joined the Fianna. He never understood war. He thought it was a waste of time."

"He *was* the god of love, after all."

"Aye." Derry's smile was soft. "He thought it strange that I wanted the Fianna more than I wanted . . . well . . . love. When I told him I was going to take the tests, he threatened to turn me into a salmon."

I couldn't help laughing again. "There's an idea."

"But he let me go," Derry went on. "Once he accepted it, he was a little too helpful. Finn had to bar him from the tests."

"What were the tests?"

"You had to know the twelve books of poetry. Then you had to dig a hole up to your waist and stand there with a shield and a hazel rod while the others cast spears at you. If one hit you, you weren't fit."

"What were the twelve books of poetry for?"

He flashed me a grin. "Finn likes to hear it. He had five Druid poets at one time, so he could choose one according to his mood. And knowing the tales meant you could at least try to predict what a god or fairy might do."

"What else?"

"You had to run through the woods with the others chasing. If you were hurt, or your hair came unplaited, or a single stick cracked beneath your foot, you were out. Then you had to leap over a stick your own height, bend under one no higher than your knee, and take out a thorn from your foot while you were running."

"Was being one of the Fianna worth it?"

He shrugged. "'Twas a good life, when we were home."

"I suppose so. All those Druids to do your bidding—"

He snorted. "A Druid? Not likely."

"But you said Finn had Druid poets. And there was Neasa—"

"No one could make Neasa do what she didn't want. The only one I ever saw her listen to was Glasny, and she didn't do that half the time."

"Who was Glasny?"

"Her . . . assistant, I guess you'd call him. Her protector. All the *veledas* have one."

"All the *veledas*? I guess that's something else that was lost through time."

He eyed me thoughtfully. "Maybe not."

His words sent a shiver through me. As did the way he looked at me, as if he were remembering last night. He seemed to be implying that *he* was my protector, but protectors didn't kill the one they meant to protect, did they?

I said, "I could like someone who did what I told him."

"Then you wouldn't have liked Glasny. He thought Neasa should listen to *him*, and Neasa thought otherwise. Finn didn't like him. He thought Glasny interfered too much, but really it was just that Finn was always trying to make Neasa do what *he* wanted. She didn't do that either, even when they were lovers."

The way Finn had taken a strand of my hair between his fingers, the way he'd looked at me as if he wanted something he didn't know how to ask for—suddenly, it made sense. "Lovers? You never told me that."

"Does it matter?"

"No, I guess not. It's just . . . you said I looked like her."

I felt him thinking, considering. "You do. Finn saw it too. But you're not Neasa, Grace. No one would mistake it."

"Because she had so much power and I've none?"

"Because you're *you*." He halted, stopping me with a light touch. "Here we are."

We stood before a warehouse fronting the river. The building looked abandoned, the loading dock ramshackle and sloping, the great doors closed. As we drew closer, I saw that the doors bore large, rusted padlocks. When we stepped up to the dock, Derry came up behind me and put his hands on my waist. When I started to protest, he said, "Can you get up there by yourself?" and then, without waiting for an answer, lifted me onto the dock, jumping up after. He went to one of the giant doors and kicked the padlock, which broke easily beneath his force.

"I think that sort of thing is against the law," I said.

His expression was wry. "You think Patrick won't have the whole police force after me once he finds out where you are? And I'm a thief, too, as I recall. If I'm going to hang, it doesn't much matter how many other laws I break."

"Don't say things like that."

He raised a brow I could only just see through his hair.

I said, "I won't let them arrest you."

"Some things even a *veleda* can't promise." He put his weight to the door, and it slid open with much squealing and creaking. "Come on. But be careful. This place is falling apart."

The doors on the river side were closed as well, and the building was cavernous and vacant, with deep shadows in the corners. Pieces of the roof were missing, and morning light slanted through the holes. There was a fluttering rush of air and noise, and a flock of birds rose squawking, sending bits of straw and dust scattering down from the beams. I heard the scrabble of rats.

"How do you know of this place?" I asked, following him inside, stepping over the parts of the floor where planks had crumbled to reveal the water below, lapping against the tarred pilings that supported the warehouse.

"Hugh told me about it. He said they come here sometimes to avoid police. Or to have a party." Derry kicked at an empty whiskey bottle, which rolled sloppily across the floor before it plopped through a hole into the water. "A good place to be away from prying eyes."

It was too silent. Eerie. Now that we were here, I wished I hadn't come.

Derry said, "There's still time to go if you want. If you've changed your mind, just say the word."

I shook my head. "No. I want to do this."

Half the loading door on the river side had sagged away, and I walked over to it. He came up beside me, pushing the rotting timbers so they fell onto what was left of the dock below. I looked out over the water, at the full sails of one or two schooners, thin gray plumes of smoke from the steamers, and beyond them Governors Island, the high round walls of the fortress called Castle Williams.

My dread grew by the moment. "When will they come?"

Derry pressed his hand to the small of my back. I went tingly and hot, as if waves of light had rushed into me all at once. "Before you'll want them to," he said quietly. "Before you're ready."

"But I am ready."

"No, you're not. Grace, listen well. Their words have more than one meaning—always trust the worse one."

"All right."

"Let them do what they want to me. Don't ask them to do you a favor. Don't be in their debt."

"They won't be turning you into a stag if I have anything to say about it," I said firmly, surprising myself at the strength of my protectiveness.

Derry seemed surprised as well, and I waited for him to tease, but he only said, "There are ways to turn me back. Or there were. Ossian will know, and Finn. They'll know who to look for to help anyway. They did it once before, with Ossian's mother. And if that's what the *sidhe* want, you won't be able to stop it, not without trading too much. Remember what I said? The more you want something, the more it will cost, and they already know you don't wish me changed. Bargain with them for the archdruid. That's what matters."

Those cunning faces. Deirdre's beautiful but expressionless eyes. That terrible, terrible draw, as if they meant to suck away my soul. What made me think I was ready for them? I couldn't ever be ready for them. "I should have left you back there. I should have done this alone. I didn't think; I forgot about the stag," I said.

"At least there's no hunting allowed in the city."

"Don't joke. Please."

He laughed softly in my ear. "I'm happy to know you care—truly I am—but don't care too much, lass. *Don't let them know it.*"

I heard a sound. A rasping behind us. Derry stepped away, whispering, "The archdruid. Don't let them distract you from it."

I felt the loss of his warmth and his reassurance, but he was right: I had to stand alone. I heard voices, whispers and giggles and singing, and then I felt their longing for my power, as strong and compelling as it had been in the alley. I was drowning in their song. *Come to us. Let us touch you. Let us have you* . . . My blood prickled with the call of magic. I swayed toward them.

"You can do this, Grace," Derry reminded me.

I gathered my strength and my will and turned to face them.

They emerged through the dimness in a solid mass. Ten, perhaps more, all glowing faintly silver. The children of the *sidhe*, beautiful and lithe. *"Monsters don't always look like monsters,"* Derry had said, and though he'd been talking about the Fomori, he could just as well have been referring to the *sidhe*.

I said to them, "Come closer. I wish to speak with you."

They stopped, parted like the Red Sea, and Deirdre came from their center—my opposite in every way, everything I was not. She moved so smoothly that I felt clumsy and awkward in comparison, an embarrassment to the name Grace. Straight blond hair rippled to her waist. Her blue eyes were an exceptionally clear color.

The others followed closely as she approached me. She stopped only a foot away, and then she glanced at Derry and said, "Ah, sweet Diarmid. Handsome as always. You would still make a good stag."

The archdruid, I told myself. "I'm the one who has business with you today."

"You wish a gift from the *sidhe*?"

"Not a gift. A trade."

"What have you to trade?" Another glance at Derry. "Your beautiful boy, perhaps? I would like that." She stepped up to him, pressing herself against him while he held himself rigid. She laid her hand upon his chest as she'd done in the alleyway. "Ah, the things I could do to him."

Their longing for me shifted. Now it was him they wanted. *She* wanted. Her thoughts whispered in my head. *And he wants me, too, don't you see it? You see how he must clench his fists to keep from touching me?*

And I did. I saw it. Fingers clenching.

Give him to me. He knew one of my sisters, did he tell you that? They lived in a house on a hill and he loved her for a time. He has always loved the sidhe. *He wants to love me too. Can you feel it?*

I could. I did. I saw how his eyes darkened. Deirdre played with the buttons on his shirt, and he let her and he wanted her. She was so perfect that I felt a sinking despair. How could I begin to compete with such a creature? Jealousy flooded me. He'd told me to let them do what they would to him—because this was what he wanted? He wanted *her*?

He was mine. He belonged to me. *"The more you want something, the more it will cost."* Suddenly, I didn't care if I gave them everything. She could not have him.

"Grace," Derry rasped, and it was as if I woke from a dream. This was a glamour. That wasn't desire in his eyes but wariness. His fists were clenched in anger.

Don't let them know how badly you want it.

I was startled at how easily the fairies had read me. But no, these feelings weren't real. Not my desire, and not my jealousy. Deirdre had only met one enchantment with another.

I said, "He's free to do as he likes. He doesn't belong to me and I can't bargain for him. There's something else I need from you."

Deirdre turned from him. Her blue eyes glittered. "What is that?"

"What do you know about the archdruid?"

Deirdre dropped her hand from Derry's chest and backed away. I tried to hide my relief. The others murmured. Their silver glow pulsed. *"Come with us. Let us touch you."* I shut my ears to the song and kept my eyes on Deirdre.

She flicked her hand and their song faded to a hush. "We will do you this favor and tell you what we know."

I felt Derry's alarm. "No favor," I said. "A bargain. We each get what we want, or there will be no trade."

"What have you to give us?"

The murmur again. *"Let us touch you. Come with us."*

Again, the prickle in my blood, my fingers itching with it. "What do you want? Besides my power—that I cannot give you."

"We could simply take it."

Derry said, "You could try."

"Are you so dishonorable that you would take from me what I've no wish to give you?" I asked. I looked at Derry. "Perhaps we should search out another group. One more . . . accommodating."

"Wait," Deirdre said. "We can bargain, *veleda*."

"Another story," said one of the fairies, drawing out the word in a wicked hiss. He stepped forward, his dark eyes flashing. "We wish a story, Deirdre."

She cocked her head at me. "Hmm. Perhaps. We liked the story you told the other day."

"The story I told?"

"Though perhaps you made Diarmid too good."

I understood then which story she meant. The Pursuit of Diarmid and Grainne. If the *sidhe* had heard it, that meant they had been close to the tenement. Derry hadn't wanted them near where we're staying, and neither did I. Too late.

Deirdre said, "You have made of him something he is not. He's like every other boy, clumsy and selfish. You are fated to be with him, but perhaps not in the way you wish. Do you feel how bound you are? Has he compelled you as he did the other one?"

"There was power in the tale," whispered the boy, licking his lips. "I would drink another."

"Yes, we feasted well on it," Deirdre said. "Though we'd heard it before."

"Another one," said the boy, and the others took up the call. *Another one, another one,* unspoken words in my mind, a rush of noise like flapping wings or wind through branches, growing louder until I wanted to put my hands to my ears.

Deirdre said, "We'll trade for another story, but this time it must be one we have not heard."

The noise died. A story they hadn't heard. It seemed easy enough, but I made myself parse her words the way Derry had advised. What other meaning could I read in them?

I felt their desire for my power and the burn of the response in my blood. This could be another trick. But through their song I heard something else, whispers of notes, so soft I had to concentrate to hear it, and even then it was distant and disjointed. Another song, one that didn't belong to them, one that said, *Trust . . . She will . . . not fail you.*

It told me to believe her, and I did. I could not have said why. "I agree."

As if ruled by one mind, the fairies sat in a circle on the planked floor of the warehouse, lifting their faces to me like children. I racked my brain, trying to think of a story they might not know. Then it came to me.

"This story is about a lady under a curse," I began, and their halos shimmered brightly with approval. "She was a fairy herself, and she lived on the island of Shalott, in a tower that overlooked Camelot, where King Arthur lived with all his knights. She was told she could never look directly down on Camelot or she would be cursed forever. She was only to look in a mirror that showed her what was happening in the castle and about its lands."

I went on, telling them every detail of the Tennyson poem I loved. How the lady watched the fishermen and farmers, pretty girls picking flowers and young pages with crimson cloaks, couples courting and knights whose armor shone in the sun. As I spoke, the glow that surrounded the *sidhe* grew brighter.

"But the mirror showed only a reflection of life, not life itself, and the Lady of Shalott grew weary of watching shadows. She was alone, and lonely."

The halo shimmered so that it was hard to see the fairies within it. I felt as if the air were pulling me, touching, tasting, licking, sucking. My skin stung.

"Then one day, she saw a handsome knight in her mirror. He had coal-black hair and rode a horse with a saddle covered in jewels. It was Lancelot, the most loyal of King Arthur's knights, riding out from Camelot. The Lady of Shalott fell in love with him so suddenly and completely that she left the mirror and went to the window to look at him, and the mirror cracked. The curse fell hard upon her."

The glow was so bright now I could not see them. I realized that they *were* feasting on the words, as Deirdre had said, drawing the power I put into them. *My* power. But this was the bargain I'd made, and so I let them do it, and while I was afraid of what Derry had told me about the way the *sidhe* could suck a Druid dry, I felt in control of how much of me they took, and it was bearable.

"She left the tower and climbed into a boat, letting the river carry her from the island. The Lady of Shalott looked upon the Camelot she had only ever seen in the mirror. She smelled the clean, fresh air and watched the farmers and the girls playing along the riverbank. Her heart grew so full and sad at the thought that she had never truly lived, she sang her last song, and in singing it, she died. Her curse was that she must only view life from afar, but she chose to follow her love instead, and to die rather than live a life of shadows."

I let the last words fade. There was silence. Birds gathered again on the beams. The halo around the *sidhe* pulsed and turned soft at the edges, sated.

Deirdre sighed. "'Twas a good tale. Do you think she regretted her choice?"

"No," I said.

Deirdre glanced at Derry, and then back to me as she rose in one fluid, impossibly lovely motion. She gestured to the others. They began to leave.

"I would have your part, Deirdre," I said. "The trade. Or do you not keep your promises?"

She said, "I know nothing of an archdruid. Nor do any of us. But I know of one who might."

"Who?"

"He lives by the sea. Not far from here. There are powerful spells there—or there were. They have diminished. We do not go there anymore."

"Where? By what sea?"

"We do not pay attention to names." Deirdre's smile was coy. "Those are for mortal folk."

"That's not good enough." I tried not to sound desperate. "I gave you a good story. You owe me more."

"I can tell you what I remember of it. There were many people. Mortals bathing. Smoke. A roaring—'twas like angry kelpies—from cars on silver ribbons. And . . . there was a sign." She furrowed her beautiful, smooth brow. "A sun and a moon. A shadowed sickle. Ah . . . 'tis all I remember."

It had been a bad bargain after all. "It's not enough!"

"'Tis all I have to give you, but for my advice: Do not trust in love. 'Twill prove your undoing."

Her words sank into me, a warning and a curse. When she turned again to leave, I said, "There's something else, Deirdre. Something I *would* ask a favor for."

She stopped. "A favor?"

"Grace, no," Derry protested.

"Can you take back a gift that another has bestowed?" I looked at him.

"You're asking me to remove the *ball seirce*?" Deirdre asked.

I heard Derry's gasp.

My fierce hope died the very next moment, when Deirdre shook her head.

"I fear not, milady. I did not give it, and I cannot undo it."

"I see." I did not dare look at him now. "Thank you, then. There's nothing else."

I stood there wordlessly as the *sidhe* melted back into the shadows and vanished, and I was alone with him again.

THIRTEEN

Moments later
Diarmid

It was done.

It had been all he could do to stand there, to say nothing, to do nothing. Grace had been calm and clever, and in the end there had been a confidence in her that reminded him again of Neasa. He hadn't been sure what would happen when Deirdre had pressed herself against him and he'd felt Grace's fear and anger. He'd expected to find himself a stag. Yet Grace had made a decent bargain, and he was proud of her.

Grace's request to take away the lovespot unsettled him, though. It bothered him that he didn't know why she'd asked. And his fear that Deirdre might do it surprised him. He'd had the *ball seirce* most of his life. He'd used it—sometimes without thought or question—and he had spent the last years regretting it, hating it. Yet . . . who would he be without it? Himself? Or someone else entirely?

Grace said, "That wasn't at all helpful."

"You didn't ask me if I wanted it gone." The words came out before he could stop them.

"I don't care if you want it gone. It's a mean-spirited gift. Did the fairy who gave it to you dislike women so much?"

"I don't know," he said honestly. "I think 'twas only that she liked me."

"It's unfair. Has any girl withstood it? Ever?"

He wanted to say yes. He wished he could say yes. It *was* unfair; he had always known it. "No."

Grace looked away. "Deirdre couldn't do it anyway. So I suppose it doesn't matter."

He didn't want to tell her that it did. That it would have given him a reason not to keep his promise to Finn. "You did perfectly. I was proud of you."

She seemed troubled. "Perfectly? Hardly."

"We've some clues. More than we did."

"Yes."

Something was wrong. "What did she show you? What was the glamour she tried?"

"You mean you don't know?"

He shook his head. "Only that she was doing it. I was too busy imagining what it would be like as a stag. You looked angry, that's all I know."

"It's odd, isn't it? The way they can look right into you."

"They see what you most want," he agreed.

She looked even more troubled. "Do you think so?"

"I know it."

He led her silently from the warehouse, back into a day that was growing hotter and brighter by the moment.

She said, "I thought they would know where the archdruid was. But the things she said . . . she didn't know anything at all."

He pulled the huge, squealing door shut, and left the broken padlock dangling. "I think she told us what she knew, and it's a start."

"A start? Somewhere by the sea? People bathing? A sign with a sun and a moon and a sickle?"

He went to the edge of the loading dock and jumped down, then turned to help her. Distractedly, she let him lift her. Diarmid took advantage, holding her closer than he had to, letting her slide down his body. He heard the catch of her breath. She stepped back quickly.

It made him think of last night. How she'd let him touch her. He was afraid of how powerful his longing was, despite his best intentions. The fairy had said that he and Grace were bound. He knew it was true—his fate was tied to hers just as it had been to the first Grainne—and the irony over their shared name wasn't lost on him. But this felt different, the way Grace eased his loneliness, the force of his desire. For the first time he wondered if the *geis* that Manannan had laid was meant to be a lesson. Diarmid of the lovespot, ruined by love—there was a grim sort of justice in that.

"A sun and a moon and a sickle." Grace's voice broke into his thoughts as they walked. "A place by the sea."

"She said it wasn't far."

"Silver ribbons . . . kelpies . . . oh, what does that mean? It could be anywhere!"

Cars on silver ribbons. A sound like roaring kelpies. Diarmid knew just the noise Deirdre meant: a belching, growling, rumbling sound. Like the horse cars in town, and the trains.

Trains. Steam cars.

"Coney Island!"

"What?"

"Coney Island," he repeated. "Where mortals bathe. By the sea. Smoke from the steamers. And there are steam cars— the Coney Island railroad. Cars on silver ribbons. Which sound just like angry kelpies."

She stared at him. "Angry kelpies. You would know this."

He shrugged. "Aye."

"You're certain?"

"No, not certain. But 'tis a place to start. Unless you have a better idea?"

"No." She shook her head. "Coney Island. How do you know all these places? You've only been here since May."

"Well, we had to know where we were, didn't we?"

"Yes, but . . . I've lived here my whole life, and I've never been there."

He thought of the pretty row house where she lived, the rooms empty now, but not always so. A little yard and a cast-iron fence. A good neighborhood. "Why would you? 'Tisn't a place for people like you."

"People like me?"

"It's for working people who don't have a country house upriver to go to for a holiday."

She went pink. "I'm not rich."

"Not anymore. But you were."

"My family isn't like that. My father would have loved Coney Island—"

"'Twasn't meant as an insult."

"You don't think I see anything. You think I'm oblivious to all this." She gestured to the slums around them. "But I'm not. I know I . . . I know I thought my life was bad, but I'm not blind or dead—not yet, and—"

She stopped short, and then she just . . . gave way. Her shoulders shook, and she pressed her hands to her face, and without thinking, he took her into his arms. She buried her face in his chest, and he held her, saying nothing. The last few days she'd been so calm and strong that he'd forgotten how strange all this must be to her. He knew what it was like to wake up one day and find the world changed. To be told that you had power, that you held the burden of the world, that you had to die. It was a miracle she hadn't fallen apart before now.

She whispered against him, "I miss my life. I never thought I'd say that, but I do. I wish I were blind again. I wish I'd never seen you, or that you were just a stableboy, or . . . or something. I wish Patrick had never called you."

His heart squeezed. "I know."

"I don't want any of this. I want to go back to the way things were."

"You can't. No one can. There's only going forward." He wished it wasn't so, but to say otherwise was a lie, and he'd already told too many. Her anguish made him feel helpless. How was he supposed to comfort a lass who'd just told him she wished she'd never laid eyes on him? He told himself to back away, to turn away.

But then she said, "I'm so afraid," and her vulnerability, along with her bravery in admitting it—that honesty he'd always admired even as it slayed him—tugged and tangled him. He felt himself falling even harder, and he could do nothing to stop it.

"'Tis all right," he managed. "The *sidhe* are gone now. You're safe."

She gave a shuddering little laugh. "Not because of the fairies. Well . . . yes, them, but . . ." She looked up at him. "I'm afraid I *am* the *veleda*. I felt something when they called me. Like a . . . stinging in my blood. And when Deirdre promised to help, I heard this . . . music that told me I could believe her."

"It was music?"

"Yes. Does that mean something?"

"The Druid spells," he explained. "They all sounded like music. 'Twas the way they were spoken."

She leaned her forehead against him. "I don't want this."

"'The *veleda* sees; she weighs; she chooses,'" he quoted the prophecy softly. "'Tis what you're meant to do, Grace."

She pushed away. He let her go, fighting the urge to pull her back again, to kiss away the glistening trail of tears on her cheeks.

She said, "I must find this archdruid."

"We'll find him. We'll follow this clue of Deirdre's to the end. I promise."

The hope in her eyes blindsided him.

"You mean we'll go to Coney Island?"

"Tomorrow," he told her.

He felt her strength restored with every step as they walked in silence back to the tenement—and he made no mazes this time. He didn't even think to do it.

Once they were there, he played ball with the children and ran the Dun Rats through more drills. But he had to force himself to concentrate on training, to remind himself of his brothers, who expected the best of him. They had to be ready. It had been four days since the fire. He hadn't yet heard from Finn, but he knew he would.

In the alcove that night, Grace seemed restless and distracted. He heard her whisper—less than a whisper, the veriest hush of sound, a murmured cadence—and he asked, "What are you singing?"

She quieted as if he'd caught her by surprise. "It's not a song. A poem. It comforts me to hear it, even in my own voice. I miss my books."

He remembered the reason they'd gone to the secondhand shop: a book to ease her boredom, which they hadn't returned with. He hadn't thought of it since. "Tell it to me, then. I'd like to hear it."

"It's all right, Derry. You don't have to pretend—"

"I like poetry. And you learn to admire it when you're made to write some yourself."

"You had to write poetry?"

"Schooled by Druids, remember?"

"Tell me one of your poems."

"You don't want me to do that. I've no talent. Truly. I'm not just saying it."

"I don't have any talent either," she said wistfully. "I wish I did. I'd love to be a poet, but even the dogs would howl and skulk away when I read mine out loud. Aidan never laughed so hard. Patrick was kind enough to listen, though, and he never even winced. He understood how I felt—"

She broke off, and in that silence he heard her missing Patrick Devlin, and her brother, and everything Diarmid had taken her from. Softly, he said, "Tell me the poem you were whispering."

She rolled to face him in the darkness. "'Ask me no more: thy fate and mine are seal'd: I strove against the stream and all in vain: Let the great river take me to the main: No more, dear love, for at a touch I yield; Ask me no more.'"

The stanza was beautiful and strange. He felt *her* in the words, which struck him with both heartache and hope, reminding him of that time in her bedroom when she'd asked him if he could change the world for her, and he'd been afraid of how much he wanted to, how much she demanded of him, how she made him want to be better than he was.

She said tentatively, "That's Tennyson. He's one of my favorite poets."

"'Tis beautiful, lass," he answered with a tight throat, a tender bruise in his chest. "Beautiful and sad at the same time. Like longing."

"Yes. Exactly like longing." There was wonder in her voice, as if she hadn't expected him to comprehend. The air between them went taut. He felt her waiting and wondered what she would do if he touched her again. If he kissed her the way he wanted to—

A knock at the front door shook the walls. Diarmid jerked up. Grace asked, "What's that?"

He scrambled over her. The boarders were stirring and complaining. He grabbed the dagger from his boot at the same moment he hissed over his shoulder, "Get back into the shadows." He was relieved when she did.

Bridget yelled, "Stop the noise, I'm comin'!" and the pounding stopped.

Diarmid waited, thinking of how to get Grace away. The fire escape was the only way out besides the front door, and—

"It's Oscar!" Little Joe called out in excitement.

It was a moment before the name registered. Diarmid shoved the dagger back into his boot, saying to Grace, "Stay here. I'll—"

But she was already rising, clutching the blanket. "I want to know what's going on."

She pushed by him, a glimmer of white in the darkness, and he followed her into the other room, where Oscar stood, his bright blond hair hidden by a brown scarf. His green eyes

lit with pleasure as they came into the room. He strode over
to Diarmid. "You look well, man."

"What's going on? Why are you here?"

"Such a welcome! Not even a 'how glad I am to see you.'"

"How glad I am to see you," Diarmid said. "You're lucky
I didn't gut you before I heard who it was. What're you doing
here in the middle of the night?"

Oscar nodded at Grace, and then at Bridget and the children. "'Tis best said in private."

"Outside," Diarmid said, gesturing to the door.

Grace said, "Wait. Does Patrick know where I am? My
mother? And Aidan—how is Aidan? And my grandmother?"

Oscar looked uneasily at Diarmid.

"Come now, kiddies, back to bed, eh? 'Tis none of your
business," Bridget said.

"But Ma, that's *Oscar*," said Little Joe.

Oscar said, "Aye, and I'm afraid I'll be agreeing with your
mama, lad. Off to bed with you. 'Tis late."

The boy's eyes went round. He scampered off to the
mattress behind the curtain, and Bridget motioned toward
the other room, where the boarders were settling in again.
"Prying ears don't help no one."

Oscar waited until Bridget made her way behind the curtain with the other children, and then he motioned for Grace
to come close. "Aidan's fine. Stranger than ever, if you ask me,
but he's with us, and Finn won't let him near the ale. And as
for your mama, and your grandma . . ."

"She's all right, isn't she?" Grace asked anxiously. "I know Mama must be worried sick, and Grandma was so—she is still . . . alive, isn't she?"

"As far as we know. Devlin's moved them both into his house."

"Why?" Diarmid asked.

"They know she's with you, Derry. Sweet little Rose couldn't keep her mouth shut, it seems. Devlin and the Fenians have put word out that Grace has been kidnapped. There are 'Wanted' posters everywhere, and a reward offered for her safe return. They've named us, and police are everywhere, looking for us. They're coming down on the other gangs too. Devlin's told the newspapers that he's taken Grace's family under his wing to protect them, that he's afraid of reprisals in case the other gangs decide to defend us."

"Will they?" Diarmid asked.

"Aye. They're hungry and they want work. They're looking for a reason to fight someone. And they don't like police tactics." Oscar looked at Grace. "But Devlin's made it personal. He's told the papers that you're his fiancée. The Fenians are hoping to buy sympathy—a pretty, young lass kidnapped . . . The whole city's in an uproar. Finn thinks some will turn against us. Offer enough money, and people will do almost anything."

"Then you'll need me," Diarmid said.

"Didn't you hear me? The whole city's looking for the two of you. Finn says not to move. You're safe here with the Dun Rats. For a while anyway."

"I don't like it."

"What I don't like are all these boarders knowing you're here," Oscar told him.

"They hardly pay attention. They come here to sleep. That's all."

"You don't suppose a reward might open their eyes?"

"I've seen no posters here."

"It won't stay that way. Rose told them you were on the Brooklyn ferry. You need to be very careful now, my friend. I have to be getting back. Walk with me outside."

Where they could talk privately.

"Wait. What about the archdruid?" Grace asked. "Have you found him yet?"

Oscar looked at Diarmid.

"Her grandmother told her about him," Diarmid explained.

"You mean the old woman knows something?"

"She did," Grace said softly. "But now . . ."

"She's mad," Diarmid finished.

"Ah. How mad?" Oscar asked, raising a brow. "Stark-raving or just a wee bit?"

Grace glared at his humor. "My mother says she won't get better. Whatever else she knows . . . I'm afraid it's gone."

"Does Patrick know this?"

"Yes. He knows everything. I told him everything."

The trust she'd put in Patrick . . . Although she'd let Diarmid touch her and comfort her, it didn't change that she was engaged, nor that she trusted Patrick. More than him.

"What's 'everything'?" Oscar pressed. "What did your grandmother tell you?"

"That there's an archdruid. That the *sidhe* can help me find him. And some other things, about keys and being broken and seas . . . I couldn't make sense of it. But about the archdruid and the *sidhe*—she was very clear about that."

Diarmid stared at her. "Keys? Seas? You've said nothing of that to me."

"Because I don't know what any of it means. I told you she said a great deal of nonsense."

Oscar looked thoughtful. He said good-night to Grace, and Diarmid walked him out. Once they were in the yard, Oscar said soberly, "I won't lie to you, Derry. Things are bad. We've managed to find a new panny, but who knows how long it'll be before they hunt us down. There're spies all over. Devlin and the Fenians . . . they've got a finger in every pie, and Fomori warriors are everywhere. We've been trying to find the archdruid, but the *sidhe* we've questioned seem confused. I don't think they've found him yet." Oscar paused. "This fight, when it happens . . . we'll need all our allies. Are you training the Rats?"

"Every day."

"Have you learned anything from Grace? Does she know anything?"

Diarmid shook his head. "I don't think so. If she knows the incantation, it's hidden deep."

"But she knows who she is?"

"Patrick told her. She didn't believe it at first, but now . . . I think she does now."

"Does she know about the choice? The sacrifice?"

Diarmid felt sick. He nodded.

"And about you? Does she know about the *geis*?"

"I don't know." Diarmid looked up at the sky and saw only leaning buildings, one or two candlelit windows, most of them quiet and dark. No stars and nothing else to show they were even in the world. "She's said nothing of it. But if I were Patrick, I would have told her. I would have wanted her to be afraid of me."

"Is she afraid of you?" Oscar asked.

Oscar's real question was obvious, and Diarmid chose not to acknowledge it. "She tried to escape me the first day. Ran right into a group of the *sidhe*."

"Sweet Danu—you've told her how dangerous they are?"

"Grace believes what her grandmother said about the *sidhe* being able to help, and she thinks the archdruid might know some other spell, something that means she doesn't have to die."

"Have you told her 'tisn't likely?"

"Aye, but . . . but what if there is one? Patrick and the Fomori have promised Grace to find it if it exists."

"They have?" Oscar sounded impressed. "'Tis a good play. Does she believe them?"

"She'd go back to Patrick in a moment if I let her. She trusts him. And the Fomori have charmed her."

"And you haven't." Oscar's green eyes glimmered in the darkness. "You haven't used the lovespot. I could see it when I walked in the door. Why not?"

Diarmid knew Oscar would never understand this. His friend was a warrior first and foremost; Oscar liked girls in his bed and then he liked them gone. Even Etain—Oscar's long-ago love—had not changed that. What could Diarmid say to explain how he felt? That he wanted to know real love for once? That he wanted a future with a girl he was bound to kill? Or that her name was Grainne and he didn't want to live that story again and he was as big a fool as he'd ever been and he knew it?

Oscar said, "By the gods. You're in love with her."

Diarmid could say nothing.

Oscar threw his arm around Diarmid's neck, jerking him close. "Are you mad, Derry? Why would you do this?"

"'Twasn't as if I asked for it," Diarmid protested.

"You should have guarded against it. You should have fought it," Oscar said furiously. "You know how much depends on this. It isn't just you. It's all of us."

"I haven't forgotten."

"So was Finn right to doubt you? Will you be able to kill her?"

"I'll do my duty. I've told you I will."

"But that was before you were in love with her—"

"I said I would do it."

Oscar released Diarmid. "If Finn knew this, he'd be here on the next boat. He'd seduce her himself and make sure 'twas well done."

Oscar was right. Diarmid couldn't bear the thought of it.

Oscar went on, "Derry, we need to know that you can do this. Tell me that I can trust you. That I don't need to tell Finn."

Diarmid took a deep breath. "You can trust me to do it, if I must."

"If you must," Oscar repeated. "Don't put your hope in this archdruid, Derry. This kind of magic—"

"Believe me, I know."

"Then you'll—"

"I'll convince her to take our side. And when the time comes . . . I'll kill her."

Diarmid felt the way Oscar was measuring him. He was relieved when his friend said, "I'd do anything for you, you know that."

"I know it."

"And I believe you'd do anything for me."

Diarmid nodded. It was true. It had always been true.

"Very well then. I'll say nothing to Finn. For now. But if I see you falter"—*there* was the voice that belonged to the best warrior of the Fianna, the one Diarmid trusted at his side in battle—"you know I don't want to do this, but there's too much at stake. Think of me. Think of the others. None of us want to die."

"I understand."

"The next time I see Grace I want to know she's mad for you. Make her forget Patrick Devlin. Use the *ball seirce*. Make it easy on yourself."

"She has a mind of her own," Diarmid warned. "And she's not convinced we're the best choice. Love might not be enough to sway her."

"We have her brother," Oscar said. "And the rest of us can be charming enough when we want. If she loves you, she won't want to see you die. Or your friends." He clapped a hand on Diarmid's shoulder. "I expect it will be only a few days before we can guarantee her safety and Finn sends for you. Don't disappoint him—or me."

"I won't," Diarmid promised.

FOURTEEN

The same day
Patrick

Patrick had done everything he could think of to find Grace and Aidan. He'd had hundreds of 'Wanted' posters plastered on every telegraph pole in the city, and in Brooklyn too. He'd kept Grace's kidnapping in the paper. They'd planted a story about receiving a ransom note from Finn's Warriors. The mayor decried the growing lawlessness of the city gangs: *"We WILL bring these enemies of peace to justice!"* The *New York Times* and the *World* had both published Mrs. Knox's pleas for citizens to be watchful and vigilant: *"Please return her to us. Grace, if you're reading this, try to escape them. We love and miss you. Please, my darling, I am praying for your safe return."*

But there had been nothing, not a single sighting. How was it even possible? Where could they be that *no one* saw them?

His anxiety wasn't helped by his dreams, which had grown more intense. In them, Patrick strode through unfamiliar halls painted with Celtic symbols, into a room filled with smoke from oracle fires, searching for a woman who wasn't there. Her peril grew every moment. He must find her. *Aidan will know. Find Aidan.*

Patrick woke every morning more confused than ever. *Find Aidan.* Bres had little advice. He told Patrick it was just a dream and that there were other, more important concerns. Lot agreed: *"'Tis only that you're worried, my darling,"* she'd said. *"He's a stormcaster. He can take care of himself."* Patrick hadn't bothered to explain that it wasn't worry that drove him, but a compulsion he couldn't ignore.

"Patrick?"

Grace's mother looked strained. He knew her fear for her children ate away at her, and he wished there was some way to relieve it.

"Mrs. Knox," he said, trying to smile. "It's still early. You should be sleeping."

"I couldn't." She came into his study. "Patrick, if you wouldn't mind . . . if you have a few moments. I've wanted to speak with you before now, but you've been so busy. It's about Grace."

"I'm doing everything I can to find her."

She nodded weakly. "I know that, but I wanted to tell you about a conversation we had before she disappeared. I think it may matter. She's under the delusion that she's living some legend. One of her grandmother's Irish tales. The myth of the *veleda*—do you know it?"

Patrick remembered Grace telling him that her mother didn't believe it. "Yes. The legend of the Fianna. The prophecy."

"She's convinced she's this *veleda*. She claimed that you believe it too." She looked at him imploringly. "I must tell you—in the last month before she slipped into this state, Grace's grandmother was quite mad. The stories she told Grace . . . I'm afraid they affected her strongly. I've told her none of it's true, but she's determined to find—oh, I know this sounds ridiculous—an archdruid. I fear she set off looking for him."

Patrick was silent.

"I hope you can understand. It's been a difficult time for her, what with her father's death, and Aidan, and . . . and our troubles. I know she'll be fine, but . . . I thought it might provide a clue as to where she's gone. Perhaps this Druid she imagined might have something to do with it."

"Wherever Grace is, she didn't go there of her own accord," he said. "She was kidnapped, Mrs. Knox. We have Rose Fitzgerald as a witness. But we'll get her back, and then she and I will be married. Did she tell you that we'd set a date?"

"A wedding date? Oh, no, I—"

"She hadn't the opportunity, I suppose. December first. It's soon, I know, but I believe she'll return long before then. Perhaps you could begin planning things in her absence? It would be a help to me if you would."

Mrs. Knox frowned.

"Does the date not please you?"

"Oh yes," she said, though her frown didn't ease. "But if it *is* a gang who's taken her . . . everyone's heard of how ruthless they are. Of what they've done to innocent girls . . ."

It occurred to him what she was really saying—she was talking about gossip, and rumors, of what people would think. She was afraid he would abandon Grace. He had to remind himself that she didn't know the truth.

"I don't believe they'll hurt her," he said. *Not yet.* "They won't be able to collect the ransom otherwise."

Mrs. Knox looked relieved. "I pray that's true. But"— worry crept into her voice again—"even so, the things that will be said about her when she returns . . . I would hate for anything to come between you."

"I would never abandon Grace. Never. I love her. If I have to take her away for a time until the rumors die, I will. We'll go to Ireland. Perhaps you could come with us."

"Ireland? Oh no. Thank you, but . . . no. You must under-stand, Patrick. I've spent a lifetime trying to escape Ireland. When I was a child it was very difficult to be Irish. You couldn't know, of course. Your father worked hard to make certain you and Lucy would never feel the struggle, just as my husband did for Aidan and Grace. But for me . . . well, Ireland holds nothing but pain. Though I suppose Grace might enjoy visiting. She's always had such an affinity for the tales . . ."

Patrick took her hand, squeezing it. "Please, Mrs. Knox, I'd be so grateful if you would let me worry about this. Plan a beautiful wedding for us."

"Thank you, my dear. I will. Hope is so much better than fear."

But as Patrick watched her leave, his own hope wavered. He felt as if things were moving beyond him, things set in motion he couldn't predict or control. He told himself that with the Fomori on his side, everything would turn out for the best. He had to believe it. Any other thought meant only despair.

"Mr. Devlin?" It was the maid, with an envelope. "This just came for you, sir. The messenger said it was important."

The handwriting was unfamiliar to him, but when he tore open the envelope, he saw the note was from Aidan.

Battery Park. Two o'clock today. I'll meet you at the flag-pole. Tell no one.

Aidan

Patrick broke out in a cold sweat of relief. *Aidan was all right. Thank God.* But that relief was followed closely by anxiety. Patrick glanced at the clock on his desk. It was nearly noon. He hurried to dress in his oldest suit coat and a hat that hid much of his hair, and called for his carriage. He didn't want to be recognized or for word to get back to anyone. The urge to protect Aidan was so strong it was easy to follow his order to say nothing.

He had the driver wait with the carriage blocks away and walked the rest of the distance to the park, which was full on this hot summer day, women lifting their faces to the cool breeze coming off the water, children playing. Most of the men were of the poorer sort, homeless, jobless. Patrick scanned the crowd, the people standing at the seawall, staring out over the water.

Then he saw him. Aidan leaned over the wall, his back to Patrick, his dark hair fluttering in the breeze. Patrick realized he'd been looking for the Aidan he'd known, the one in decent dress, wearing a top hat and shined boots. His childhood friend. But this Aidan looked like any immigrant—no hat, worn pants, a too-small coat stretched at his shoulder blades.

Patrick walked as casually as he could toward the seawall. When he was past the flagpole, Aidan turned, looking over his shoulder. Patrick saw when Aidan recognized him. He leaned back against the wall, waiting as Patrick approached.

"Coming down in the world a bit, Patrick? I haven't seen that coat in a while."

"I wanted to blend in."

"You'll have to do better than that. Perhaps you could try not eating for a couple of days. Or selling that watch chain."

"Where's Grace?" Patrick asked.

Aidan glanced away.

"At least tell me she's safe." *And not under the spell of the* ball seirce. *Please.*

Aidan laughed. "Safe? Are any of us?"

"We've been worried for you. For both of you. Your mother—"

"My mother is willfully blind," Aidan said bitterly "She's brought all this on herself."

Patrick thought of Mrs. Knox, frail and fearful. "You're being cruel. If you could see her as I do—"

"She's not sleeping. She's despairing and wan. Yes, I know. It's how she's been the last two years, while she's had Grace handle everything."

"Because you wouldn't."

"I had other things on my mind."

"Like what? Lightning coming from your fingertips?"

"Aye."

"*Aye*. You sound like Diarmid and the others. That's where you are, isn't it? You've joined with the Fianna."

"I have."

"Why? They're greedy and arrogant. They'll bring this city to its knees."

"They didn't call *themselves*, did they?"

"I was wrong about them," Patrick admitted. "Why did you ask me here?"

"To tell you it's the Fomori you're wrong about." Aidan's long, shaggy hair blew into his face. He shook it back. "There's still time for you to change sides. We could use you."

"This isn't the fight I wanted. It's because of the Fianna that we're enemies. They were ready to fight for Ireland until they learned of the Fomori. *They* refused to join with us. They've created this mess."

"You should have waited for them to find you."

"I waited three weeks. *Three weeks*." From the corner of his eye, Patrick saw a lean boy approach. He was pale and dark eyed, dark haired. He stopped only a few yards away, watching them. Patrick lowered his voice. "I want only Irish independence. I don't want this gang war in our city streets."

"You don't know what you're talking about. You're so wrapped up in your idealism you can't see what's really happening."

"I can see it well enough. Do you think I don't worry over it every day? Do you think I don't know how much danger I've put Grace in? We're looking for an archdruid to save her life. Will the Fianna do the same? Or are they interested only in her choice?"

Aidan cast a sideways glance at the watching boy, and squinted as if the sun hurt his eyes. "You really think you can save her life?"

"I hope so. It would be easier if she were here. Does Diarmid have her? At least tell me that. Has he . . . ?" He couldn't bring himself to say the words.

"She's safe enough. Stop looking for her."

"No! I can't just leave her to him—"

"She needs him, Patrick. Right now, she needs him more than she needs you. But I don't know if that will always be true."

"I don't understand. How does she need him?"

Once again, Aidan glanced past him. He paled and put a hand to the wall to steady himself. He looked ready to swoon.

Patrick followed his gaze to the boy. Now there was another one, a blond, but with the same eerie dark gaze. They were doing nothing, only standing, only watching, but Patrick felt danger like a creeping fog.

Aidan put his hand to his eyes and swayed. "Ah. *Patrick.*" It was a sound of pain. "Don't let me—"

He took a lurching step toward them, as if weakness had overtaken him.

Get him out of here.

Patrick grabbed Aidan's arm, looking for a place to hide him—

Hide him?

Aidan stumbled. Patrick tightened his grip, pulling Aidan after him. Those boys—"The *sidhe,*" Aidan gasped. "They're all over."

The sidhe. *The key to finding the archdruid.*

Do your job. Keep Aidan safe. The thought exceeded everything else. Patrick whispered urgently, "We have to get you out of here. You'll have to run. I'll keep them from following. *Run*, Aidan. And don't look back."

Aidan nodded tensely. "I'll find a way to get in touch with you again."

"Just go." Patrick pushed him.

When Aidan dashed off, Patrick spun, blocking the path of the two boys following. "Leave him alone."

The boys—the *sidhe*—smiled at him, and Patrick felt their magic, the terrifying pull of it, as he'd never felt anything in his life.

"You cannot stop us," said the dark-haired one, dodging him.

Patrick gripped the boy's arm. He felt a rush of adrenaline; he threw the *sidhe* to the ground as if he weighed nothing.

The boy cried out as he tried to get up, then collapsed again, his leg twisted beneath him.

Patrick looked at the blond. "Care to try?"

The blond lunged. Patrick knocked the boy's legs from beneath him with a swift, well-placed kick. The fairy fell, then scampered up again, loathing in his eyes, and ran. Patrick let him go—he was running in the opposite direction from Aidan.

A policeman approached, one Patrick recognized as a Fomori warrior put onto the force by the Brotherhood.

"What's this?" the man asked. "A nasty fairy, is it?"

The dark-haired boy looked frightened now. "We didn't mean any harm. None at all. We just wanted to touch—"

"Shut up," the police officer said. He grabbed the boy, jerking him from the ground. "Should I be tossin' him into the sea for you, sir?"

"Take him into custody," Patrick ordered. "Question him. See if he knows anything about an archdruid."

"Let me go!" the boy shouted.

"Come on now," said the officer, taking him away, and suddenly Patrick smelled smoke and . . . and hemp. The smell from his dreams. But there was no sign of smoke nearby. He felt light-headed. He stumbled to a bench, trying to remember what Aidan had told him. The wrong side. No one safe. *"Right now, she needs him more than she needs you. But I don't know if that will always be true."*

The words that troubled him more were the ones that had been in his own head: *Do your job.*

My job.

Patrick looked up. The sun was blinding, the sky cloudless and hotly blue, the water beyond dotted with schooners and steamers and plumes of smoke. And Patrick felt the peril of the day sink into him, beautiful and deadly as the eyes of the *sidhe.*

FIFTEEN

July 24
Grace

I woke cradled in Derry's arms. He was awake too; I felt it. I lay there as still as I could while my heart pounded. He touched my hair gently, as if he was afraid to wake me, and then he kissed my shoulder. I felt it like an electric shock—it was all I could do not to jump. *A lie*, I told myself for what seemed the hundredth time.

I pretended to stir, and he released me so quickly it was as if he hadn't been holding me at all. I stretched and murmured, opening my eyes. When I looked at him, he sat up, not meeting my gaze.

"It's about time," he said brusquely. "The morning's half gone. You'd best get dressed. We need to be going."

He grabbed his shirt and boots and brought me some of the water that Molly or one of the boys fetched daily from the public pumps. Then he left me alone to wash and dress. With him gone, I didn't have to guard my emotions so closely, and it was too easy to think of last night, of the things I'd seen in him that I'd never suspected. His reverence of Tennyson's words, the way he'd understood. It left an ache in my heart that lingered still.

When I went out to the main room, he was sitting at the table, talking with Bridget as she sewed.

"You two enjoy yourselves today," she said. "Have a beer for me."

"We will," Derry said, smiling back at her, so charming and easy. We stepped into a simmering-hot day and a blue sky hazed by smoke from the gasworks and the rendering plants along the waterfront. Children laughed and yelled in the yard.

"It's a bit of a walk at first," he told me. "But then we'll take the steam car."

"A steam car? But won't that cost money?"

"I've still some coin left. Grace, stay close, will you? I think Deirdre's folk are finished with us, but there will be others. Tell me if you see anyone glowing."

"I will."

"The moment you see it. Don't stop to wonder if it's real or just the sun."

I nodded. We went up one street and down another, through the alleys littered with offal and garbage to streets that grew wider, lined with houses now instead of tenements, and yards decorated with hedges and flowers wilting in the hot day. There was garbage here, too, and overflowing ash cans, but it was better than where we'd come from, and the streets were at least swept—there weren't inches of soft silting dust covering everything.

When we finally got to the station, it wasn't crowded, but there were still plenty of people waiting for the train. Derry slowed. "Anyone glowing?"

Ordinary people, every one of them, as far as I could see: Families with children and picnic baskets; men looking impatiently at their pocket watches; couples enjoying the day together. But mostly there were roughs smoking cigars and looking arrogantly about. One of them winked at me as we approached. "No one."

Derry let out a breath—it was only then I realized how tense he'd been—and bought our tickets. The conductor called that it was time to board, and Derry grabbed my hand as the crowd surged, some pushing women and children out of the way to get a seat. Derry tripped the one who'd winked at me, and we slipped into the hard-backed wooden seat he'd been going for.

I glanced at Derry, and he gave me a wide-eyed, innocent look. "What?"

"You did that on purpose."

"I don't know what you mean," he said, but his expression became smug. He stared out at the steam dummy, belching smoke, that pulled the cars. "I'd let you sit by the window, but I hear 'tis a dusty ride."

There were no windows, actually. It was open as a street-car, and the men smoking cigars had taken seats in the front so their choking smoke floated obnoxiously back. There was a whistle, a lunge, and the car jerked into motion. The chugging grind of the steam dummy was loud enough that people had to shout to talk to one another, and we were drowned in other people's conversations about business meetings and getting a new cat and whether or not to eat the fried chicken now or wait for the beach.

"This is what angry kelpies sound like?" I asked.

He smiled so his dimple showed. "Close enough. The kelpies are a bit louder, though, and crosser. You don't want to be near one, trust me."

The road curved, and the cars went so fast that at times it was almost frightening, but soon we were passing through the countryside. We sped past farms dotting rolling hills, fields of tomatoes and cabbage, and villas sitting in the midst of green acres. Soon the dust of the city was mostly gone. Derry stared out as if he couldn't get enough of the landscape, and I said, "It's beautiful, isn't it?"

"Reminds me a bit of home."

"Yes. I imagine it does. I know how much you miss it. You must want to be back there."

"I doubt I'll ever see it again."

"Why do you say that?"

"I don't know. A feeling I have, I guess. Things aren't what I thought they'd be. And who knows what will happen?"

The weight of what we were doing, everything that was at stake, hit me again and we fell into silence. I remembered the power I'd experienced with the *sidhe* yesterday, and my fear. I remembered how it felt to be in Derry's arms as he comforted me, as if I belonged there. That was how it had felt to kiss him—something I'd tried to forget. It was becoming so hard to remember it was a spell. It all seemed so real.

But this was how Lucy felt, too, I knew. I only needed Derry's help, and that was all. There could be nothing more between us.

It wasn't long before we were at the Coney Island depot, and miles of open shore and blue water stared back at me. There were flags and signs everywhere advertising "Clams of All Styles," "Roasted Corn Here," "Lemonade," "Beer!" and "Come Inside for the Best Ice Cream in Coney Island!" In every direction, you could see black-clad swimmers bouncing in the waves. Bathing houses, beach umbrellas, and blankets adorned the sand, along with a barrier of cardsharps and swindlers you had to cross before you could get to the water, their one-legged tables pushed into the sand, and men crowding around for their chance to lose at three-card monte. Organ grinders played lively tunes while their foolish monkeys jumped about and made people laugh. There was a shooting gallery, and a puppet show on a little makeshift stage at the corner. Restaurants, saloons, and hotels lined the road fronting the beach, and the smells of clams and saltwater, beer and smoke filled my nose.

Down the beach a short distance was the steamer landing from Manhattan, and next to it was a huge enclosure of several hundred bathing houses, and beyond that a wooden platform where people who weren't swimming stood drinking beer and looking out over the water. The breeze was cooling. I lifted my face to it.

"Oh, I love this," I said, laughing. "I love it."

Derry smiled at me, his eyes looking very blue in the glare off the sand and the water. The moment held, again I felt shivery and strange, and it was a relief when he looked away. "Well, we should be looking for that sign, don't you think?" he said.

"A sun and a moon and a sickle. I don't even know what kind of shop that would be."

"Diminished power, Deirdre said. Probably a Druid of some kind that they sucked dry. Maybe . . . we found Cannel at a sideshow. He was the fortune-teller there."

"A fortune-teller." I glanced at the row of shops and hotels and restaurants stretching along the waterfront. "I don't see anything like that here, do you?"

"Not here." He looked at the buildings snaking away from the depot. "'Twould be something small, I think. Someplace out of the way."

We started to walk. I was hungry—we'd eaten nothing this morning, and not much for days before that—and the smells of clam chowder, melting sugar, and grease made my stomach growl. It was loud enough at one point that Derry said, "We'll get something to eat soon. Let's see what we can find first."

"Don't you ever get hungry?"

"I'm getting used to it," he said, and I thought of the way he lived now, in tenement rooms, on beds of straw or the hard floor with stinking blankets.

"You're no better than I am, you know. You were one of the elite bodyguards of the king. You had soft beds and plenty of food. Why, you were probably richer than I ever was."

He sighed. "Aye, that's true. We spent much of the time in battle, though, and away from home. You learn to suffer hardship quickly enough. We've a talent for it, you might say. But you're right; there was always the thought of home. 'Tis easy to bear misery when you know it's not permanent."

"And now? Do you think it's permanent, the way you live now?" Then I realized: He couldn't know that, could he? It was all up to the *veleda*. Who won and who lost. Who lived and who died. *It is all up to me.* "No, never mind. I . . . I wasn't thinking."

"'Tis a good lesson, whatever comes of it. We weren't always good at remembering who we served."

Arrogant. Greedy. The reason for the *veleda*.

I thought of what it must've been like for him to wake to such a foreign place, no longer wealthy and beloved, and I couldn't help wondering what would happen to him when this was all over. If he would even still be here. The thought that he might not be saddened me—no, much more than that. Suddenly I was no longer hungry.

We had walked several blocks from the depot, and now the restaurants and hotels became booths and weather-beaten buildings and saloons. Signs advertised fishing and beer, and we had just passed a saloon called the Sea Keg when Derry stopped.

He was staring down an alleyway where a sign hung askew, one of the ropes that held it frayed to almost nothing. "Lewis Corley, Fortune-Teller and Mystic." Below the words was a faded painting of the moon orbiting the sun, and the silhouette of a sickle.

I started toward the shop.

Derry caught my arm. "Be careful."

"Deirdre said they don't come here anymore."

"That doesn't mean it's safe." He led the way to the door instead, opening it as I followed. The door creaked as if it hadn't been oiled in a long time. Inside smelled of mildew and dust. There was a small round table with two chairs. The walls held framed drawings, some of them foxed with mildew.

Derry said, "Those are the pictures on Cannel's divination cards."

"Tarot cards," I noted. At the back of the room was a doorway covered with a curtain. I called out softly, "Mr. Corley?"

The place felt profoundly empty.

"He's not here," I said, disappointed. "There's no one here."

Derry shook his head. He gestured for me to stay as he went to the curtain. He stood at the side and slowly drew it open.

There was a whistling sound. Something shot past me so quickly I jumped back. An arrow pierced the wall next to the door.

"Oh my God!" I cried.

Derry was already through the curtain. I heard a tussle, someone groaning, and then he was coming through again, hauling an older man holding a bow. Derry twisted the bow away, tossing it aside as if it were a toy. He shoved the man into one of the chairs.

"I'm sorry, I'm sorry!" said the man. "I thought you were them! No one ever comes here but them! I didn't mean to—did I hurt you?"

Derry grabbed him by the collar. "You could've killed her. I should cut your throat for that alone."

The man shrank back. His long gray hair fell into his face. "I didn't mean to! I didn't mean to! It's them! They come here, and they're evil! They . . . she . . ." He looked at me as if he'd only just seen me. "Why, you have power."

Derry's expression was as grim and forbidding as I'd ever seen it.

"You have power!" the old man repeated, panicked. "You must leave this place. They'll sense you're here and come back. Please, you must go! I can't . . . I can't bear it!"

I tried to calm him. "We mean you no harm. I only need to ask you some questions."

"He's useless, Grace." Derry kicked the leg of the chair so the whole thing shuddered and the old man cowered. "There's a reason they don't come here anymore. Look at him—they've sucked him dry."

"They have, they have," the man agreed.

"We're looking for an archdruid," I said. "Do you know where he is?"

"An archdruid?"

"He doesn't know anything, Grace," Derry said.

The old man whimpered. "If he exists, he's gone already. They would have found him. They are always hungry."

Derry leaned close to him. "He would be Irish. Very learned. There might be others around him, but he would be the one in charge. He would have spell books. Divination tools."

"No, no." The old man's eyes were nearly rolling back in his head in fear.

Derry exhaled loudly. He peered around the room. "I'm going to search. Ask him what questions you will, but you'll get nothing from this one."

He disappeared behind the curtain. I went up to the man, kneeling beside him. "Think hard, please. This is very important. Anything you know . . . anything you can remember . . ."

He pushed his face into mine. "She is cunning and mean. She will kiss you, but 'tis not a kiss at all. A long slurp, a drink of power, and she'll make you ask her to do it again. And again. Till there's nothing left." Tears welled in his eyes. He began to tremble. "I can't even read the cards! Thirty years, and I can't make sense of them!"

I felt sorry for him. I knew what Deirdre was like; I knew that terrible temptation to surrender. Seeing him made me understand Derry's fear.

The old Druid was no help. Lewis Corley began to sob, helpless and heartbreaking, and I left him to go to Derry, who searched the room beyond the curtain. There was a narrow bed and bureau and shelves piled with knickknacks. He pulled down the few books sitting on the shelves and handed them to me. "What do they say?"

"*The Origin of Species*," I read. "*Principles of Geology*." The other two were no better, nothing at all to do with magic. "There's nothing here."

He had already moved to the bureau and was going through the drawers.

"What are you looking for?" I asked.

"I don't know. Anything." He jerked his head at the cubbyhole near the door. "See if there's anything there."

"How will I know?"

"You'll know."

From the room outside, I heard Lewis Corley muttering, "Go away. Flee, I tell you!"

The shelves in the cubbyhole held five different hairbrushes tangled with strands of gray hair, a shaving razor, a strop, a mug of shaving soap, several bits of different-colored sea glass, three seagull feathers, and a deck of stained and tattered tarot cards. I held the cards up to Derry. "These?"

He glanced over his shoulder. "Do you feel anything in them? Any power at all?"

"Would I?"

"The ogham stick burned you."

"Yes, but—"

"You would feel it."

I put them back, reaching deeper, finding handkerchiefs and a pair of cuff links shaped like Irish harps and stones that looked as if they held tiny snails locked inside of them.

I touched something flat and wooden, like a ruler but with what felt like holes punched into it. I curled my fingers around it. It was warm, and then—

"Ouch!" I jerked my hand back.

Derry twisted. "What is it?"

"It burned me." In spite of the pain, there was not a mark on my skin. A burn that wasn't a burn. *Just like Patrick's ogham stick.*

Derry was beside me in an instant. "What?"

"In there. In the back. Something wooden. Be careful, it's—"

He pulled it out and laid it flat on his palm. The holes I'd felt were markings, runes—again like the ogham stick.

I said, "It doesn't hurt you at all, does it?"

He shook his head, turning it over in his hands, studying it.

"Is it another ogham stick?"

He nodded.

"You can read this?"

"Aye. For once."

"What does it say?"

"'Tis puzzling, but then, all these things are. It doesn't make any sense unless you know what it's for. They wrote that way on purpose: to keep those like me—who can read ogham but aren't Druids—from understanding. Wasn't a Druid alive who didn't think he was better than everyone else." A glance at me, and then a grin.

"Sounds like someone else I know."

"It's hard to read in here. Too dark." He pushed aside the curtain and we stepped out. He cast a contemptuous look at Lewis Corley.

Corley trembled. "Take what you want. Whatever you want. None of it's any use to me. They stole it all. They stole it all."

"What does this stick do, Mr. Corley?" I asked.

He tucked his chin into his chest and said nothing.

Derry said, "It's not a spell. It's a prophecy."

"A prophecy? How can you tell the difference?"

"There's nothing to call. No incantation. But if they wrote it down, it's important. It says: 'The sea is the knife. Great stones crack and split. Storms will tell and the world is changed. The rivers guard treasures with no worth. To harm and to protect become as one, and all things will only be known in pieces.'"

"The sea is the knife. To harm and to protect are as one." My grandmother's words. I stared at Derry.

"What?" He frowned. "What is it?"

"Those are the things my grandmother said. I thought . . . I thought it was nonsense."

"To harm and to protect," Corley repeated.

Derry's frown deepened. "Where did you get this?"

Corley peered at us as if he were half-blind. "It isn't mine."

Derry held out the stick. "You don't recognize this?"

The old man shook his head. "They left it one day. She did. Something for the future, she said. And she said . . . she said it needs a key, but she never said where it was. I don't know what it is. I don't know what it says. Take it! Take it!"

"My grandmother said that too," I told Derry. "She said something about a key. And . . . and Aidan says it in my dreams. 'We need the key.' Over and over again."

Derry looked back to Corley. "Who is the *she* who left this? D'you mean Deirdre? Did the *sidhe* leave this? Or someone else?"

"Was it an old woman?" I asked. "Or . . . perhaps not old. Her hair was once nearly black, like mine——"

"I don't know!" he shouted. "I don't know! Go. Please go before they come back."

Derry said to me, "We'll get nothing more from him."

I knew he was right. The *sidhe* had damaged Lewis Corley beyond repair—and I might have become like him. I still could, if I wasn't careful. Derry shoved the stick into his pocket and we left. I could hear Corley sobbing long after it should have been possible.

"It doesn't make any sense at all," I said as we started back to the depot. "Why would my grandmother have said the same words?"

"Had she any Druid training?"

"Druid training?" I gave him an incredulous look. "From who? Where? Have you forgotten what time we're in?"

"A time when there are Fianna and Fomori and *sidhe* walking about," he said wryly. "It doesn't seem such a bad question. We're looking for an archdruid, remember."

"The next thing you know, we'll be hunting Minotaur and basilisks too."

"What are they?"

"Don't worry. They don't exist. They're only stories."

"Ah," he said, quirking a brow. "The way the Fomori exist only in stories. The way *I* do."

That made me pause. "You have a real gift for reassurance. Has anyone ever told you that?"

He laughed.

I sighed. "Truthfully, I don't know what is real anymore. Archdruids and *sidhe* and mysterious ogham sticks that need a key when there's no lock to open—"

"A key to decipher it, maybe. Like a kind of code."

"How would we ever find such a thing?"

"You said you were dreaming about a key—have you seen anything to tell you what it might be?"

"Only Aidan telling me we need one."

"Aidan said once that your dreams might hold answers."

"Answers? Ha! He *would* say that. More like riddles. Mazes. Labyrinths. If there's some power trying to show me the way, it should give better directions."

"We should be careful about chasing after things that don't matter, lass. There's not much time. This might have nothing to do with the archdruid."

Not much time. Samhain. It was nearly August already. But I felt that the stick had something to do with me. "My grandmother said these same words when she told me to find the archdruid. And I'm *dreaming* them too. It seems too big a coincidence."

"We could puzzle over it for years. 'Tis what they meant mere mortals to do. Without a key, we've no hope of deciphering it."

"But it could be a clue."

"About the archdruid? It might have something to do with the *veleda*, but it's the archdruid we need just now."

My throat tightened. "What if we don't find him? What if we never discover the right incantation? What will happen then?"

He was so quiet that the *thud* of our footsteps on the boardwalk sounded thunderous. We were coming back onto the beach. I saw Derry's reluctance to tell me, but finally he said, "If the ritual isn't done on Samhain, the Fianna die. Never to return to any world."

I felt a distress I didn't want to look at too closely. "And the *veleda* too?"

"I don't know. I never heard what would happen to the *veleda* if the ritual doesn't happen, but 'twill be nothing you can just walk away from." He gave me a small smile. "We're not the only ones looking. We'll find him, Grace."

I wasn't reassured, not until I looked at the edge of the ogham stick poking from his pocket. Not until I thought of what Lewis Corley and my grandmother and my dreams had all said. I knew the stick could tell me where the archdruid was. I didn't know how I knew it; only that I did. The key would unlock it. Once I had the key, I would know what to do and where to go.

All I had to do was find it.

The cries of the vendors became louder as we approached the rail depot, along with the shouts and squeals from the water. The sun beat on my shoulders and my face, reminding me that I had no hat, that my skin was no doubt turning pink, and my mother would have my head for it—

Homesickness washed over me. Oscar's news last night had eased my worries over my family somewhat, but I still wished I could see for myself that they were all right.

Just then Derry said, "Let's not go back yet. We've done what we meant to do, and the whole day's still ahead of us. Why don't we get something to eat and walk along the beach for a bit? Let's just forget it all. The archdruid and the stick and who you are and who I am, and just . . . be. You and me at the seashore. Just for the day."

The thought of spending the day here without worrying over burdens I didn't want and couldn't carry sounded wonderful. To just be myself, to forget . . . I wanted it almost more than I'd ever wanted anything.

"Yes, let's," I agreed.

His smile was so dazzling I could not help smiling back.

"Come on then," he said.

He bought a paper cone full of roasted clams, and we headed toward the water, accosted all along the way by men begging us to try our hand at cards. At one point Derry pushed a man hard in the chest and said, "Leave us be," and the man retreated as if he'd seen something that frightened him; I knew what it was: Diarmid Ua Duibhne, Fianna warrior.

I reminded myself that we were forgetting everything, and let it go. We walked along the shore, sucking the salty, peppery clams from their shells—I'd never tasted anything so good in my life—and dodging children who rushed dripping and laughing and screaming from the surf. I knew I'd never forget this: the hot sun and my hair blowing into my face, the sand squishing beneath my boots, licking the clam juice off my fingers; Derry walking beside me, his hands shoved in his pockets, his collar fluttering in the breeze; the roar of the waves and the whistles of the steamers and the shouts of swimmers.

We dodged a dead possum washed ashore, and steered clear of something a group of children poked at with a stick. Sandy seaweed tangled in clods, drying in the sun, buzzing with sand flies. It was best not to look too closely at it, I realized, when I bent over one only to see it glistening with what looked like a horse liver, probably dumped into the bay from a rendering plant.

Mostly, though, it was beautiful. Seagulls dipped and cawed, and when we were done with the clams, Derry emptied the shells out on the beach and the birds flew down in a mass to fight over them.

"Do you want to swim?" he asked. "I think they rent bathing costumes, if you want."

I shook my head. "But I would like to go wading."

I plopped down on the sand and unlaced my boots, drawing them off. Without thinking, I pulled up my skirts to roll down my stockings, and when I looked up, he was watching me with an expression that made my stomach do a funny little flip. I pushed my skirts down again and unrolled my stockings from beneath the fabric, and he grinned.

"Aren't you going to wade?" I asked.

"Water makes me nervous."

"You're worried about sea champions and monsters, is that it?"

"Nothing good ever came out of the sea."

"Fish," I said. "Lobster and clams. Crab and salmon and cod."

"Sea serpents and kelpies," he said, playing along. "Cliodna's Wave, which swept everything away. Fomorians."

I looked at families lounging on the sand and women tiptoeing into the surf and men plunging in with gusto and tried not to think of the mythical tidal wave he'd mentioned. "I don't see any Fomorians. Do you?"

"Not a one."

"Take off your boots. Wade with me."

I stared pointedly at him until he surrendered and pulled off his boots. I piled my stockings and boots on the sand, and then I lifted my skirts to run into the surf, squealing when the cold water hit my calves and splashed up to my knees. I stood there while the ocean sucked at my toes, my feet sinking into the sand with each retreating wave.

Derry came up beside me so tentatively it made me laugh, his trousers rolled to just below his knees. "Look at you—where's the brave Fianna warrior now?"

"I'd rather go up against Lochlann's entire army." He looked disdainfully at the surf foaming over his feet. "It's cold."

"Don't be a baby." I kicked, splashing his trousers.

He jerked back. I saw him open his mouth to protest, and then this look came into his eyes—this teasing, calculating look—and I knew what he was planning the moment before he bent to splash me, and I turned and ran through the water, tossing over my shoulder, "Oh no you don't!"

He caught up with me before I'd gone more than ten feet. He grabbed me around the waist, lifting me until my feet were free of the water and my skirts dragged wetly against my legs, swinging me around to face him, pulling me close. "Shall I drop you?" He grinned evilly, loosening his hold just enough that I gasped and grabbed onto him.

"Don't you dare," I said.

"Or . . . 'tis a little deeper out there. What d'you think? D'you fancy going home soaking wet?"

"Let me go right now," I said, trying not to laugh. "Or I'll scream."

"Everyone's screaming. No one would care."

"All right—I'm sorry I splashed you. I won't do it again. Now put me down."

He laughed. "You think I'm so easily fooled? If I put you down, you'll soak me."

"I promise I won't."

"Ha!"

"Derry, put me down this moment."

His arms tightened around me. "Ask me nicely."

"And then you'll let me go?"

"Aye."

"Please. Please let me go."

And he did. He released his hold so suddenly that I plunged into the surf. A wave swept up to smack me, and I was soaking from the waist down, my sleeves wet to the elbow. I glared up at him, and he laughed so hard he doubled over. I jumped up and pushed him, and Diarmid Ua Duibhne, pride of the Fianna, went down like a sack of potatoes, flailing in the water, sputtering in surprise. It was so comical I burst out laughing too.

He rose, looking down at himself, his soaked shirt clinging, droplets of water sparkling in his hair, and then before I realized his intention he strode through the water and pulled me into his chest, and he shoved his other hand into my hair to anchor me, and then he kissed me in a way that turned me inside out.

The kiss was just like the one before, a leaping, pulsing fire, a force that rushed into me, breaking me apart, and all I wanted was more. I told myself to push him away—but I didn't. I couldn't. I felt myself sigh into him, and his mouth urged mine open as he deepened the kiss. It was as if every touch and glance between us had spiraled down to just this one thing, as if we were fated for this. I tasted saltwater and clams and the grit of sand, and before I knew it I was curling my arms around his neck, pulling him closer.

I heard a catcall, someone hooting and laughing, and I sprang away. I felt myself go red as two young men thrust their hips suggestively as they walked by us.

Derry let me go with a smile, barely glancing at the roughs who'd teased us, and then he said lightly, as if he hadn't just ravished me in front of everyone, "We'll be here for hours now, you know, drying off."

"The sun's hot. Perhaps it won't take so long." I walked back to our boots, and he followed. The dry sand clung to my bare, wet feet. I glanced down at my skirts, my second-best gown, streaked with dirt and dust as it hung lank and wet, the hem encrusted with sand. "Oh no. My dress is probably ruined."

"I like it better. You don't look so untouchable." He met my gaze. "Now you look like you could belong to me."

The way those words hit me . . . I felt the spell of him strengthen and hold, that urge to touch him possessing me until it was the only thing I wanted to do. His hand came to my waist. His other hand cupped my cheek, and he brought me close and kissed me again. His mouth moved to my cheekbone, sliding to my jaw, my throat, and I went weak. I thought I might melt, just a puddle of desire and yearning shimmering on the sand.

I managed, "Not here. People are watching."

He murmured against my skin, "No one's watching."

"They will if you don't stop."

"I don't want to stop."

"Please, Diarmid."

His eyes were dark. "I like the way you say my name. Say it again."

"Not if you don't let me go."

"Then I guess I don't want to hear it that badly." He grinned.

I grinned back. Like the most stupid girl alive. Which I was. I flattened my hand against his chest. The heat of him radiated through his wet shirt, and I didn't want to pull away.

I love him, I thought.

It stunned me. For a moment, I couldn't even breathe. I forced myself to think. No, it was the lovespot, I *knew* that.

No matter how real it felt.

He means to seduce you and kill you. That was the truth. And it was working. He *was* seducing me, and I was letting him. I was no different than Lucy—I'd seen him kiss her just this way. It meant nothing to him; *she* had meant nothing to him, a means to an end only. *Just as I am.*

He was helping me find the archdruid, and perhaps he did want to save my life, but if it came down to saving me or sacrificing me for his brothers, he would choose them. He belonged to the Fianna. He wanted to be one of them more than he wanted love.

I should be home, with Patrick, who truly meant to help me; with my mother and grandmother, who needed me. I shouldn't be here, letting this enchantment grow. I had to find a way to escape before I stopped caring that it was a spell, before Diarmid completely bewitched me.

"I'm thirsty," I said, as brightly as I could.

"You'd rather have a beer than kiss me?"

"Lemonade. And I'm *very* thirsty."

He sighed, but he released me. "Lemonade it is, then."

We put on our boots. He slung his arm around me as if he couldn't bear to let me go for even a moment, and I liked it—which only frightened me more. We walked back to the crowds, to the wooden booths and bathing houses near the pier, and I saw the steamers loading passengers to take back to the city, and I knew how I could escape him.

I needed only a few moments and enough coin for a ticket. A few cents, which he had in his pocket. But how to get them, and how to get to the steamer . . . that was the problem. He would never leave me alone in such a crowd. Then, when we reached the booths and restaurants, the signs advertising clam chowder, ice cream, and lemonade, I had an idea.

I turned to him so suddenly he stumbled. I used against him what he used against me—I smiled up at him flirtatiously, feeling a surge of victory when he looked a little stunned. "I want to give you a surprise."

"A surprise?"

"Yes. But you can't look. And I . . . I need some money."

"For what?"

"If I told you, it wouldn't be a surprise." I trailed my hand upward, curving it around his neck, tangling my fingers in the thick hair curling against his collar. "Go get the lemonade, and I'll get this and meet you back here."

"It's too dangerous—"

"I haven't seen a single fairy."

"There are roughs everywhere. And the monte dealers—"

"I'm just going to a booth. Just over there. I won't go near them." I went onto my toes, *me* kissing *him* for once. I'd never been so bold, and I liked it a bit too much. It strengthened my resolve to escape him. I whispered against his mouth, "You'll like it. I promise."

"I can't let you go alone." But I heard him wavering.

"It's only for a moment. I'll hardly be more than a few yards away. And if you let me do this, I'll let you kiss me all you want. I won't say a word to stop you."

He swallowed, his warring emotions clear in his eyes. I felt guilty for doing this to him.

Then I thought of what he'd done to me, the reason I was here in the first place. I pressed against him. "It's just a little surprise. What can it harm? Don't spoil the day. It would make me so happy. Please, *Diarmid*."

The name he liked to hear, and I knew by the look on his face that he was going to ignore his warrior instincts and let me go.

"All right," he said. "But just a few moments, Grace. No longer. I'll get the lemonade and meet you back here. Five minutes."

"Of course."

"How much d'you need?"

"I'm not certain."

He reached into his pocket and gave me a few coins, which I clutched tight. "Five minutes," he said again. "Right here."

I nodded and then—only because I needed the ogham stick—I gave him a last, hungry kiss, pulling the stick from his pocket as I did so. It was hot within moments. I twisted it in my skirts before I drew back.

"By the gods," he muttered, caressing my jaw. "I don't want to leave you for a moment."

I smiled and nudged him. The ogham stick was hot even through the fabric. "Go on. I'll see you soon."

He threw me a final reluctant glance as he went to the lemonade booth. I didn't waste a minute. I dodged behind the booths, and then, when I was certain he couldn't see me, I ran toward the ferry station and salvation.

SEVENTEEN

Moments later
Diarmid

He didn't like leaving her even for a moment, and before he'd walked three yards, Diarmid changed his mind. But when he turned back around, she was already gone. He craned his neck, searching, but the booths were crowded together and there were too many people. He told himself it would be all right. It would make her happy, and that was what he cared about, because he knew now that she wanted to kiss him as much as he wanted to kiss her. He knew that she felt the same longing to keep touching, to never stop. He'd seen his hunger reflected in her eyes.

He strode to the nearest lemonade booth. He bought her drink, and then went to the booth next door to buy a beer for himself. He started back, passing a restaurant plastered with broadsheets and advertisements, some fluttering loose with the ocean breeze, some half ripped away.

And he saw his face.

Diarmid halted. The beer and the lemonade sloshed over his hands. A drawing of him, with large black letters banded at the top of the broadsheet. He couldn't read it, but he knew what it was. A 'Wanted' poster. He remembered Oscar saying they'd been put up all over the city.

Then Diarmid realized what was tacked beside it. Another broadsheet, this one with a sketch of Grace.

He'd been a fool to come here. He'd been so distracted by her that he'd forgotten that the entire city was looking for them. There was a reward for their capture, and he had brought her to a place where there were a thousand people or more needing money, all of them passing these broadsheets.

He dropped the drinks and broke into a run back to where she'd promised to meet him. He pushed through the people, ignoring their startled looks and their *hey!*s. When he got there, she was nowhere in sight, but he scanned the crowd, telling himself not to worry. Had it even been five minutes yet?

There were roughs everywhere. Monte dealers and swindlers. He remembered how she'd been caught by Billy's Boys in Manhattan and broke into a cold sweat. By the gods, he would never find her here. There were too many people, too many places. By the time he checked the booths and the restaurants and the beach, she could be—

Diarmid dashed into the crowd again. She wasn't at the ice cream booth or the puppet stage. Not where they sold taffy or at the shooting range. He saw a crowd of young men shouting as they gathered around something, and his heart seized until he realized it was just a dogfight.

He raced to the bathing houses—there were hundreds of them, impossible to search and she hadn't wanted to swim anyway. He went to the rail of the wooden platform overlooking the surf. There was no dark-haired girl in a green dress on the beach. Nothing. Only girls in bathing costumes and families and couples, and over there the steamer dock—

The steamer dock. The way back to Manhattan. Diarmid saw what he hadn't seen before, what he'd been too aroused to notice. The way she'd pressed against him. She'd told him once that she didn't like it when he flirted with her, but today *she'd* been the one flirting. She'd turned him inside out with it. *"I'll let you kiss me all you want. I won't say a word to stop you,"* when despite the obvious fact that she wanted him, too, she'd never stopped fighting it.

She'd been on her toes, playing with his hair. *"I want to give you a surprise."*

Then he discovered that the ogham stick was no longer in his pocket, and he knew she'd played him completely. She'd blinded him with her kisses. She'd bound him the same way the first Grainne had, tangling his weaknesses into a noose. *"It would make me so happy."*

He was a fool. Once again and forever. Diarmid's anger erupted, along with a terrible fear. He rushed from the platform to the steamer docks. One boat was already pulling out, its whistle piercing the roar of the waves. He'd let her go. He'd even given her the coin to buy a ticket. She could be on that ferry, and he would never see her again—because he knew without a doubt that if Patrick got hold of her, the Fianna were done. *He* was done. Finn would never forgive him for this, and Diarmid would never forgive himself.

He reached the station, grabbing the doorjamb, slinging himself through the open door and into the depot. People stared at him; one or two women leaned to whisper warnings to their children. He ignored them. Grace wasn't near the ticket booth, nor sitting on the wooden seats in the outside foyer. He ran to where passengers were boarding the next boat.

There she was. Standing on the stairs, fanning herself with a ticket. His relief was overwhelming.

And on its heels came his fury.

She turned at just that moment, nervously, as if she were afraid someone—he—would come after her. Her brown eyes widened when she saw him. She whispered something urgently to the young woman ahead of her, who moved out of her way, and Grace began to hurry up the steps.

He ran to the stairs, heedless of the complaints of those he shoved as he took them three at a time, jerking people out of his way. He heard a man below say, "Now there, young man— you can't do that. You must wait your turn—"

She was just before him. He grabbed her arm, yanking her to a stop. She said in a low voice, "Diarmid, I'm going home. You can't stop me."

"I just did." He dragged her back. When she tried to pull away, he said between his teeth, "Don't try me, Grace, or I'll haul you over my shoulder. I don't care if you scream. Just let anyone try to stop me."

He saw when she understood he was serious. When he pulled her with him back down the steps, she didn't fight him. He ignored the scandalized glances, the frowning men who seemed as if they might intervene in the moment before they saw his face and thought better of it. At the bottom of the stairs, he snatched the ticket from her hand and gave it to a young woman standing near the ticket booth, saying, "We won't be needing this."

Once they were out of the station and away from other people, he spun to face her. "Quite a surprise. But I thought you said it would be one I liked."

"I had to try. Don't do this, Diarmid. Let me go."

"Why? That's what I want to know. Haven't I been helping you the way I promised?"

"I *had* to! You know how things are. I *don't* belong to you. I'm engaged to be married."

Jealousy and misery put an edge on his anger. "That doesn't matter anymore. It can't. Or do you kiss Patrick the way you kiss me?"

"The way I kiss you is a lie. We both know it. You're trying to convince me to choose the Fianna. You plan to . . . to seduce me. You've bewitched me, but you don't mean any of it. All this is just a means to an end—"

"No." He said the word almost desperately, as if it erased everything Finn had ordered him to do. "No. If anyone's bewitched, it's me."

"Don't lie to me," she said. "Please. You owe me that. None of this is real. At least admit it."

His anger faded at her plea. "I wish it were that easy. 'Twould be better, wouldn't it, just to say that I feel nothing? That this is all some game to win you to the Fianna's side. And I'll admit that's what my brothers want of me, what Finn wants. But that's never . . . that's never been what *I* wanted of you, Grace. Not from the start. You were just a lass and I liked you. I don't want you to be the *veleda*. I wish I could change everything."

She shook her head. "I can't stay with you. Please, Diarmid. If I have any chance at the life I want, any chance at all, you have to release me. Patrick has my family. He's told the whole world we're engaged. And he truly loves me, I know he does. He'll find the archdruid for me, because he doesn't want me to die."

"Why do you believe it when he says it, but not when I do?"

"You're not telling me the truth. You never have. I don't know what you really want or what you really think. When you tell me things, I don't know what to believe."

And then he said, helplessly, "I love you. You can believe that."

He saw the flash of something in her eyes—joy, perhaps?—chased by wariness and fear. She didn't trust him, and she was right not to, because while he'd told her the truth, he hadn't told her all of it. A giant lie of omission was sitting right between them: *I love you but I have to kill you.* And there was no way around that.

"I *don't* believe you. You would say that too. Just so I would choose the Fianna."

"D'you think so? Then tell me why I feel set afire when I touch you. How is that a lie? Why do I feel as if we're fated to be together? Why do you run every time I kiss you? Is it because you feel the same? Why are you so afraid, Grace?"

"Because it doesn't matter how you feel about me! You'll always choose the Fianna."

He stared at her.

She went on, whispering, "You regret the only time you didn't. You regret Grainne, and you will always regret her. You'll do whatever you must to make it up to Finn. Whatever it costs you. Or me. That's why I'm afraid. And that's why I want you to let me go."

"I can't." He had to force the words. "I have a . . . duty to keep you safe. To protect you. And I . . . I do have to convince you, Grace. I have to at least try. Finn expects it. They all do. Whatever happens with the archdruid, you'll have to choose. Whatever you think of me, I need for you to see the truth of what we are."

She made a sound—frustration, fury—and threw the ogham stick at him. "Here, take it. I can't even hold it. Look at me! I don't understand it, and I'll never find the key, and I can't do *anything.*"

Diarmid picked up the stick, sliding it back into his pocket. Very carefully, he said, "I can't bear the thought of you dying.

I can't. I said I would help you find the archdruid, and I will. If it takes my last breath, I'll find him. Just please . . . stay. Let me help you. I know I can."

She considered his words, but gave nothing away.

He continued, "You say Patrick will find him for you, but he wants you to sit in his parlor and drink tea while everyone else is searching." By her expression, he knew he'd landed on the truth, and he pressed his advantage. "He'll have the Fomori looking, but whatever you think, they're lying when they say they want to save you. What they want is the incantation. Patrick's not strong enough to control them, Grace. The whole of the Brotherhood isn't. The Fomori will do what they want, and they'll say whatever convinces you to choose them."

"Just as you will."

"Don't make the mistake of thinking they care, Grace. Not like . . . not the way I do. This quest belongs to you. Don't let Patrick take it away. You'll never trust the truth if you don't see it for yourself. You told me that already, and you were right. You should hear what this archdruid has to say about your power and your fate. Patrick won't let you do that. I will."

She was quiet, and he waited tensely.

Finally, she said, "For now, I'll stay. Only because you're right about Patrick—about the fact that he won't let me search. And my mother doesn't believe the legends. She'll want to plan a wedding I don't even know if I'll be alive for, and neither of them would let me out of their sight, and . . . and you're right that I need to learn the truth for myself. You know how to manage the *sidhe* and I think you can help me find the archdruid, and so I'll stay. But there's one condition."

"Anything."

"I don't want you to speak of love anymore. And you won't touch me. You won't kiss me."

His relief turned into something heavy and rotten.

"I'll have your word, Diarmid. Promise it. Or I promise you that I'll keep trying to escape, and I promise I'll never forgive you when I get home again. Which I think you don't want, however you truly feel about me."

He nodded. "As you wish."

She was staying with him. Together they would find the archdruid, and he could convince her to choose the Fianna. It was what he'd wanted. He'd won.

Why didn't it feel like victory?

EIGHTEEN

The same day
Patrick

The Fianna weren't there?" Bres asked. He seemed calm but his voice was icy, and Patrick saw the anger in his flinty blue eyes. "I thought you said the information was correct."

Balor didn't look the least bit cowed. "We were lied to."

"We require better informants. And where are our spies? Have they *nothing* for us?"

"Our spies can't penetrate the Fianna. They're too protected. But we're hearing about a riot planned at Tompkins Square. The Fianna will be leading it."

Patrick asked, "What about the *sidhe* boy we captured? What has he said about the archdruid?"

"The boy escaped before we could get him to the police station." Balor folded his massive arms across his chest so he looked like an immovable boulder. It didn't stop Patrick from challenging him.

"Escaped?" Patrick echoed in disbelief. "From Fomori hands? How is that even possible?"

Balor shrugged. "They're cunning creatures."

"There will be others," Bres reassured him. "We've seen the *sidhe* all over the city. They'll find this archdruid eventually."

"You mean to just *watch* them? That's no plan at all! It's almost August. Samhain is coming. We need the spell to save Grace."

Bres steepled his fingers and smiled at Patrick. "Yes, indeed. There's no need for concern. I promise you we have things well in hand."

Bres's smile reassured Patrick. He was too tense, jumping at everything. He'd had too many strange dreams and was sick with worry over Grace and her mother and Aidan, especially after that meeting in the park, when Patrick had seen the *sidhe*'s effect on Aidan. Patrick had told the Fomori that he'd gone to Battery Park to walk and think, but he hadn't mentioned his meeting with Aidan. He wasn't certain why. Something in him told him to wait. Aidan had said nothing of importance anyway.

Daire Donn appeared in the doorway. "Downstairs we've a witness who saw Diarmid and the *veleda*."

Patrick was out of the meeting room almost before Daire Donn finished his sentence. He heard Balor and Bres and Daire Donn behind him as he ran down the steps, rushing into the clubroom to see Lot, luminous in pale-blue silk, and

Rory Nolan. In a chair, flanked by two Fomori policemen, sat a young man.

"You saw them?" Patrick blurted.

The young man nodded. "I'll say I did. He tripped me. Put out his boot and took my seat. Smiled when he did it too."

"Where?"

"The Coney Island steam car."

"They were on the car?"

The man nodded again. "Went to the beach same as the rest of us."

Balor stepped forward. "You're certain it was them? The same two on the drawings?"

The young man's eyes widened at the sight of him. His hands clutched nervously at the armrests. "Yeah. 'Cept she was prettier—and dirtier. But that was him; I'd swear to it. I saw the poster and went right to the police. When do I get my reward?"

Balor growled, "If your information leads to their capture, you'll get it."

The man looked pleadingly at Patrick. "Hey, that weren't the deal. I gave up my only day off for this. I could still be at the beach with my friends."

"Give it to him," Patrick ordered.

"We already knew they were in Brooklyn," said Bres.

"Just give it to him. There's more if we need it."

Balor reached into his pocket and pulled out a small purse. He took out a gold coin and handed it to the man. Balor jerked his head at the police. "Take him away."

They took the boy out, and Balor closed the door.

"We've got Manhattan and Brooklyn blanketed with spies, and Diarmid's enjoying the day at Coney Island," Patrick said.

Balor settled his great bulk on a settee that looked as if it might collapse beneath him. "We'll have her back within hours. But you'd best expect to find her changed, at least for a time."

"I'll win her back," Patrick said, with more certainty than he felt. "It's me she loves. And then we'll find the spell to save her."

Lot's eyes were dark with pity. "I know you mean to do what's right, but I think it's time you considered that society will never accept her now. The rumors . . . well, I'll be blunt: People will think you a deluded fool if you marry her. Diarmid has already compromised her. Most believe she ran off with him of her own accord. She'll be shunned. Perhaps . . . perhaps 'twould be better for you both if she dies in the ritual as she should."

"*What?*"

"Lot isn't wrong, my friend," Daire Donn said gently. "The *veleda* will never outlive the rumors."

"What do I care for rumors?" Patrick couldn't keep his voice from rising. "I'll take her to Ireland. That's where our fight truly is. What do I care what society here believes of her?"

"Think of *her*, darling," said Lot. "A woman needs the support of society, of friends. Things will be very difficult for her. Perhaps she would not *want* to be saved."

"Of course she wants to be saved! She's seventeen. Her whole life is ahead of her. A life with me."

Lot came over to Patrick, pressing his hand, filling his nose with the scent of water lilies. "I'm sorry to speak of such difficult things, my darling, but I merely mean to warn you. We will save her life. But she may wish we hadn't."

"I'll let her make that choice herself," Patrick declared.

"But first we must find her," said Balor.

Patrick's step was heavy as he walked home. There were voices in the parlor—his mother and Lucy and Mrs. Knox. He thought of the news he had and wished he could leave it unsaid.

His mother looked up with a quick smile as he stepped through the doorway. "Patrick! You're home early. Won't you come and have tea with us?"

He shook his head. "I just wanted to let you know: a witness spotted Grace at Coney Island. We've sent men over. We're hoping to have her by tomorrow."

"Oh thank God," Mrs. Knox gasped.

Patrick's mother touched her shoulder. "It will be a happy time indeed when Grace is brought home." But Patrick saw the doubt in his mother's eyes.

Lucy asked, "Was she with Derry?"

Patrick hesitated, but there was no way around the truth. He nodded.

"What were they doing at Coney Island?"

"I don't know," Patrick said.

"Swimming, perhaps?" Lucy's voice was touched with hysteria. "Taking in the sights? Having a good time?"

"Lucy, please," said their mother.

"It's true, isn't it, what everyone's saying?"

"What are they saying?" Patrick asked, though he knew.

"That it wasn't a kidnapping. That she went with him willingly. That she doesn't want to escape him. She's run off with him. You all know it. She's in love with him and she's run off with him and I don't know why none of you will admit it!"

"Lucy!" their mother scolded.

"Well, it's true. It's true! She pretended to help me and all the time . . . all the time she was——" Lucy looked at Mrs. Knox and clamped her mouth shut, and then she ran sobbing from the parlor.

"Maeve, dear, I'm so sorry. Lucy's just so sensitive these days . . . you know how it is with young girls."

Patrick didn't stay to hear the rest. He didn't want to think about his own fears, or Lot saying, *"Perhaps 'twould be better for you both if she dies in the ritual . . ."*

He went to his study, to the glass cases, and braced his hands on one, staring at the illustration he'd shown Grace not so long ago. The painting on bark of a young, dark-haired man offering a handful of berries to a blond woman. Diarmid and Grainne. Grace's favorite of the old legends. *"Let me be your Diarmid,"* Patrick had said to her that day, before either of them had known that the real Diarmid was here, and Grace had already met him.

It almost felt . . . fated.

"Right now, she needs him more than she needs you. But I don't know if that will always be true."

It was all he could do not to fling the relic across the room. *No.* Grace wanted to come home. She wanted to be with him. She wanted Patrick to save her.

And he would find the archdruid if it took everything he had. He could not lose her. Not to Diarmid Ua Duibhne.

And not to fate.

Patrick was just finishing dinner—alone, because he was in no mood for company—when Daire Donn arrived.

"The *sidhe* are good for something, it seems," he said, striding into the room with a victorious smile. "Our men came upon three of them near the waterfront in Brooklyn. They were talking of a Fianna warrior who's training a gang in a tenement there. The Dun Rats."

"And?" Patrick asked.

"The Dun Rats are known to be allied with Finn's Warriors. The *sidhe* were also buzzing about a girl with power."

"Grace," he breathed.

Daire Donn nodded. "Yes, my friend. We know where they are."

"I t's getting late. We should go back."

Grace nodded. After that, she didn't say anything at all, and frankly Diarmid was relieved. The beach had lost its appeal. The day seemed distant already, like a dream he couldn't quite remember—leaving behind only his damp trousers, the itch of sand, and saltwater against his skin.

The sun was dipping toward the horizon as they went to the depot. Mostly families waited there—the roughs lingered on the beach, drinking and carousing until the last train and the last steamer, and so he and Grace didn't have to fight for a seat.

She sat silently beside him, but he heard what she was thinking as if she shouted it: *Don't touch me. I don't trust you. You're lying to me.*

He was suddenly so tired he didn't think he could move. He wanted to close his eyes and sleep during the journey, but he stayed vigilant as always. They passed nothing more threatening than a lowing cow. By the time the cars pulled into Brooklyn, dusk had fallen. No one bothered them as they walked to the tenement. Bridget was sewing at the table, while the boys and Molly played cards and Sara played with a train made of spools. The room was sweltering.

Bridget raised an eyebrow as they came inside, obviously seeing the tension between them. Diarmid was too exhausted to care. Let her think they'd quarreled—they had. "Long day, eh?" she asked.

"Yes," Grace answered, the only thing she'd said in more than an hour. Diarmid threw himself into the only empty chair, slouching until he could lean his head against the rickety spindle back, closing his eyes.

"Don't go anywhere," he told her.

"I won't." She sounded sad. He told himself he didn't care. She'd rejected him—*again*—and it hurt, no matter that he knew he deserved it. He tried to remember if a girl other than Grace had *ever* told him no. Never. Not once, whether he'd used the lovespot or not.

Finn's orders circled in his head: Use the *ball seirce*. Make her fall in love with you. Diarmid was tired of calling himself a fool. Tired of being one. He'd made a mistake and fallen in love with her. He should never have allowed himself to ignore the *geis*. All he could hope now was that he could convince her to choose the Fianna. Then, Finn might forgive him for not using the *ball seirce*, because Diarmid wouldn't now. It was the time to do it—she was clearly never going to feel for him what he had hoped she would—but he knew himself well enough to know that if he used it, it would only make things worse. He wanted her too badly. If she made a single move toward him, he would be more helplessly in love than ever.

He had to protect himself and his brothers. They were his life, and he meant to keep it that way. He had to be able to kill her. He couldn't count on an archdruid or anyone else to change things, no matter how much he hoped. Which meant that he had to somehow make himself stop loving her—was that even possible? She'd given him the chance to try. No talk of love. No kissing. No touching.

But he didn't want to try tonight. Tonight he was tired of everything.

He fell into a restless sleep where he dreamed about her. Part of his mind heard the talk in the room, the children laughing—and yet, he wandered into a dream at the same time, the dream he'd had once before: kissing her, and then screaming and a knife flashing. He jerked awake so abruptly he nearly fell out of the chair as Miles rushed into the room, breathless and wild-eyed.

"They're here," he said to Diarmid. "You and Grace got to go!"

Diarmid was immediately alert. "Who's here?"

"You got to go *now*. The police—"

"The police?" Bridget looked horrified.

Diarmid heard a commotion below.

"They're looking for you and Gracie. They know you're here. Get out!"

Diarmid sprang to his feet. Grace sat on the floor beside Sara, and he was there in two strides, grabbing her arm. "The fire escape," he said tersely.

Miles slammed shut the door of the flat and braced himself against it. Bridget said to him, "You go with them. Show them where to hide. I'll take care of the police."

Shouts came from the stairs, and blows—the Dun Rats trying to slow the police. Diarmid half pushed Grace out the window onto the metal platform and leaped out himself, jerking loose the ladder, which crashed and squealed as he lowered it. Miles was just behind them.

"Go down," Diarmid told Grace. "I'll be right behind you."

She looked back, and he knew what she was thinking. The police. The Fenian Brotherhood. *Patrick.*

Fiercely, he whispered, "You promised. You promised to stay."

Her gaze grew distant for a moment, as if she were listening to something far away.

Miles shouted, "Hurry!"

Grace came to herself and started down. Diarmid went after her, their combined weight making the flimsy metal shake. When she was on the ground, he jumped the last few feet. Miles scurried after.

Someone shouted, and Diarmid saw police coming around the corner with a group of Fomorian warriors.

"Stop!" a policeman shouted. "We've got you surrounded!"

"No he don't," Miles muttered, dodging the other way, toward the cesspool. "This way!"

Diarmid yanked Grace after him as he followed Miles. They skirted the cesspool and the leaning privies and ran to an alley between two tenements. Miles plunged into it. The alley was very narrow, less than a foot and a half wide, so they couldn't really run, but then they were through and on the next street over. He heard shouts and thudding footsteps—too close. Grace stumbled—the skirts and corset were impossible. Her breathing was ragged. He ordered, "Don't you dare slow down."

Miles dodged into another mazelike corridor. Where he was taking them, Diarmid had no idea, but there was no time for questions. Night was coming on now; they ran past two lamplighters so quickly and close the men had to leap to avoid them.

But they couldn't get enough of a lead to hide in the growing shadows. Grace was having trouble keeping up, but Miles didn't slow and neither did Diarmid. He only tightened his hold. Finally, she jerked back, trying to free herself, panting. "Diarmid . . . I can't . . ."

More shouts behind them. Miles called, "Come on! Hurry!"

"Leave me," she gasped. "They . . . won't . . . hurt me."

He said, "Get on my back," and bent to take her piggyback. One moment of hesitation and then she did as he asked, and when he had a tight grip, he ran again.

The warriors were gaining; Diarmid was slower now, carrying her. Her arms clutched around his throat. The ogham stick in his pocket jabbed into his thigh. Adrenaline pumped through his veins.

He'd been known for his speed, and it didn't fail him now, even carrying Grace, but the Fomori met every turn and twist, dodged through every narrow passageway. They were always just close enough that there was nothing to do but run.

They careened around a corner. The waterfront was before them. Miles dashed down a dock. It was nearly dark. All Diarmid could see was the looming shadow of an old oyster sloop at the end. Miles raced up to it, sliding to a stop when a man stepped out of the gloom holding a pistol.

"We need Battle Annie," Miles gasped. "The Dun Rats ask for sanctuary. Hurry! The police're just behind."

The man put up his pistol and launched into action. He called over his shoulder, "Let's take 'er out, boys!" Suddenly, the dock swarmed with young men unmooring the boat. River pirates.

He reached to loosen Grace's choking hold, and she protested, "Diarmid—"

"Get on board!" Miles cried.

"We'll fight 'em off, lad," the man with the pistol promised. "We welcome it."

Diarmid hated boats and the water, but he could see no other way. The river pirates formed a wall protecting him and Grace from the approaching Fomorians. He heard the hiss of blades drawn from belts and scabbards. A boy on board the sloop yelled, "Come on!"

Diarmid raced up the gangplank, which was lifted the very next moment.

Again, Grace said anxiously, "Diarmid, no—"

"We've no choice." The boat was moving already. The clash on the pier was loud, the grappling boys turning to shadow in the darkening twilight. Fomorian warriors, river pirates, and Miles. The police shouted, "Stop that boat! We order you to stop!"

But the sloop kept on. Diarmid let go of Grace. She slid down his back, gaining her feet. Her fingers bit into his arm; her face was very white. "Diarmid, they're *glowing*."

He stared blankly at her, his blood still pounding, dizzy at their near escape.

"They're *fairies*," she said.

He looked at the boys on the deck and saw what he should have seen before. Their pale skin in the darkness. The way they watched her as they readied the boat to sail. Their beauty.

The sails raised, catching the wind as the boat raced into the channel. They were trapped with the children of the *sidhe*. There was no escape.

TWENTY

The next moment
Grace

No," Diarmid said softly. He raced to the railing, gripping it, staring off toward shore and the fight across the
water. "No, no."

We were moving quickly; within minutes I could no
longer hear the fight and the shore became just twinkling
lights, the sails huffing in a steady wind that breathed the
yearning of the *sidhe*—that seductive song I had to struggle
to resist. *Touch us. Let us kiss you and hold you. We will give
you everything.*

I wished I had fallen or hung back. That I hadn't heard
Aidan's voice in my head—the voice from my dreams—saying, *Stay. You need him*, that had made me keep the promise
I'd made Diarmid. I wished I was with the police, on my
way back to my family, instead of standing here fighting the
sidhe's yearning, and Diarmid's—

And my own.

It had been bad enough before he'd told me he loved me. I hated how much I wanted to believe him. I hated that I must remind myself every second that he was a liar. *But what if he's not lying? What if it were true? What would it change?*

I didn't know. I loved him, and I was afraid of what I might do because of it. I was already on the verge of not caring that it wasn't real. His kiss made me forget it entirely.

But my family needed me. They were depending on me. Patrick needed me. I had to go back. I had another life to live.

Assuming I could live it.

Yet . . . I couldn't help anyone without the archdruid, and to find him, I needed Diarmid. The faint silver glow from the *sidhe* sailors working the sloop brightened the night. A fey boy stood beside me, watching me with greedy eyes as he coiled a heavy rope, and I remembered what Miles had asked for. Battle Annie and sanctuary.

I said, with as much dignity as I could muster, "Take me to Battle Annie."

The boy said, "Oh, you'll see her soon enough."

"We've asked for sanctuary."

"And you have it." Tentatively, he reached out—

"Touch her and you'll be missing a hand," Diarmid snapped, striding over from the rail.

The boy drew back, glaring at Diarmid. "What a great warrior you are. You are on our property now. You have no say in this."

"Maybe not. But you'll still be missing a hand."

I touched Diarmid's arm. He stiffened, but went silent, and I said to the *sidhe* boy, "We would see Battle Annie now."

He glanced at Diarmid, and then back to me. "This way."

He led us across the deck. I felt the hunger of those we passed, pressing, almost unbearable. The boy took us to a slightly raised cabin at the center of the boat, down a short flight of stairs, into a hallway that glowed even with no lamp. The hall opened into a room with a low, bowed ceiling and trapdoors set in the floor opening to the hold. Stacked hammocks swung from a double row of beams on either side; some of them held sleeping boys. They woke as we passed, raising their heads to watch, their shining gazes glued to me, their hunger like a fine mist stinging my skin.

At the far end, the boy stopped and knocked on a door. "Our *guests* request a word, milady."

From the other side of the door, I heard a woman's laughter. "Send them in."

The boy stood back to let us enter. I had to stoop to keep from hitting my head. Diarmid had to bend nearly from the waist. We'd no sooner stepped inside than the door slammed shut behind us with a hard, grinding *click*.

The room was bigger than I expected. It ran the entire width of the sloop. There was a bed, a table covered with rolled charts, a stool, and an open trunk exploding with clothing. In the middle was a desk. A woman stood behind it, with two boys flanking her.

"Well, well," she said. She, too, was haloed with a pulsing silver glow, brighter than the others. She wore trousers and a shirt with the sleeves cut off. She was tall and her arms were as muscled as a man's; she looked stronger than any woman I'd ever seen. Her black hair was looped in braids, some of which had been tied in knots while some dripped down her back. She had tied feathers into them. Her sloe eyes were bright blue, and her skin was pale and marked with ink—a double stripe on her left cheekbone, and crossed swords on her shoulder. She wore huge golden hoop earrings—three in each ear—and at least ten necklaces, beads and chains and shells. Shoved in her belt were three daggers and a club. There was a pistol on the table, along with a flagon of wine and a cup.

"'Tisn't often I host one of the Fianna. And the *veleda* too. Quite a day. Quite a day." She smiled at Diarmid—a terrifying smile that revealed two front teeth filed to points. She jerked her head to the two boys standing behind her. "Disarm him."

They were on either side of Diarmid before I had time to draw a breath. He lifted his arms, but didn't fight them as they patted him down, removing a dagger from his belt, another from his boot. One of them pulled the ogham stick from his pocket.

"No, you can't—" I began.

Diarmid gave me a quick shake of his head.

The boy put the stick on the table before Battle Annie, who picked it up, turning it in her hands. It didn't seem to burn her any more than it had Diarmid. She spat, "Druid words. What does it say?"

Diarmid said, "Nothing. 'Tisn't a spell."

"Not a spell? What do you take me for? Why would you have it if it means nothing?"

"We got it from a Druid at Coney Island. Your folk had already ruined him." Diarmid's voice rang with disgust.

"Deirdre sent us there," I said. "She thought he might know of an archdruid. There's one in the city and we need to find him."

Battle Annie's blue gaze settled on me. "Why?"

Diarmid tensed. I wondered what was safe to tell her, but in the end my need to find the archdruid was too great. "*I* need him. For the prophecy."

Battle Annie stepped around the table, still holding the ogham stick, and sauntered over to me. I smelled her sweat and her perfume—ylang-ylang and sandalwood. I felt her hunger for my power as an itching in my fingers and in my blood. I saw it in her blue eyes and heard her singing in my head: *Let me. Let me touch you.*

She shoved the ogham stick at me. "What do the words say?"

I didn't take it. "I can't read ogham."

"You're a Druid priestess. Tell me what it says!"

"I told you I can't read it."

She shoved the stick into my stays. Even through the layers of whalebone and cotton, the stick burned, radiating, hotter and hotter. I stepped back, shoving her away without thinking. "Don't touch me with it!"

Her gaze narrowed. "It burns you."

Diarmid broke in. "It says nothing. 'Tis a prophecy, but one neither of us understands."

She looked at him. "Ah yes, I'd forgotten. *You* can read it."

"It means nothing."

"Do you think me a fool, Diarmid Ua Duibhne? If it's meaningless, why does it burn her? Why does she protest when it's taken away?" Battle Annie threw the ogham stick to the table, where it skittered nearly to the edge. "What does the stick say, lad? Who knows—perhaps my boys and I can help."

Diarmid didn't answer.

Help. That was all I heard. Perhaps they *could* help, just as my grandmother had said. "It says something about the sea being a knife—"

"Grace," Diarmid warned.

"—and things being broken. To harm and to protect become as one, and everything is in pieces."

"*Grace.*"

"Perhaps she knows what it means," I hissed. I turned to Battle Annie. "The man who gave it to us said it needs a key. But we don't know what that is, or what the stick would tell us if we found it. I hoped it had something to do with the archdruid."

Battle Annie was thoughtful. "You are not what I expected, *veleda.*"

"If you help me, I'm willing to bargain."

"No," Diarmid said. "No more bargains."

"I have to find him."

He ignored me and said to Battle Annie, "We've asked for sanctuary. Safe passage out of Manhattan and Brooklyn. In return, I can offer the thanks and loyalty of the Fianna."

Battle Annie smiled, as terrible as the first time. "Unless things have changed very much, Diarmid, that means little."

"You have my personal guarantee. I'll swear to it. On Danu's name."

"Your guarantee means nothing. The *sidhe* have favored you, but that is in the past. And as for your oath—Danu is a long-ago god and a mother I no longer serve."

Her gaze came back to me. I felt the sliver of it beneath my skin. Then she looked at him. I felt the communication between them, though she was silent and so was he, and I had no idea what she was telling him, what she was showing him. A glamour or something else? I saw him go taut. I saw a misery in his eyes that hurt. And then she said:

"I might accept a more meaningful promise."

The blood left his face.

Battle Annie laughed. "Ah . . . how precious is the life of your *veleda*? I must confess yours is an interesting game to watch. Which way will it go, I wonder? Choices, choices . . ."

"No more of this," Diarmid said. "Will you grant us safe passage or not?"

"Perhaps. But I won't bargain with you. One cannot trust the Fianna, even now. What will you give us for safe passage, *veleda*? Your coin is worth something, at least."

"No. Grace, no."

"It's my choice to make," I told him.

"No."

He was so adamant. I didn't know what he saw that I missed, and in my silence, Battle Annie said, "As you wish."

She snapped her fingers at the boys, who rushed forward, along with others who emerged from the shadows. Four of them grabbed Diarmid. Two were on me, their hands on my arms, their craving trying to pull my power through my skin, drawing on me, drinking . . .

"By the gods, stop them!" Diarmid shouted.

I felt dizzy, delirious. *"She'll kiss you . . . and make you ask her to do it again."* I understood what Lewis Corley meant. I wanted it to stop, I wanted it to go on forever.

"Leave her as she is, you fools! She may be of some use to us."

At Battle Annie's order, the draw stopped suddenly and I stumbled, disoriented. Battle Annie gestured, and they took us out, back down the hall, to the crew's quarters. There was the bang of a door, a scuffle, and then I realized someone was lifting the trapdoors of the hold. Diarmid fought them, but they shoved him over the edge, into the hole, and then they shoved me too.

It wasn't far to fall—perhaps four or five feet. I fell on him, heard the grunt of his breath as he caught me, and then the doors slammed shut and the darkness was complete.

TWENTY-ONE

Late that night
Patrick

T hey've escaped."

Patrick listened as impassively as he could as Daire Donn told them the news.

Simon MacRonan asked, "How exactly does a river gang escape the Fomorian god of the sea?"

"Tethra and his men were blinded by a fog."

"A fog," Patrick said flatly.

"Aye. 'Twas a glamour."

"A glamour?" Simon asked. "Set by river pirates?"

"They aren't just river pirates," Daire Donn said. "They're children of the *sidhe*."

Patrick jerked upright in his chair. "You've let Grace fall in with *fairies*?"

"'Tis not the best situation," Daire Donn admitted.

Simon sputtered, his eyes bright with alarm, "I would say that's an understatement, given all you've told us."

"I think we can trust that Diarmid will do everything in his power to keep her safe." Daire Donn looked uncomfortable as he said it.

"He's a warrior, not a magician." Patrick lurched to his feet. *Protect her, keep her safe. Do your job.* The words spun in his head.

"We're pursuing them even now, through the fog . . ."

"You're telling me a *god* can't sweep away a fairy glamour?" Simon asked.

"These are . . . very strong *sidhe*," Daire Donn said.

"How strong?" Patrick snapped.

Daire Donn grimaced. "The strongest we've seen in the city. Truthfully, the strongest we've seen for some time—but they are not stronger than Tethra. We should have your fiancée and Diarmid by morning."

"And in the meantime, what could the *sidhe* do to her?"

Daire Donn's smile was thin. "I suggest you don't think of that, my friend. Remember, the Fianna cannot afford to lose her either. I think we can trust Diarmid not to fail. As we will not."

Patrick's fear only grew. The *sidhe* had Grace. They were after Aidan. What of the rest of the family? He went home quickly. Though he had Fomorian guards at every door, they had proven how unreliable they could be.

Even after reassuring himself that everyone was safe, Patrick didn't sleep. He slumped in a leather chair in his study, staring unseeingly at the cold fireplace.

"Right now, she needs him more than she needs you."

But why? The question plagued him. The need to see Grace's brother again was so strong Patrick imagined he saw Aidan materializing before him. He shrugged away the fancy. A pink-edged dawn crept through the window. When the urge came over him to go into the park, he obliged it restlessly and went out the back door. The guard there started, raising his rifle until he saw it was Patrick. "Good morning, sir."

"Good morning." Patrick went to the gate, stepping out past the climbing rose that shielded the backyard from the park. Delivery wagons rattled in the distance, but the square in front of him was empty. He followed the path to the gazebo, which was sheltered by overhanging trees. He was not surprised to see someone already sitting there, nor was he surprised to find it was Aidan. In some part of his mind, he'd known Aidan was waiting; he'd come here to meet him.

Grace's brother was throwing little threads of purple lightning from finger to finger, spinning them about, weaving a web of electricity. Aidan said casually, "I'm trying something new. I wondered if I could do it, if I could just call you like this."

Patrick sat beside him on the bench. He found himself mesmerized by Aidan's light play, unable to look away.

"When did you first know you had this power?" Patrick asked him.

Aidan closed his hand, banishing the threads. "I've always felt there was something . . . not right about me. When Papa died, it got worse. Then, about three months ago, I began to feel as if I were burning. It was like . . . like being on fire from the inside out. The only thing that eased it was drink and laudanum. And then the dreams started—dreams that came true. Things I knew that I couldn't know. But the lightning—the sparks—that didn't start until I met Finn. He told me I could do it. He knew just by looking at me."

"How did Finn find you?"

"He didn't. The night Diarmid found me in that gambling hell, I meant to get drunk and throw myself off a dock somewhere. He saved me. Believe me, I didn't want to be saved—but then . . . he took me to your stables and you called him Diarmid and . . . I'd had a dream about him and Grace. It all fell into place. I followed him to the others. Finn told me I'm a stormcaster, that our family is descended from the *veleda*, which I knew anyway, because of Grandma, and that our ancestor, Neasa, was a Druid priestess of great power. He said he could see it bursting out of me the same way it did from her."

Patrick was amazed at how easily he accepted this, as if he had known it all along. "What about Grace?"

Aidan looked down at his hands. "I don't know about Grace."

"You said she needed Diarmid."

"She does."

"He's led her into a *sidhe* trap."

Aidan's head came up. "The *sidhe*?"

"She's on a ship with *sidhe* posing as river pirates. Some of the most powerful fairies the Fomori have seen."

Aidan's breath hitched.

"So what I need to know is: What do I do? What do you see? What can you tell me?"

"I can only talk to her in dreams," Aidan said. "And then not very much. I don't think Grace knows yet that it's real. Darkness keeps closing between us. She needs a key—what that would be, I don't know, though I think . . . I think Diarmid has something to do with it. I know she's afraid."

Grace afraid. It pained Patrick to think it. "Of him?"

"Perhaps." Aidan exhaled deeply. "But there's something else too. It's just . . . there's something wrong, Patrick. Nothing's as it should be, and I don't know why. There are all these . . . these loose pieces, and I can't bring them together, no matter how I try. Grandma said there was a curse—"

"A curse? You mean the *sidhe*?"

"She never said more. And now she never will."

"There's still a chance she'll wake up."

"No," Aidan said sadly. "Even if she does, she'll know nothing."

"Why do you say that?"

"Because she gave it all to me."

Patrick stared at him. "She *gave* it all to you?"

"I have her visions," Aidan explained. "I know they're hers. But they're jumbled and confused. Things don't make sense. It's as if . . . as if her madness is distorting what's true. I can't make heads or tails of it."

A suspicion nagged at Patrick, one he couldn't quite grasp. Here was Aidan, spinning lightning, having prophetic dreams, speaking with Grace through them, inheriting his grandmother's visions. Aidan, with ancestral power of a kind Finn had recognized.

Patrick asked, "What has Finn said about Grace? He's met her, hasn't he?"

Aidan nodded. "Diarmid brought her to the tenement one night. I wasn't there, but I've heard about it."

"Did Finn see any power in her?"

"She knew how to say the spell on the ogham stick that called the Fomori."

Patrick realized then what hope he'd been harboring. Grace had said, *"What if you're all wrong?"* He wondered . . . Aidan was bursting with power, and Patrick had seen little of it in Grace. Still, the ogham stick had burned her. She'd seen the Fianna glow. She'd known how to say the spell.

But was it enough? Grace's bits of power felt like scraps, an inheritance passed piecemeal.

"Cannel divined that she was the *veleda*," Aidan said, as if reading Patrick's thoughts.

"Her blood was on the *dord fiann*," Patrick remembered, feeling as if he snatched at straws. "She'd cut herself on it. The Fianna can't be called without the *veleda*'s blood, isn't that right?"

"That's what the spell needs. And . . . there's something else you should know, Patrick. Cannel sees something else in Grace."

"What's that?"

"He sees her aspect in threes. Two days ago he came up with a theory about why that is."

"'She sees; she weighs; she chooses,'" said Patrick. "That's what the prophecy says. The triune has always been part of the *veleda*."

"It's true of goddesses too. Brigid. The Morrigan."

"Are you saying Cannel thinks Grace is a goddess?"

"He thinks she's that powerful. More powerful than she should be."

"But—"

"I think this key—whatever it is—unlocks her power." Aidan met Patrick's gaze.

The power of a goddess.

If Cannel was right, the kind of energy Grace's death would release would be immense. Whoever held it would be unbeatable, just as the prophecy had said. Patrick's own ambitions beckoned. Freeing Ireland. Everything he'd worked for. That kind of power—what he could do with it, what he could achieve . . .

No. It wasn't worth her life. It would mean nothing without her. Nothing.

He was shaken by the ferocity of its temptation. "The Fianna know this? They know what kind of power Grace might have?"

"They know it," Aidan said.

"Then they'll have no wish to try to save her life."

"They're looking for the archdruid because they need the incantation. Grace doesn't know what it is and neither do I. But you said the Fomori are trying to find another spell, one that will save her?"

Lot and the others had tried to reassure Patrick, and he wanted to believe them. He said, "They tell me they're looking for the archdruid for such a spell, but I don't think they suspect the kind of power you're describing."

"Do they think it likely that another spell exists?"

"They said it is possible."

"Did they say it just to appease you? Or to win Grace's trust?"

"Whatever they think, *I* have to believe in it. I love her. I have to save her."

It had been years since they'd been close; those childhood days of playing with tin soldiers and sharing secrets were gone, but Patrick saw a pity in Aidan's eyes now that reminded him of those times, when Aidan had known him better than anyone. He was surprised to find the connection still existed, that he understood Aidan without words.

"You don't believe there is another spell," Patrick said.

"I want to believe it. Like you, I *have* to believe it. I love my sister, and no one else is looking out for her. Only you and me. Perhaps Diarmid, but it's hard to be certain. I know he's attracted to her. Perhaps he cares for her. I told you: there's something between them, and it's important. But he's Fianna through and through, and in the end, he'll do what Finn asks of him."

"You mean the *geis*."

"Yes. So you and I need to form our own alliance. One dedicated to saving my sister's life. Whatever else we do, we need to be together in this. Are we agreed?"

Patrick felt immeasurable relief. Here was the ally he needed. A man who only two months ago seemed like the most unreliable person on earth, and who was now the stormcaster for Patrick's enemies. But he felt Aidan could be trusted, that he was somehow *meant* to trust him.

"We're agreed," he said.

TWENTY-TWO

July 25
Grace

A re you all right?" Diarmid asked.

"Yes. I think so." I pulled away from him, still shaken from our encounter with the *sidhe* and the fall into his arms. I could see nothing at all, not even his shadow. I heard something scrabbling beyond—rats. "This is terrible."

"It's not good," he agreed. "You should have let me handle things."

"Because you were doing so well."

"At least I wasn't offering them everything."

"Neither was I."

"Aye, but they were taking it anyway, weren't they? I told you to be careful. I told you not to trust them and not to let them touch you."

"I didn't have much choice," I said.

"You can't let them take your power."

"What does it matter? Someone will take it. If not them, then the Fianna—or the Fomori. All for some stupid war."

"It's not a stupid war."

"Isn't it? Do you even know what you're fighting for?"

"To keep the Fomori from devouring every Irish soul," he said tightly.

Wearily, I closed my eyes. There was no difference between that darkness and the darkness we sat in, and so I opened them again. "And what will the Irish get if you win?"

"Their lives, for one. And their freedom."

"And they'll pay for that with eternal devotion, won't they? The Fianna will be heroes again. Everyone will love and admire you. There'll be nothing in the city you can't have. Money . . . power . . . women . . . and it all starts over again. How long before you're as corrupted as you claim the Fomori to be? No one believes you aren't already. Battle Annie wouldn't even bargain with you. The rest of the *sidhe* doubt everything you say. Why shouldn't I doubt it too?"

"Because you know me."

The way he said those words, so softly . . . they felt so true. Once again I wanted to trust him, to believe him, to love him.

"Grace—" There was a movement in the darkness.

"Don't touch me. You promised."

He sighed so heavily it seemed to drag the dark down with it. "You shouldn't have told her about the ogham stick, you know."

"I was trying to find out if they knew anything about the archdruid."

"We don't even know if the ogham stick has anything to do with him."

"I think it does. What did Battle Annie show you? What did she tempt you with? Was it a glamour?"

"You don't want me to speak of it."

"I wouldn't have asked you if I didn't want to speak of it."

Very deliberately, he said, "She tempted me with you. The glamour she raised showed what you and I could be together if you only"—a self-deprecating laugh—"ah, never mind. She knows how I feel. Everyone believes in that, it seems. Everyone but you."

"Oh."

"Aye." I heard him move, his footsteps. The ship rolled; water slapped against the hull. I felt it vibrating beneath the wood under my hands. Diarmid kicked something; there was a quiet thud and a scrabble of tiny claws that made me shudder.

The sound of rustling. "There're some burlap bags over here. They're empty, but they'll serve as blankets. 'Tis a bed of sorts, if you want."

"Where will you sleep?" I asked.

"Well . . . it might be a while until Annie gets over her irritation."

"So?"

"So we might be in for a bit of a stay. There're a dozen rats or more in this hold. I don't know what else is down here, but ship rats aren't something you want to mess with, I hear. I'm guessing you won't like them nibbling at you in the night any more than I will."

"And you can protect me from them, is that it?"

Another sigh. "I don't know what Annie or the rats have in mind, Grace. But I'm tired. Truly, it feels as if I could sleep a year. I don't want to be jumping awake at every movement because I don't know where you are and I can't see. I'd sleep better if you were beside me, and maybe you would too. In any case, it'll be more comfortable than the floor."

The idea of it was tempting, and that was dangerous. But as long as there was nothing more than sleeping . . .

"All right." The ship pitched. I had trouble keeping my footing as I made my way toward where I thought he was.

His hand brushed my arm. "Here," he said, pulling me down onto rough burlap. He brought me close, one arm around me, so my head rested on his shoulder. His other hand was light at my waist. I felt his heart beating against my cheek. I'd been building walls around myself, and now they dissolved as if something in me knew I had no more need of them.

I closed my eyes, and let the lullaby of his breathing rock me to sleep.

I was awakened by a shaft of bright light coming from the open door. Two faces peered down at us, and I realized in that moment how entwined I was with him, my legs tangled with his, his hand twisted in my hair. He cursed beneath his breath—something Gaelic—and pulled his hand from my curls, sitting up.

"Battle Annie wants to see the *veleda*," said one of the boys.

"Alone," said another.

"No," Diarmid said. "She does nothing without me."

I touched his arm. "It's all right. I'll see her."

"Grace, no—"

"I said I'll see her." I pushed my hair out of my eyes. It was a knotted mess, and my unwashed skin felt itchy and sticky with salt and sand. My corset pinched.

He whispered urgently in my ear, "Don't be a fool. You don't know them as I do. Insist that I come too."

"I can get us out of here. I know I can." I pulled away, walking to the square of light and squinting at the boys above. "How do I get up?"

There was a clatter; I stepped back as a slatted ladder unrolled into the hold. It swayed as I caught it and set my foot upon it.

"No bargains and no favors, Grace," Diarmid said.

"I know."

I went up the ladder. When I was at the top, the boys gathered it and me and let the door of the hold fall closed.

Now that I was alone with the *sidhe*, I didn't feel so confident. I would have to be clever. I would have to be alert.

"This way," one boy said, and I followed them to Battle Annie's quarters.

"The *veleda*, milady," the other boy announced.

Battle Annie sat at the desk. Behind her stood her courtiers. A bowl of apples and some fluffy white bread was before her, along with a steaming cup that smelled like chocolate. My stomach growled. The last thing I'd eaten had been the clams at Coney Island.

She gestured to the chair opposite. "Please, sit. Join me."

I knew the stories. Never eat with the fairies, never drink with them. I sat down, but when she shoved the chocolate toward me, I shook my head.

"'Tis human food."

"How do I know that? How do I know it isn't glamoured?"

"I've no wish to drain or enslave you, *veleda*. You're more useful to me in other ways."

That only made me more nervous. "What ways are those?"

Battle Annie took an apple from the bowl. She drew one of the daggers from her belt and sliced a piece, handing it to me. "Take it. I think when you do you will know the truth."

"The truth?"

"Whether 'tis glamoured or no."

I laughed. "And how should I determine that?"

"Use your power."

I didn't want to tell her that I didn't know how to do that, or even if I could. She was waiting, and she looked as if she would wait, apple suspended, forever, and so I took it. I wasn't going to eat it. I didn't trust her any more than I'd trusted Deirdre.

Battle Annie said, "Close your eyes. Listen."

The apple slice felt like any other apple slice, but that didn't mean it wasn't fairy food. "Listen?"

"Aye. Listen. Tell me what it says."

"It's an apple—"

"Listen!"

Well, what could it harm? Obediently, I closed my eyes. Nothing. Or . . . wait . . . I heard the song of the *sidhe. Let me touch you. Let me kiss you. Let me.* The whole room pulsed the melody. My blood burned in response.

"The apple," Battle Annie urged.

I tried to focus on it, the way it felt: a crisp sliver, its juices wetting the tips of my fingers, sticky and sweet, the way the flesh gave just a bit when I pressed it. But I heard nothing.

And then there was something, a strange music that bade me *Listen. Listen.* The same music I'd heard before, hazy and faint, telling me to trust Deirdre. So far away, so hard to hold. I struggled to hear. The more I tried to grasp it, the more it fell to pieces. Then it was gone.

But I'd heard its message. The apple was unglamoured. "You're telling the truth," I said.

Battle Annie sat back in satisfaction. "Ah. As I thought. I believe we can do business." She pushed the rolls toward me. "Now will you eat?"

My doubts about whether or not I was the *veleda* disappeared. "I don't understand. I've never been able to do any of this before a few days ago. Why is it happening now? What changed?"

"I've no understanding of Druid ways. Eat, and you and I will talk, *veleda*. I have a proposition for you."

I was wary, but I ate the apple, which was juicy and sweet, snapping between my teeth. It may have been the best thing I'd ever tasted. Battle Annie carved another slice, handing it to me, and I ate that, too, and then broke one of the rolls into pieces. Soft, fresh bread—something I hadn't had in what felt like forever.

I said, "No bargains and no favors."

Battle Annie grinned that terrible grin. "You speak with Diarmid's voice."

"He's warned me to be careful. He's had dealings with the *sidhe* before."

"Aye. But he is just a warrior; he has no power of his own but strength and strategy. Useful to you, I think, but his only value to us is his beauty."

"He was right, though, wasn't he? He told me you'd try to take my power. Your minions already tried."

"And I stopped them, did I not? 'Tis true we're hungry for your power, but to drink it will only appease my hunger for a time, and then I would be hungry again. No, I don't want your power. I want use of it. Do you know the story of Cormac's Cup?"

Cormac's Cup. The High King of Ireland, Grainne's father, received a cup from Manannan that told truth from lies. A lie told over the cup broke it into three pieces; a truth told over it welded it together again. When Cormac died, the cup disappeared.

"I know the story," I said.

"What the cup once did—that task belongs to the *veleda* now. Your job is to discern truth from lies."

I thought of Diarmid. Of Patrick. Of the Fianna and the Fomori and my whole life hanging in the balance. "I think that particular power has been lost over the years."

Battle Annie gestured to a pretty girl courtier, who gave her the ogham stick. Annie set it on the table between us. "I will help you find this archdruid you speak of."

"Why?"

"Because a *veleda* without training is of little use to me."

"How is a *veleda* with training of use?"

"Every day, I am besieged with requests. Decide this, debate that. I could use a Cormac's Cup for myself. In lieu of that, a *veleda* would do. You can already judge some truths. With training, you would be better. We could be allies. Battle Annie's strength in return for your judgment."

"I may not have much to offer you. There is the prophecy to consider. On Samhain I must make a choice. There will be no power left after that." I didn't want to say the rest. I didn't want to *think* it. "*I* may not even be left."

"'Tis a risk I'm willing to take."

I felt a piercing hope. "Then you think perhaps I don't have to die?"

"All things are possible, *veleda*. And fate is ever-changing, is it not? You may yet influence it."

The same thing Diarmid had said to me about divination: what was foretold was only what would happen if nothing changed. But if something did . . .

"I may influence it," I repeated. "How?"

"Arm yourself—not with weapons, but with training. How can you hope to change the world without knowing the forces that bind it?"

"An archdruid could teach me those things?"

Battle Annie nodded.

"Then there is one here in the city?"

"I have not heard of any archdruid here for many years. Then again, I have not looked for one."

"But my grandmother told me he was here. She said the *sidhe* could help me find him. Are you telling me her words were madness after all?"

"Sometimes truth and madness are the same. But I warn you, *veleda*: Be careful of those who claim that truth is certain. It is anything but."

"You mean . . . what Diarmid tells me."

"That one struggles. He loves you and knows he should not. As you love him and know you should not."

My heart pounded in my ears. "What about Patrick? And the Fenian Brotherhood? The Fomori? The Fianna? Which of them is right?"

"We have always found your mortal insistence on certainties strange. Nothing is as clear as you wish it to be. You have walked your path blindly until now. Time to open your eyes."

How perfectly, annoyingly unhelpful.

She pushed the ogham stick toward me. "Now I will return this to the one 'twas meant for."

"I don't know what to do with it," I admitted. "I don't know what it means. Without the key, it's useless. I don't suppose you have any idea where such a thing might be?"

Battle Annie only looked at me thoughtfully and said, "Have we a deal? Your judgment for my friendship?"

"Listen well," Diarmid had said. I heard no threat here. Battle Annie and her gang could be powerful allies. I had more faith in the *sidhe*'s ability to sniff out the archdruid than in my own. Truthfully, who knew whether I would even be alive to live up to my part of the bargain?

"We have a deal."

She held out her hand, and I shook it. Then she pushed back from the table and said to her boys, "Fetch Diarmid. Bring him here and let him eat. We'll make for Governors Island."

"Why Governors Island?" I asked.

"Something you will need is there."

"Something to do with the archdruid?"

She cocked her head. The beads in her hair clicked as they fell against one another. "Would you prefer I return you to Manhattan?"

Home. My old life. *Go back. Be who you were.*

But Diarmid was right when he'd said no one could go back. There was only going forward. If I meant to change my future, I had to face the dangers before me, including the Fianna warrior who had made himself my partner in this.

Time to open my eyes.

I looked at Battle Annie and said, "Governors Island it is."

TWENTY-THREE

Later that morning
Diarmid

He sat there in darkness, listening to the rats and the slap of water against the hull and footsteps passing overhead, waiting for the steps to pause. He expected it so often that when they finally did, he didn't believe it. Then there was a *creak*, and the hold door opened. The slatted ladder came tumbling down.

"Battle Annie will see you now, Diarmid Ua Duibhne."

The moment he set foot above, the *sidhe* grabbed him, holding him fast. "Where's Grace?"

"She's with milady," one of them said. "You've nothing to fear."

"I don't quite believe that."

"Believe what you want," said another. "'Tis nothing to us."

They led him to the captain's quarters and shoved him inside. He saw Grace at the desk with Battle Annie, sliced apples and bread before her. Horrified, he said, "You didn't eat it. Tell me you didn't eat it."

Grace said, "It's not fairy food."

"It's glamoured, Grace—"

"No." She rose and brought him to the other chair. "Sit down and eat. It's not glamoured."

He sat and shoved the plate away. "You've eaten it, and I'll never get you off this ship now. What did I tell you?"

Battle Annie smiled. Her pointed teeth gleamed. "Don't be a fool, lad. I have more to gain by making her a friend. Glamours are for fairies like Deirdre, who want only to play. I've bigger plans."

Grace said, "I've made a deal with Battle Annie. She's going to help us find the archdruid."

He should have known it. When had Grace ever done what he told her? She was as infuriating as Neasa had been. He asked, "And in return?"

"Annie believes I have a power that can help her."

His dread became crushing. "What have you done, Grace?"

"Made a good bargain," she said. "They're giving us safe passage to Governors Island."

"There are troops all over it."

"Not many, and they keep to Fort Jay. You can avoid them if you stay to the shore," Battle Annie advised.

"'Twould be better to go somewhere else. Somewhere—"

"She said no to Manhattan. I would have taken her there if she'd wished it."

He looked at Grace in surprise. "You said no?"

"I made you a promise, didn't I?"

"Aye, but . . ." There was something else here. Something he didn't understand. He felt as if he'd turned a corner and the world had upended. He said to Battle Annie, "What did you do to her?"

The river pirate queen only pushed the ogham stick toward him. "She cannot hold this without pain, but I return it to you. 'Tis useless to me."

He took it before she could change her mind, shoving it into his pocket.

"Now will you please eat?" Grace asked. "I know you're hungry."

"When we're ashore. If I can really get you off this ship, I'll eat."

"Always so cautious," Battle Annie said. "Such arrogance, to assume that you know what is right all the time. Does it not get wearying? Do the Fianna never guess wrong?"

"Rarely."

"Your *veleda* truly has a hard task then." She rose, gesturing to her courtiers. "Pack this up for them to take ashore."

"Don't trouble yourself," Diarmid said.

Grace said, "Thank you, Annie. We'll be happy to take it."

He glared at her. She returned his gaze, and he saw her confidence, as if she'd come to some decision. But what? What had she traded, exactly? He felt at a disadvantage, slow and muzzy-headed.

"Come then," Annie said. "We'll be there shortly."

She left the cabin, her necklaces and earrings and beads jangling, the feathers in her braids fluttering. They followed her to the stairs leading to the deck, and the light changed; instead of oil lamps, there was an almost-blinding fog, as if the sun were encased within it—a fairy glamour, he realized, and one that now and again pulsed with blue light. Battle Annie said, "We were pursued all night by Fomorians, but they won't see where we leave you, and with any luck, they'll continue to pursue us for another day or so."

Maybe. Or maybe not. The thought of the Fomorians just outside that scrim of fog made Diarmid nervous. The flashing blue must be Tethra's lightning bouncing off the glamour, trying to break through it.

It was time to get off this ship, and as quickly as possible. On land, Diarmid felt he could keep Grace out of their hands. On the ship, there was nowhere to escape if Tethra got through that fog—and he would, eventually.

The sails luffed; a faint breeze ruffled his hair. Out of habit, he checked the heavy forelock covering the *ball seirce*. Grace said, "It would be nice to see your eyes. They're such a pretty blue." A compliment. And the way she looked at him . . .

"What did she do to you?"

"What?"

"Battle Annie. What did she do? What glamour or . . . or spell did she cast on you?"

"I don't know what you mean."

"Something's different."

"It's your imagination."

"No," he said firmly. "It's not my imagination that you chose to come here instead of Manhattan, when all you've been doing since we left is try to get back there."

"I decided it would be better to stay with you."

Now he was certain there was an enchantment. "I'll make her take it off." He turned from the rail. "I'll—"

She grabbed his hand. "Don't be stupid. I'm not bespelled. Not by her."

"Then by who? Tell me and I'll—"

"Oh for God's sake, Diarmid. Why can't you believe that I know what I'm doing?"

He paused. "'Tis just that they take you away to meet with a fairy, and I can't do anything but go mad wondering what's going on. Then when I see you again, you're looking like you have all the answers, and you call my eyes *pretty*, and—"

"I'm sorry I said it. Here, how's this: I can't stand the way your hair hangs in your face. Is that better?"

"It's only that . . . you're suddenly . . . very confident."

"Which is not what you're used to, I know. I forgot—only the Fianna are allowed to make decisions."

"That's not what I said."

"But it's what you meant. You don't trust that I can make a good one on my own."

He felt as if he'd stumbled into a trap and couldn't get free. She'd gone from compliments to prickliness in a moment. He tried to placate her. "You haven't had many dealings with fairies, that's all."

"And you've used *your* experience with them so well?" Her eyes were blazing now. "All your prettiness and your . . . your . . . charm haven't bought you trust among them."

He stepped back, bewildered by her scorn. "Grace—"

"They *do* trust me." Her gaze was steady and unrelenting. "They believe in me. I've made a good bargain, whatever you think. At least with Battle Annie, there's the chance of . . ."

"Chance of what?"

"Something I can do with myself if I survive this." She looked into the bright fog.

"I thought you already knew what you wanted to do with yourself. Save Ireland with Patrick Devlin—wasn't that it?"

Her hands tightened on the rail. "I don't know. Perhaps."

Diarmid's hope soared. *It means nothing,* he told himself. "Is that right? What then?"

"I suppose that depends."

"On what?"

The fog parted magically. Before them was Governors Island, trees and short clay cliffs sloping steeply to the shore; what looked like an abandoned building—a boathouse or a storehouse—cradled in the trees. Someone shouted from the bow; the sails went slack, the ship slowed.

Grace said, "On whether I'm still alive."

The hope he'd felt withered. Once again, he wondered if she knew about the *geis* and his role in her sacrifice. He didn't know what to say except the truth he hoped for: "We'll find the archdruid, Grace."

She said nothing.

The island was small, but they were on the side opposite the armory of Castle Williams. Fort Jay and its barracks and parade grounds at the top of the island's slope were hidden from view, shielded from the beach by a thin band of woods. Battle Annie's crew had taken them to the only place on the island where it might be possible to elude discovery. He heard the plunge of the dinghy as it went over the side.

Battle Annie appeared behind them. "The boat's ready. You'll be safe enough if you keep in the trees."

"Can you get word to Finn about where we are?" Diarmid asked.

She glanced at Grace as if asking permission, which irritated him. His irritation grew when Grace nodded, giving it.

"Aye," Battle Annie said. Then, to Grace, "If you've need of me, you have only to call."

"Call? And how am I to do that? Just shout across the harbor?"

Battle Annie's smile made Diarmid shudder. "Just listen."

Grace's slight smile in return told Diarmid it was a joke between the two of them, and he didn't like that either. He would be glad to be rid of the river pirate queen. Grace went down the ladder to the rowboat first, holding the leather bag of food and supplies that Battle Annie's courtier had given her. Diarmid followed. There were only three of them—Diarmid and Grace and a *sidhe* sailor, but still the rowboat rocked beneath Diarmid's weight as he boarded, and he sat uneasily, gripping the sides. The water was very close. Fog blanketed them, muffling and echoing the *splash* of the oars.

"You see?" Grace told him. "I'm off the ship. The food wasn't glamoured."

"But not off the boat," he pointed out. "If you can set foot on land, I'll believe you."

The dinghy tipped and jerked in the waves. Diarmid's stomach lurched. When they got close to shore, he wanted to jump out immediately, but he couldn't risk that. This could all be a trick. He'd be standing on the shore watching the sailor row her back to the ship. He watched as the *sidhe* boy helped her over the side, her boots splashing in the shallow tide, the hem of her gown dragging. Diarmid didn't move until both her feet were on solid ground.

"You see," she said.

He stepped into ankle-deep water, and was relieved as he watched the boy row away.

Grace sat on a large rock at the base of the bare clay scarp and held out an apple. When he took it, she teased, "Be careful now . . . perhaps it's glamoured still."

He rolled his eyes and bit into the fruit. He was famished; it was all he could do not to swallow it whole.

She said, "Battle Annie told me there was something I needed here. Something to do with the archdruid."

"Did she say anything more? Like what to look for? Or where?"

"No. Where would it be, do you think? Where the soldiers are? I don't suppose they have fortune-tellers at Fort Jay."

Diarmid laughed. "No. And trust me, we don't want to go anywhere near those soldiers."

"I suppose not." She glanced over her shoulder at the treed slope. "We'll have to sleep in the woods, I guess."

He finished the apple, so hungry he ate the core. "Better than a tenement closet. But I'm thinking of that storehouse. It looks like no one's been there in a while."

She reached into the bag and drew out his daggers, which she handed to him, along with a roll. "Here. You might need these."

He shoved the daggers back into his belt and his boot and ate the roll in two bites. "Stay here. I'll make certain no one's inside."

She looked alarmed.

"Don't worry. I won't leave you alone for long. I don't want to come back to see you've changed your mind and gone to the city."

"How would I do that?"

"I'm no match for *sidhe* magic."

"I'm not going anywhere. I want to stay with you."

Move, he told himself. *She means nothing by it, and you're resisting her, remember?* He started off down the beach. He felt that every moment he was away from her would change her more, and he had a hard enough time already keeping the two Graces straight in his head—the one who kissed him as if she could not get enough of him and the one who wanted him to leave her alone.

He had to climb through brambles and trees to get to the storehouse, which was as abandoned as it had looked from the shore. There was a door on the water side, blocked by brambles;

he tugged them out of the way, their tiny thorns and prickles scratching and biting at his bare hands. Finally, he managed to open the door wide enough to wedge himself inside. It was dim and empty; there were old crates lying about, some rusty chains, and a few bales of dusty straw smelling of must and mildew. Resting against the far wall were two sets of broken oars. Open slats just below the roof let in light and air. Dust and sand covered the floor, undisturbed. He wondered if the army even remembered this place was here.

He hurried back to her. She sat against the big rock, her face raised to the sun, her eyes closed. For a moment he just looked at her, his longing almost suffocating him before he forced himself to say, "It's empty. I think 'tis safe enough."

She opened her eyes. He saw again that disconcerting resolve. What had Battle Annie said to her? What had happened in that room?

"I'd feel better to be out of the open. Come on." He held out his hand to help her up. She grabbed it, the rocks shifting beneath her feet, slipping and rolling, and she fell into his chest. His breath simply left him.

Was she breathless, too, or was he just imagining it? She looked up at him, and he saw fear in her eyes before she pulled away. *Fear.* Why fear? He'd done nothing to make her fear him. Unless she knew about the *geis* . . .

He led her to the storehouse. Inside, she walked about the room, thoughtful again, withdrawn. He sat against the wall, pulling the ogham stick from his pocket, reading the runes, trying to make sense of it.

The sea is the knife. Great stones crack and split. Storms will tell and the world is changed. The rivers guard treasures with no worth. To harm and to protect become as one, and all things will only be known in pieces.

Druids and their wretched cleverness! He couldn't figure it out. He would have dismissed it as nothing if not for Grace's grandmother, because Grace was right—it was too coincidental. The same words, the archdruid—this had to mean something, but without a key, it was meaningless. And where to find a key? Where even to look? It would be easier just to follow the *sidhe* until they found the archdruid.

Easier, but more dangerous. He thought of how Grace had leaned into their touch at Battle Annie's, that expression of pleasure and desire, just as when he kissed her—

"What are you doing?"

He started. She stood before him.

"Trying to decipher it," he said.

"I asked Battle Annie if she knew anything about a key."

"She didn't."

"How do you know?"

"The fairies drink Druid power, but they don't like Druid magic. They prefer to be the cleverest in the room."

"Something they have in common with the Fianna," she said, but she smiled to soften it. "Is that something you learned from the twelve books of poetry?"

He shook his head. "That I learned from a fairy I knew."

"The one who changed from an ugly hag into a beautiful girl? Who built you the house that you lived in together—until you made her angry by reminding her too many times that she'd been ugly?"

He was surprised once again by the stories people told. That tale—where he'd been stupid and wrong—would not cast him in a very good light. Then again, he would have thought that about Grainne, too, and people had built a romance from it.

Grace sat beside him. "I know your whole life, I think. It must seem unfair to you, since you don't know the same things about me. But I guess it evens everything out."

"Evens everything how?"

"You'll always have an advantage, won't you? You're so . . . the way you look, and you . . . you have the *ball seirce*. I need *some* defense against you."

That terrible hope again—it was impossible to pretend it wasn't there. "Why do you need a defense, Grace?" he whispered. "What's wrong with giving in? You know how I—"

"Sssh. You promised."

He let out his breath in frustration. "You're turning me into a madman. You kiss me one moment and push me away the next. How can I convince you that I mean what I say? What do you want from me?"

She twisted her fingers together. "When I was with Battle Annie, she said some things . . ."

"What things?"

"That I needed to open my eyes. That I had been blind." She paused. "I'm the *veleda*."

Her words confused him. "Aye."

"No, I mean, I *know* I am. These last days, I've felt a power in me and . . . it's all true. The prophecy. The choice. All of it."

"We'll find the archdruid, Grace. We'll—"

"And I know you're the one who has to kill me."

He felt as if she'd struck him.

She said quietly, "Patrick told me about the *geis*. Though you haven't—you've been keeping it from me. But it's true, isn't it?"

He had trouble finding his voice. "Aye."

"And you mean to do it. You'll do it because you belong to the Fianna. Because to belong to them is all you ever wanted. More than love, you said."

"Grace—I want to save your life as much as you do. If there's a spell that says you don't have to die, or a way I don't have to kill you . . ." Her expression made the words die on his tongue. "What is it? Why are you looking at me that way?"

"I wish I could tell whether you're lying the same way I knew that food from Battle Annie wasn't glamoured, but I . . . I can't. When you kiss me I believe you, but I know that's only a lie and—"

"It's not a lie."

"Of course you would say that. But I've only ever kissed one other boy, just Patrick, and . . . and I don't know enough to tell—" Her cheeks pinked with embarrassment. "Oh, I'm making a muddle of this. I don't even know what I'm saying. It's just that in my dreams, Aidan keeps telling me I need you, and I . . . I can't run away from you, though I know I should.

The truth is . . . you frighten me. More than anything I've ever known."

It was not what he'd hoped for, but he understood, because she frightened him too. Because he should run from her as well, and he couldn't. He felt fate's hand again, that sense of needing her beyond the *geis* or the prophecy or anything else. Worlds hung in the balance—his own and hers and that of the Irish, and it was both bigger than anything he'd ever known and as small as the two of them.

"I know. I feel it too." He brought his hand up to touch her, and then he remembered his vow and let it fall again. He saw her swallow. He waited for her to tell him it was all right, to say, *Touch me. Kiss me.*

Then she looked away, and he knew she meant to stick to the deal they'd made, and it felt so . . . wrong. Disastrously wrong. Tragically wrong. As if each moment that they didn't touch put everything farther out of reach.

She leaned her head back against the wall, staring up at the open slats above, the sunlight slanting through. "Tell me how it feels to die."

It was so far from what he was thinking that it was as if she were speaking a foreign language. "Grace, it's not going to come to that. It can't—"

"Did it hurt?"

"Grace—"

"Tell me the truth," she said. "I want to hear a truth I can believe. Please."

He closed his eyes, unable to bear her implied admission—*I know I have to die*—or his own fear. He forced himself to be as honest as she wanted him to be. "Aye, it hurt. At least at the beginning. But I'd been gored by a boar. More than once. There are less painful ways to die."

"You said 'at least at the beginning.'"

He kept his eyes closed. He and Grainne had been visiting her father. It was the first time they'd been there since their elopement. There was a feast planned, a celebration with family and friends—including the Fianna . . . and Finn. Diarmid had been anxious and nervous; he'd slept restlessly. He woke near dawn to the howling of his dogs. Grainne murmured, *"'Tis nothing, my love. Go back to sleep."* He'd tried to, but the noise only grew louder with the sunrise. Finally, he got up to look. *"Take your great sword and your red spear,"* she'd said, but it seemed too much. The dogs had probably only cornered a fox. Why would he need the great spear and sword for that? So he'd taken the smaller ones instead, and he'd been halfway out the door when Finn waylaid him in the hall.

He hadn't seen Finn since Aengus Og had brokered the uneasy peace between them. And so when Finn told him the dogs had a boar, and it was best that Diarmid not go after it—*"'Tis the boar prophesied to kill you, my friend. Why else did Aengus put a geis on you never to hunt boar?"*—Diarmid was annoyed. Finn telling him what to do once again, and besides, he'd known nothing of any *geis* about boar. How would Finn know of a prophecy that Aengus hadn't told his own foster son? Diarmid suspected that Finn had made it up just to taunt him, and so he ignored the warning. He asked for the use of Finn's best dog, which Finn refused. Diarmid had been angry, and determined not to show any weakness when he faced the Boar of Ben Bulben—that was actually his own half brother shape-changed and fierce with hatred and jealousy. Diarmid's vanity had blinded him to the truth. Because of pride, he'd lain dying on that high, grassy plain, bleeding through many wounds.

He didn't open his eyes as he told Grace, "I remember being thirsty. I was thirsty more than anything else."

"And Finn brought you water," she said. "It would have saved you, but he hesitated."

"He was still angry with me. But I didn't trust him either."

"Three times he let the water run through his fingers, until the others begged him to save you."

"Ossian and Oscar." He saw Oscar leaning over him, tears in his green eyes, the morning sun haloing his hair.

"By the time Finn finally brought you the water, it was too late."

"'Twas like falling into a dream." It was as though a veil had covered the world. "Like being . . . released. I suppose that's the best way to put it."

"And the pain?"

"'Twas gone. I never felt as good as that. As if nothing could weigh on me or trouble me again."

"You were happy?" she asked.

"Not happy. Not sad either. Just existing, and everything moving around me. The past and the present and whatever was meant to be. I—" He opened his eyes as a sudden memory seared him, something he'd forgotten. "I saw you."

"You saw *me*?"

"Aye." When he'd seen her then, he'd thought her only a comforting spirit sent to welcome him to the Otherworld, where layers of time wrapped around him, life as it had been and as it was and as it would be, all at once.

Amazed, he said, "I've always felt as if I already knew you, but—aye, you were there. Or at least, the vision of you."

"What did I do? What did I say?"

"It was brief. I don't even think I saw your face. It was more your . . . your presence. You were waiting in a place I wanted to be."

She looked skeptical—and hopeful too. "You're not just making this up?"

"I swear to you I'm not." Diarmid laughed disbelievingly. "I didn't remember it until this moment. When I was dying, I didn't know who you were. Only that I was supposed to go toward you."

"Did you? Where was I?"

"Waiting. It's hard to explain."

"Was there an Otherworld, the way the legends say? Is that where I was?"

Diarmid tried to remember. That bright silver veil; Grace waiting, something he knew he was meant to go toward. And then . . . a great yank, and the next thing he knew he was in his old body, in a room in his foster father's house, and Aengus was talking to him. Talking and talking, and Diarmid wanting so badly to return to the world where she waited, though he couldn't remember where that was.

"If there is an Otherworld, I never got there. Aengus brought my body back, and he wouldn't let my spirit go. He was grieving. He missed me too much. He kept me . . . tethered. Now and then, he'd pull me into my body so I could talk to him. And then Finn died, and Aengus sent me with the others to fall into the undying sleep." He leaned his head back, closing his eyes once more as memory washed over him. "I never saw or felt you again. Not until we woke here, and I found you swooning in Patrick's yard."

He felt her press closer. He kept his eyes closed, afraid of what he would see if he opened them. Afraid to find that she didn't want what he wanted.

He felt her lean over him, her hand on his chest. It was all he could do just to let her, to not demand, *Kiss me, Grace*—

She swept the hair from his forehead.

And then she said, "What is *that*?"

TWENTY-FOUR

The next moment
Grace

Diarmid jerked away, scrambling to his feet. I fell back,
catching myself just before I went sprawling. He was
already pushing his hair over his forehead, his eyes blazing.
"Why did you do that?"

"You had a twig in your hair. I was just taking it out.
What—" I broke off, suddenly understanding.

The *ball seirce.*

That was the mark I'd seen. The legends said it was there,
on his forehead, and yet . . . I'd never seen it before. It was a
distinctive scar; I would have remembered. Which meant—

He'd never used it on me.

No. No, I wouldn't believe that. I couldn't. I must have
seen it. Dully, hoping against hope, I said, "Did you get that
burn in the fire?"

He was frighteningly tense. "It's the *ball seirce,*" he ground
out.

No. No, no. "But . . . I've never seen it before."

"Of course not."

"I thought—I thought you'd used it on me. Before. The first time you kissed me, I thought I was compelled—"

"To slap me?" He laughed. "Aye. That's what I do. I go around compelling girls to make me miserable."

It's real. Everything I felt. I was drawn to him and I wanted him and I loved him. I didn't know which was worse—feeling that I'd been compelled to love him, or knowing I'd been so foolish as to fall for him on my own.

My words spilled out. "I love you."

"*Now* you do."

"No, I felt that way before . . . before I saw it. I don't feel any differently."

He slid down the wall, drawing up his knees, burying his face in his hands. "You think it's real, Grace, but it's not. It's the spell."

I was stung. "Don't tell me how I feel."

He lifted his head. "Yesterday you told me you didn't want me touching you. No talk of love, you said. You tried to escape me. Only a few moments ago you told me you were afraid of me. And now you're telling me you love me—after you see my *gift*."

"I've been frightened of what I feel. I've been running from it."

"And now you're not." Flat disbelief—no, more than that, as if he expected the lie.

"I'm still afraid. I don't *want* to be in love with you. It's stupid and it's dangerous. You belong to the Fianna and I can't

trust you and . . . oh, I know better than this! But I'm not compelled. No more than I was before."

"They all say that. They all like to think their minds are
still their own."

"My mind *is* still my own."

"No it's not."

"How do you know? Have any of them . . . any of the others"—how I hated to say it—"been in love with you before
they saw the lovespot?"

"What do you mean by *love*? D'you mean, did they look at
me? Did they think I had pretty eyes? Did they kiss me? Did
they want me?"

"You make me sound like a fool."

He sighed heavily. "Not you, no. I'm the fool. I should
never have let myself . . ."

"Let yourself what?"

"Nothing." He climbed to his feet. "I'll see if I can find us
something to eat."

I caught his arm. "I'm not hungry. We still have the food
Annie gave us. You don't need to go anywhere."

"Grace—"

"I don't know what to do. I don't know what I *should* do. I
love you and . . . and you said you loved me. Just yesterday you
said it. Was it a lie after all?"

"No. But what you feel for me now isn't real. And I wanted
it to be real." He paused and then said bitterly, "It will fade
eventually. You can take solace from that."

"It's not a spell," I said desperately. "It's not going to fade. Dear God . . . what do I do?"

"Grace, listen to me. *Listen.*"

His words echoed Battle Annie's, the way she'd told me to find the truth. He took my arms as if he meant to shake me, and the touch lit my blood. His gaze locked to mine as if he felt it, too, holding me prisoner so I couldn't look away. *Touch him.* I stepped closer. He didn't move. When I kissed him, he shuddered, and I knew he felt the fire that ignited between us. His arms went around me; he kissed me as hungrily as I kissed him. The fire consumed me, the light of him pouring in. *Give in. Give in.* Whatever else was between us, whatever lies, whatever obligations . . . we were bound to each other. When I was in his arms, I knew it was true. I could not keep denying it. *Give in.*

His fingers were at my bodice, unbuttoning, shoving it over my shoulders, down, dragging at the drawstring of my chemise, stumbling over the armor of my corset, and my old dream flooded back, brutal and insistent. Screaming and a knife flashing.

I froze. What was I doing here? Why was I letting him do this? The choice I had to make, the ritual and the *geis*—none of those things had gone away.

"Fate is ever-changing."

The words reassured me. Yes, fate could be changed. And I could change my own. I *would* change it.

But he'd felt my hesitation and pulled away. "I can't do this. I'm ... I'm taking advantage and I shouldn't be. 'Tis only that I've wanted you for so long ..."

"I want—"

He shook his head. "When the spell fades, you'll hate yourself for letting me touch you this way. You said you don't trust me, and nothing's happened to change that. Nothing but the lovespell. I want you to trust me, Grace. I want you to love me. But not because a spell has stolen your will."

I was so much in love with him I felt stupid with it. I wanted him to keep touching me. But he was right—now was not the time for us to be together. Not because a spell had changed the way I felt, but because of what I needed to do. Perhaps I *could* change fate, but until I had, it would be best not to trust him. Best not to love him.

I forced myself to step away. I pulled my sleeves up over my shoulders and buttoned my bodice.

"I'll be back." He went to the door. "I won't be far. Call if you need me."

Then he left me there alone.

I sat against the wall and stared up at the light streaming through the slats, watching it change to gold with sunset. The evening was so quiet I heard the lap of water on the shore and the whistles of steamers in the distance.

I spent the time building barriers against him, wanting to be strong enough to resist him, wondering if I could.

The words from my dreams played through my head, and I resisted those too. I wished I knew what to do.

The ogham stick rested on the floor where Diarmid had left it. Such a small thing, yet I knew it held the answer if I could only find it. Carefully, I touched it. The burn was quick and intense. I jerked my fingers back. How was I to discover anything if I couldn't even touch it? *We need the key.* But there wasn't a single clue—

I heard a sound, the cracking of branches, the brush of brambles beneath a foot, and the door pushed open. Diarmid came inside, looking weary. I reached for the leather bag and fumbled for an apple. I held it out to him. "I promise I won't ravish you."

His smile was small, his eyes haunted. He came over and took the apple, squatting, close, but not too close.

"You remind me of a wild animal who's afraid to get near," I teased. "Perhaps . . . a stag."

His laugh was small too. He looked down at the apple. "I'm sorry."

"For what?"

"For the *ball seirce*. For trying to . . . tempt you. I had no right. I should never have told you how I felt. 'Twas wrong, and I'm sorry. But I'd thought . . . What if we start fresh? I'll keep you safe and try to persuade you to choose us, but honestly. With talk alone. Without all the rest of it."

My heart sank into a dark and lonely place, but this was what I wanted too. This was best.

I said, "Well, then, convince me your Fianna are in the right."

He was visibly relieved. He sat beside me and began to tell me the stories. Many of them I knew already, but there were new things in them, the world from his point of view, and before long we were laughing, and his arm came around my shoulders as if it were the most natural thing to do, as if he didn't even realize he was doing it, and I forgot the reasons he was telling me these things. He was only a boy I loved who was telling me about his life.

But that moment didn't last long. It was too familiar: his laughter, his warmth, and the lapping of the water against the shore. It was my dream. Except in my dream, I was touching him, I was kissing him, and the need to do so now came over me like a fever. In my head, the words circled around and around: *Give in.*

TWENTY-FIVE

July 26
Patrick

The things Aidan had said preyed upon Patrick. What troubled him most was that the Fianna believed Grace had the threefold power of a goddess.

The possibilities had tempted *him*—and he loved her. If the Fomori knew this . . . would it change their efforts to save her life?

He was disturbed at his own lack of trust. They said they wanted to spare her. They said they were looking for the archdruid. Just because they'd let that *sidhe* boy escape and seemed loath to confront any others . . . but they knew the *sidhe* better than he did. Why should he doubt them? Still, something nagged at him. Better to keep his own counsel until he knew what it all meant. Aidan was right—it was Grace who mattered now.

Patrick strode into the dining room, where Mrs. Knox picked at a late breakfast of coddled eggs and toast. The circles beneath her eyes were deep, purple shadows. Her lips were dry and chapped. Her usual elegance and delicacy now looked beyond frail—she looked as ready to topple as a house of cards.

Aidan had said, *"My mother is willfully blind."* Perhaps. But Patrick felt he was failing her. "You're not eating."

"I'm not hungry, Patrick. Truly, it's fine. My headaches..."

"Should I call the doctor? Is there a medicine you need? Something I can do?"

She shook her head. "It's only worry."

Patrick wondered what he should tell her. He wanted to ease her concerns without creating more. Finally, he settled on one thing he thought he could say. "I've some good news for you."

Her eyes lit. "Grace?"

"Not Grace. Aidan. We've found him. That is, *I* found him."

"Aidan? Oh thank God! Is he all right? Is he home?"

"He's fine. I've spoken to him. And no, he's not home. He's . . . helping us look for Grace."

Mrs. Knox asked warily, "Is he drinking?"

"No. He seems . . . good. I don't think you need to worry about Aidan." *At least not just yet.* "I'm keeping in contact with him."

"He *is* safe?"

"Yes."

Mrs. Knox sighed. "I wish I could tell you how grateful I am for you, Patrick. I wish there was some way to thank you for your kindness to my family."

"You've given me your daughter. I'll spend a lifetime thanking *you*."

The butler appeared at the dining room door, followed closely by Bres, who said jovially, "Ah, breakfast! Good morning, Devlin. Rather a late start to the day, don't you think? 'Tis nearly eleven." He bowed to Mrs. Knox. "Mrs. Knox—you're a vision this morning. Simply glowing."

"Because I've just heard some very good news," Mrs. Knox said.

Oh no. No, no.

"What news is that?"

"Patrick's heard from my son. Aidan's safe!"

"Is that so?" Bres looked at Patrick curiously. "Well, that *is* news."

"And I imagine you've some of your own," Patrick said, uncomfortably changing the subject. "Else you would not be visiting me this morning."

Bres sobered. "Aye. We've word of Finn's Warriors at last."

"You've found them?" Mrs. Knox looked anxious again.

"We believe so, madam." Bres pointed Patrick to the door. "Will you please excuse us, Mrs. Knox?"

Patrick followed Bres into the hall.

"Where are they?" Patrick asked.

"In a stale beer dive on Bleecker. We're heading over there as soon as Balor can rally a force."

"Not without me."

"This could get ugly, my friend."

"I've spent the last three years raising rebellions in Ireland. Do you imagine I just stood back and sent men to their deaths? Believe me, I can hold my own."

"Against the Fianna?" Bres raised a brow. "Need I remind you that they were the High King's elite warriors? Finn knows how important you are to us. He would target you. No one doubts your ability or your zeal, but I'm afraid I must order you to stay."

"Order me?" Patrick laughed. "Have you forgotten where you are?"

Bres's answering smile was grim. "I have not, but we can't afford for something to happen to you. It's for the good of the cause that I ask it."

"I'll stay out of the way, then," Patrick insisted. "But I'm going. Your men let Grace and Diarmid escape on a fairy sloop, for God's sake. Now I want to see to things myself."

Bres sighed reluctantly. "Very well. I'll post you a guard."

"I don't need a guard."

"The others would question my judgment if I allowed that, and I cannot have anyone distracted because they worry over you." Bres's tone was mild, but Patrick heard the underlying steel that had made the man a formidable king. "We would all feel better if you were protected. You do realize how much depends on you?"

"Yes, I know. I've connections here, and in Ireland—"

"Because of the *veleda*," Bres corrected. "Without you, she has no reason to give us her allegiance. Your love for her is the strongest weapon we have. Please accept what protection we can offer."

Patrick understood, but he hated the need for it. "As you wish."

"Now tell me, what have you discovered of the stormcaster?"

"Nothing," Patrick lied. "Grace's mother was worried; I wanted only to ease her mind. We know he's with the Fianna and that he's safe. It seemed a kindness to tell her the latter at least."

"So you haven't spoken with the lad?"

"No. Shouldn't we go?"

Bres's carriage took them to the club where Balor waited. "My troops are on their way. We'll meet them there. 'Tis certain to be a bad fight." Balor clapped his fist into his hand and grinned, which made him look more frightening than ever.

The three of them crowded inside the carriage—Balor was so huge Patrick had to squeeze against the door.

"They'll be rousted like rats from a fire," Balor said gleefully.

As they neared Bleecker, Patrick pushed aside the leather curtain to peer out the window. He could see nothing out of the ordinary, but he smelled smoke. Oracle smoke. He glanced around, wondering if anyone else smelled it. Then, the smell was gone. The carriage turned a corner. "Where are the police? I don't see—"

Abruptly, the carriage was surrounded by a swirling mass of people, police and gang boys, all holding clubs and shouting. The carriage stopped, unable to go farther. Patrick jumped out, hearing Bres call, "Patience, Devlin! Your guards! Hold up!"

Patrick didn't wait. He pushed through the crowd, and there were the Fianna. Finn fighting like the very devil, twisting and swirling, his golden-red hair flying around him. Ossian with sweat pouring down his face. Keenan wrenching the club from a police officer's hand. The mass of bodies surged and pulsed. Dust rose in a cloud. People shouted, "Leave 'em alone!" and "Get 'im, Finn!" The force of the crowd jostled Patrick. This fight was nothing like the ones he'd organized in Ireland, where there were guns and bayonets. This was a mob. The Fianna fought like dogs, lunging and dodging, biting and kicking and stabbing. These were the elite forces of the High King? These were *heroes?*

Balor pushed through into the fight. Patrick started to follow when a hand pulled him back.

Bres. Beside him were two Fomori warriors in police dress, Patrick's guards. "Devlin—think of us. 'Tisn't just the danger—the Brotherhood can't be seen as a part of this. Think of your position. We have a plan and it must be followed."

The Fomori king was right: the Fenian Brotherhood was too respected; they would never take part in a gang fight, which is how this appeared to anyone who didn't know the truth. Patrick stayed. Bres stood beside him, the guards behind. The sky darkened. It had been clear and blue moments ago, but now gray clouds gathered. An unkindness of ravens lit on the telegraph wires, cawing and rasping, and Patrick thought, *Is that all you have? Only a few birds?* Where was the great Morrigan, who favored the Fianna? Her three aspects? Where were Badb the Battle Crow, Nemain the Venomous, and Macha the Hateful?

Lightning flashed purple. Again, Patrick smelled hemp smoke, so strong it burned his nostrils. The air shivered as if it spoke only to him, and he recognized the voice in it. *Aidan.* There was another flash of lightning, striking the pavement only a few feet away. The people near him murmured in fear, easing back.

"The stormcaster," Bres breathed in Patrick's ear.

Aidan was at the edge of the crowd. He looked as thin and haggard as he had the other morning, his eyes hollowed, his hair too long. Yet he looked more like Grace than ever—and Patrick realized why. Aidan's usual distracted air had been replaced with the intensity and focus of his sister.

But it was the intensity of an apprentice trying to concentrate on something new. He wasn't aware of what was around him. Patrick muttered, "Watch yourself, Aidan." He saw Aidan frown, looking about, and he knew that Aidan had somehow heard him and was looking for him.

Patrick told Bres, "Don't hurt him. I don't want Aidan hurt."

"We're not likely to harm a stormcaster. Not when we need him ourselves." Bres gestured at Miogach, who stood a few feet away, surrounded by gang boys—some of the groups that hated the Fianna had joined with them. Miogach pulled one aside, murmuring something, and the boy shoved through the crowd toward Aidan. *A guard*, Patrick thought with relief.

Patrick felt Aidan's power grow. He couldn't take his eyes from his old friend, who moved as if he were in a dream, raising his arms, his hair whipping around his head like writhing snakes.

The back of Patrick's neck prickled. The smell of smoke dizzied him, though he couldn't see any smoke at all. He saw the police trap Ossian; Finn and Goll surged toward them.

The skies opened up.

Patrick was soaked through. Those who were there only to watch the fight rushed to escape the rain. Aidan raised his face to the heavens, and the gang boy that Miogach had sent drew a dagger. *Just to protect him,* Patrick told himself. Aidan wasn't to be hurt. But the boy advanced toward Aidan, and there was something in his face—

"No!" The thunder drowned out Patrick's warning. He plunged into the crowd toward Aidan, brushing off Bres's restraining hand. Behind him, Bres called for the guards to follow, but Patrick was already pushing through the crowd. Aidan frowned in concentration as he directed lightning that forked and split into a dozen different fingers, not noticing the gang boy intently moving toward him.

"Aidan! Watch out!" Patrick shouted. He tried to get through; the crowd blocked him. The boy had reached Aidan. Patrick gasped as someone elbowed him in the ribs. "No! Stop that boy! Stop him!"

The crowd cleared as the boy raised his knife. "Aidan!" Patrick ran toward him. "Aidan! Look out!"

Aidan spun around. Lightning flashed from his finger-tips, catching the boy and flinging him through the air. The boy slammed into Patrick. They crashed to the ground, the boy heavy on top of him. Someone screamed. Someone else shouted, "'e's dead!"

Patrick scrambled and rolled, throwing off the body. The boy *was* dead; there was no doubt. Patrick wiped rain from his eyes, looking for Aidan, but he had disappeared into the mob. The street was mud. The thud of clubs and shouting filled his ears. People shoved to get away, others to get closer; everyone was fighting. Patrick struggled to his feet. Balor stomped through the teeming mass, tossing boys aside with a single thrust of his mighty hands. Two police went down, one beneath Oscar's dagger and another under Finn's fist.

Balor snarled, "Now!" and police streamed into the crowd, forming a line, separating the Fianna's makeshift gang mili-tia from their leaders. Thunder roared. Ravens dove among the police, frenzied.

Finn and Oscar and Ossian turned to face the police and Balor, knives drawn. Finn called, "Stormcaster!"

Aidan stepped from the crowd, spreading his hands wide. Lightning ricocheted off the street, forming a pulsing electric barrier between the police and the Fianna. The police stag-gered back.

But Balor walked into the lightning. It spun and chased over his skin. People gasped and screamed. He kept going. Aidan redoubled his efforts, the lightning growing brighter, stronger, faster. Still the giant didn't stop.

"Now!" Finn shouted. He and the others raced forward, daggers flashing, clubs raised.

The crowd surged in front of Patrick. He couldn't see. He could only hear shouts and screams, thunder and the cries of ravens.

There was a crash and the earth beneath his feet shuddered. Cracks shattered the ragged cobblestones. There was more screaming, and gunshots joined the cacophony. When Patrick finally managed to push through the crowd, only Balor remained, standing over a great pothole in the street. The Fianna were gone; the gang boys had scattered.

Aidan was gone too. Gone and *safe*.

Suddenly, Bres was beside Patrick. "That was foolhardy of you, Devlin."

Patrick heard the anger in Bres's voice, and when he turned to look at the Fomori king, Bres's eyes were cold, and Patrick saw that, whatever Bres had said, the Fomori had wanted Aidan dead.

"You hadn't seen the stormcaster before today," Bres said. "Is that right?"

Patrick's own anger exploded. Rain slashed over his face, falling into his mouth as he spat, "I said I didn't want him hurt. You told me he wouldn't be. Aidan is Grace's brother. If something happened to him, whoever was responsible . . . she would remember it when it came time to make her choice."

"Ah. And is that the only reason you wish him kept safe? The *veleda*'s love for him?"

The sun burst through the clouds, too bright, glaring over the cobblestones. The police shoved people about, shouting, "Go home! Go home unless you want to be arrested! Fight's over!"

The uncertainty that had dogged Patrick returned, the sense that things weren't as they should be. "Isn't that enough reason? Besides, Aidan's an old friend."

"We all have old friends who have become our enemies," Bres said. "Your loyalty to him is admirable, but I wonder—is he as loyal to you? He is not on our side—he would harm you if he could."

"So it was me that Miogach was worried about?"

"You left your guards behind. The stormcaster was too close. He would have killed you. Remember what we fight for—old associations, old loyalties . . . sometimes they must be put aside for the greater good."

Patrick had to remind himself that the Fomori—his *allies*—knew nothing of the vow that he and Aidan had just made to each other. Of course they'd thought he was in danger. Why wouldn't they? He should not be so suspicious. He had no reason, only old stories that he knew could not be true.

Bres said, "The boy is lethal. He has more power than we thought. Or he's been trained since we saw him last."

"I thought training needed an archdruid."

"Yes," Bres said.

"You mean the Fianna have found him?"

"I don't know." Bres's glance skipped past Patrick. "Ah. Well. I imagine we'll soon find out." He smiled in triumph. Patrick followed Bres's gaze.

Fomori warriors emerged from the alley. They had someone with them, a young man whose white-blond hair dripped into his eyes as he struggled in their grip.

Oscar.

Diarmid woke to find he was holding Grace so tightly his arm had gone numb.

He'd known how difficult it would be to resist her once she saw the lovespot, but he hadn't had enough imagination to foresee the torment it actually was.

He wished he were in the city, with Oscar and the others, fighting police and the Fomori and other gangs, battle lust and anger firing his blood instead of this ceaseless, relentless wanting. Though he knew that if he were there, he would only be wishing for her.

Some god somewhere was laughing at him. Probably Aengus Og. Certainly Aengus.

Gently, Diarmid disentangled himself. Grace made a little murmur, but she didn't wake until he'd pulled completely away. She opened her eyes sleepily and smiled; he wondered what it would be like to wake to that smile every morning. In the days they'd spent together, Grace had never before given him that soft, welcoming look.

It was only the lovespell.

He looked away, hearing the roughness in his voice when he said, "Battle Annie told you something on this island would help us find the archdruid?"

Grace stared at him blankly. "Oh. Yes."

"And she gave you no idea what or where?"

"No. But it's a small island."

"Too small. Especially with a hundred or so troops about." He rose. "Well, I suppose I'll start looking. I don't know when Finn will send for us, assuming Battle Annie tells him where we are. We may not have much time."

She scrambled up. "I'm going with you."

"No, you're not."

"She said it was for me to find."

"It's too dangerous."

"You sound like Patrick now. You said yourself that this is my quest. I have more at stake than anyone."

Not quite true, but he let it be. He supposed if she were with him, he wouldn't worry about her being alone in the storehouse. So, despite his best intentions, he nodded. "All right. We should get started."

She opened the leather bag and took out two of the apples and what he knew were the last rolls. It would be good to find some food on this expedition, so he took the bag with its remaining apples and tied it to his belt to carry whatever they found. He shoved the door back into place as they left, pulling the vines to half cover it again.

He led the way down the clay scarp to the beach. Castle Williams, at the other end of the island, was barely used, an armory only; people came to the island to sightsee all the time, so he doubted he and Grace would be noticed. The tide was out, and it wasn't difficult to wend their way to the grassy slope near the fort. Diarmid heard the shouts and laughter of children. Boys and girls raced up and down the hill from Fort Jay.

"The orphan picnics," Grace said.

"Orphan picnics?"

"The city sends groups of them here through the summer so they can play in the fresh air."

"The city does that?" It seemed at odds with cutting off aid to the poor, the lack of jobs, and the increasing police brutality. The city had done everything it could to make life worse for those who had nothing; this little kindness was hard to believe. Diarmid was immediately suspicious. "Why?"

"I don't know. They always have."

Diarmid thought of Finn marshaling gangs into a militia, bending the anger and despair of the poor to his purposes. Now he watched the children racing up those hills, and he wondered if perhaps there was more to the story.

In any case, the children were a good shield. There were adults with them, along with a few older children wandering about the beach, and he and Grace looked as if they belonged with them.

Grace said, "I wish I knew what we were looking for."

Diarmid tried to remember what he knew of the island. He hadn't been the one to scout it—that had been Keenan. There was Castle Williams, of course, plus Fort Jay and the barracks, a few officers' houses that were mostly empty, and the parade grounds where the military band practiced. No shops, restaurants, or other types of entertainment. What exactly had Battle Annie thought they would find?

Diarmid led the way toward the round, red sandstone walls of Castle Williams. Children dashed about, shouting as they played hide-and-seek. A soldier guarded the entrance, keeping people out. Not that Diarmid expected there would be anything inside to find.

Grace glanced up the steep slope that led to Fort Jay. "Are we going up there?"

"There's nothing else *but* that." Diarmid began to climb. The apples in the leather bag thudded against his thigh. Children dodged past them, squealing and laughing—at one point he had to back up sharply to avoid a small boy barreling into him, and Grace grabbed Diarmid's arm to steady him. He jerked away—too hard—and saw the hurt in her eyes.

They were near the top when the music from the military band began. Groups of children gathered around the parade grounds, watching in awe. Beyond were the walls and peaked roofs of Fort Jay.

Diarmid paused. The walls of the fort were too high and smooth to climb. There were no trees. The second-story windows of the buildings gave a far-reaching view. There might be only a small military presence on the island, but they were all gathered here, and he didn't relish the thought of taking on a hundred soldiers—and for what? He and Grace didn't even know what they were looking for. They didn't know if Fort Jay held any clue at all. They had only the word of Battle Annie, whom he didn't trust.

"How are we to get in there?" Grace asked in a low voice behind him.

"We can't. At least not now. Maybe tonight."

"We wouldn't get to the wall without someone seeing us."

The band began playing "Yankee Doodle." It was an obvious favorite of the children, who clapped and cheered. One or two threw themselves into a dance.

Diarmid asked, "Are you sure Battle Annie said there was something to find here?"

"Yes. Something I would need, she said." Grace's forehead furrowed as she thought. "What could soldiers have to do with an archdruid?"

He'd been wondering that himself.

"I don't think they sit around reading tarot cards," she said.

"Maybe there's a Seer among them. It doesn't have to be cards. It could be . . . entrails or smoke. Or watching the patterns of birds."

"Entrails?" she said skeptically. "Bird watchers?"

"You never know."

"What if there's nothing here at all? What if Annie was only playing games?"

"You thought she was telling the truth," he reminded her. "You told me I was wrong to doubt it."

"But maybe *I'm* the one who's wrong. Everything feels so . . . uncertain. Perhaps I shouldn't have trusted her. We should be in the city. How will we ever find the archdruid from here? This is pointless and stupid and—"

"Grace," he said quietly. "Despair is our enemy. I've seen men so afraid of dying that they just stop fighting, and so they make their death true when it didn't have to be. You can't give up hope. I won't, and I won't let you."

She caught his gaze. The connection leaped between them, and his heart sped.

A *crack* split the air. Grace looked up. "Was that thunder?"

The sky was cloudless. There was a faint breeze coming off the bay, and none of the suffocating heaviness that usually came with heat lightning.

Another rumble, louder this time. The military band kept playing, but some of the men looked nervously at the sky. One or two of the younger children ran to a stern-looking man and woman.

Then the sky darkened, clouds appearing suddenly, in a way Diarmid recognized. The children began to shriek. The woman called, "Come, children, hurry now!"

The military band trailed off.

In the distance, Diarmid saw a flash of purple lightning above the buildings of Manhattan.

Grace said, "Aidan."

Yes, Aidan. A Druid storm, and no doubt a fight. Diarmid thought of his brothers, and a battle he should be in, instead of standing on a hill on Governors Island, helpless. The clouds boiled; the wind picked up.

Lightning scored the sky. Thunder crashed so loudly that Diarmid winced. Then the rain began, icy cold and relentless. Trust Aidan not to conjure a *warm* rain. Children raced off, trying to escape the deluge. The military band hurried awkwardly back to the safety of Fort Jay, a tuba jerking and slipping, the drummer struggling to keep the strap on his shoulders.

Diarmid motioned for Grace to follow him down the hill as he searched for some kind of shelter. But there was no safety outside the circular walls of Castle Williams, not a single overhang. He made for the trees farther down the beach, back toward the storehouse. The rain pelted hard, pitting the surface of the water, stinging his eyes. He heard Grace stumbling over the wet stones behind him in her thin, smooth-soled boots. By the time they reached a solitary tree arching over the shore, they were both drenched.

He fell against the trunk, huddling in the scant shelter of the leaves. The foliage wasn't thick enough to protect them. Grace's hair hung lank, her dark lashes spiky with rain.

"God forbid Aidan should ever do anything that doesn't affect me as well." Her face was pale with chill, her lips colorless. "I'm freezing." He fought the urge to take her into his arms.

The clouds showed no sign of parting. Thunder still roared. The fight must be fierce. Finn wouldn't have asked Aidan to cast such a storm for just a gang fight.

"It's not stopping." Grace shuddered. "What does it mean that he isn't stopping?"

"They're fighting the Fomori."

"How you must wish you were there instead of with me."

Deliberately, he said, "Aye." It was to save himself, but when he saw the hurt in her eyes again, he hated himself for it. "Grace . . . it's not so easy. You know that."

"Yes, I know."

The sky was blacker than ever. "Who knows how long this will last? D'you want to try to make it back to the storehouse?" he asked.

"I want to get out of this rain."

He set out. She slipped before they had gone three steps, and he reached back and took her hand, weaving his fingers through hers, which were cold and wet, but the heat that fired told him even that was a mistake. The clay was greasy and slippery. He pulled her with him, because those boots of hers were impossible, and she fell against him more than once. When they reached the storehouse, they were muddy and bedraggled, and yet he was burning even as he was freezing.

Grace stood in the middle of the floor, her arms wrapped around herself, shivering. The heavy fabric of her dress dripped into a puddle at her feet. Rivulets ran from her hair over her shoulders. Her skin looked blue.

He knew she needed to get warm and dry. He didn't like where that thought led him. Reluctantly, he cleared his throat and said, "You should take off your gown."

Her pause was so loud it seemed to echo. "You're always asking me to undress."

"'Tis for your own comfort. You'd dry off faster and be warmer, too, without all that wet. Just to your shift. I'll keep to this side. I won't come near."

He looked away, but he heard her fumbling. He thought of the pale cream of her shoulders and quashed the image. He undid the buttons on his shirt and drew it off, wringing it out in the corner, leaving a puddle on the worn floorboards. Then he hung it on a protruding nail. He shook his hair, which didn't do much good. It still dripped onto his shoulders. His pants he couldn't take off because there was nothing between them and his skin, but he drew off his boots, which sucked damply at his feet. He kept his eyes averted, but he heard her every movement, her soft exasperated breaths.

He wanted to take a glance but didn't let himself do it. Instead, he stared down at a scattering of straw, crumpling a piece in his fingers, and thought of all the ironies tumbling about him. He'd wanted her to be in love with him; she was. He'd been ordered to show her the *ball seirce*; he had. Everything he wanted, that his brothers wanted, had happened, and it only pushed him as far away from her as he'd known it would.

Again, he heard her mutter in frustration. He ignored it. She bit off a curse. He ignored that too.

"Diarmid, please—my laces are knotted. They're too wet. Could you help me?"

He glanced up and knew he was in trouble. She wore only her shift and corset. Her dress and her petticoats were in a pile beside her, and she was as soaked as he was, so the shift clung to her.

She looked as tormented as he felt. "Please. Just undo them, and then you can go back to your side."

He took a deep breath and went to her. She turned away, which didn't help much. He worked the knots, his knuckles brushing her back, gritting his teeth against the feel of her through the muslin. Her scent came to him—grass and clay, rain and the tang of salt. He felt choked. Diarmid closed his eyes, trying to calm himself.

"Please . . . hurry." Her voice broke.

He opened his eyes again, trying to concentrate on the knot and not the unbearable urge to touch her. Finally, he pulled the laces loose.

He couldn't move. He felt paralyzed as she undid the hooks on the front of the corset, as she let it fall to the floor.

"There," she said with relief. "That's done."

She began to step away. And then . . . he didn't know how it happened—*how did it happen?*—his hands were on her waist, keeping her there, and he was bending, pressing his lips to the hollow where her neck met her shoulder, and her gasp bewitched him.

She turned to face him, and he saw the love in her eyes. Love and desire, along with a helplessness he understood, because he felt it too. *The spell*, he tried to tell himself, but it was too late. The whole world, his life, everything, pushed him to her. He could no longer struggle against it. He let himself fall into the lie of her love.

He pulled her close to kiss her. He tangled his hand in her wet hair and the inevitability of her swept him. She wrapped her arms around him, her hands burning the bare skin of his back, and he wanted to be touching her that same way. It was the only thing he could think: *I want. I want.* He kissed her jaw and then pressed his mouth to her pulsebeat. Her heart raced beneath his lips. So like a dream he'd once had and . . . *No, don't think it.* Don't think of anything.

Only this.

TWENTY-SEVEN

The next moment
Grace

I'd resisted him all day. It had been the hardest thing I'd
ever done. But now I felt the danger of him and I didn't
care. Whatever he would be to me in the future, today he was
only the one I loved. The wet cotton of my chemise bunched
beneath his hands as he pulled it up to touch my skin, and it
was what I wanted too—more of him. There was a part of me
that whispered, *Are you certain?* A part that knew where we
were going and was afraid. I could stop this. I should stop this.

But then my dreams filled my head, and I felt as if I were
in the grip of something beyond what I could know, and my
fear disappeared. Being with him was the only thing that
made sense. This was how it was meant to be.

I pulled him closer, fumbling with the buttons at the
waistband of his trousers.

He froze, and then he gripped my hands, stopping me. His
breathing sounded harsh and labored. His face was chiseled
with desire, his words raw. "I haven't the will to fight this

anymore, *mo chroi*. I don't care what's right. I can't—" He swallowed, resting his forehead against mine. "You should tell me to stop. Tell me no."

"I don't want you to stop. I don't want to say no." I twisted my fingers loose, grazing his stomach. His breath hitched and shuddered—he trembled with the struggle to resist, and I felt a moment of wonder, of awe. This was the power I held. I couldn't call lightning or cast spells, but this . . . I could do *this* to him.

"Grace." He said my name as if it were wrenched from him, as if he were pleading for some mercy only I could give. "Be sure. We can't take this back."

I looked up at him, hot with embarrassment and need and desire as I said the words I knew I had to say. "I am sure. This is what I want. But I don't want there to be—a child. I've heard there are . . . there are ways. Do you . . . do you know how . . ."

His breath released hard. "Aye, *mo chroi*."

He kissed me, and it was gentle and sweet before it grew passionate again. After that, there was no hesitation. He pulled me to our bed of straw, and then there was nothing between us, not clothing, not the future. Though it hurt—deep and sharp enough that I cried out—I didn't let him stop. When he tried, I held him and whispered, "This is ours, Diarmid. It might be the only thing left to us. Don't take it away."

It was worth the pain. I loved him, and I loved being this close to him, and with every moment, my connection to him strengthened; a circle finally closed, an electricity that flashed and fused and held, filling me, completing me. The feeling didn't go away even when it was over and I lay cradled in his arms. I understood with a start that this was what had been waiting for me on Governors Island. This was what I'd been sent here to find.

The storm had stopped. The sun streamed through the slats near the roof, evaporating the rain into steam. I felt strong, vibrant, and alive. There was music singing in my head, the music of the water and the sun and the birds and the beat of his heart, the whole world kneeling at my doorstep, offering itself to me. *Here I am—do with me what you will.*

I said, "I feel different."

Diarmid said ruefully, "'Twasn't good this time for you, I know." Then he grinned. "But it gets better with practice, I promise."

I felt the heat of a blush, but I levered myself up on one elbow to look into his deep-blue eyes. "That's not what I mean. I feel as if there's something *more* to me. I don't know how to describe it."

He traced up my arm, a touch that made me shiver—no, it was something much more than that. This shiver reached deep inside of me and pulled, burning the way it always did when he touched me, when he kissed me, as if doors were opening, light flooding in.

I said, "I think you have something to do with it."

"I'm told I have that effect."

I walked my fingers down his sternum, till I reached the muscles of his stomach, and when he gasped, I smiled. "I guess I have an effect too."

"You always have."

"That's what I mean. I feel . . . powerful when I'm with you. Even more so now. More like a *veleda*. Why do you suppose that is?"

"I don't even know what it means," he said.

"At Battle Annie's, it was how I knew the apple wasn't glamoured. It was like a . . . a song, but it was broken and faint and I couldn't hear it well. It was how I knew to trust Deirdre too. But the song is stronger now. Louder. It's as if . . . as if it was waiting for you. I hate even to say that. It'll just make you more arrogant than you already are."

His expression grew wistful. "I hope it does make you more powerful. 'Twould make me feel better to think there was some good to come of this."

"Some good?"

"This isn't what's best for you, Grace. We both know it. You don't belong to me, and you're bespelled and . . . and I meant to protect you, from me as much as anything. I shouldn't have lost control. I should have been able to fight it."

"Don't regret this. Please. I don't. I love you."

He cupped my cheek, his thumb brushing my lips. "'Tisn't fair. You said that once, and it's true. A mean-spirited gift, you said. It makes a lass do what she might not otherwise. You can't tell me that you ever considered lying with me before yesterday."

"Considered it? Oh my—" I took a deep, steadying breath. "I dreamed about it. I thought of it whenever I was with you. And sometimes—oh, all right, *often*—when I wasn't."

I saw the doubt in his eyes, but there was hope there too.

"I did." I leaned over him, my hair falling to curtain our faces from the rest of the world. "And I fought it. I've been afraid of what I feel for you, but this is what we were meant to be to each other. You feel it too. I know you do."

"I feel it," he said simply. "But the lovespot would make you feel that, Grace. And one day the feeling will be gone, and you'll hate me for today."

"It won't be gone, because it's real. It's the most real thing I've ever felt. It's part of who I am now. It belongs to me. I promise you, Diarmid Ua Duibhne, I will never regret this."

He searched my face. I didn't know what he was looking for, but he must have found it, because the sorrow in his eyes melted away; they darkened with desire. "Then I suppose I should do what I can to make certain you don't." He pulled me down to brand me with a kiss that left me breathless.

And he was right. It *did* get better with practice.

I started awake, sweating, my heart pounding.

"What is it?" Diarmid murmured sleepily.

"Something's wrong."

He sat up, his skin gleaming in the moonlight. "What d'you mean?"

"There's something . . . I don't know. We need to go back."

"Back?"

"To the city." I grabbed my chemise. "Hurry. We need to hurry—"

He touched my arm. "You had a vision? What was it?"

"No. No vision. I just felt it. I *know* it. There's trouble. They need us."

"Grace, we can't go rushing back. Not without something more than a feeling. Finn will—"

"I don't care about Finn! They need us. Something's happened."

"Are you sure?" he asked carefully. "You're sure this feeling is about the Fianna and not about something else? Not just a bad dream? Not about the Fomori or the *sidhe*?"

"I don't know where it's coming from. It's only—" I threw aside my chemise and put my hand to my head, trying to still the panic coming from . . . somewhere. "Oh, I don't know!"

"Come now, lay down again." He tugged gently at my shoulder. "Close your eyes. See what comes to you."

I followed his directions. His fingers played over my skin, stroking, and I closed my eyes and focused on his touch. Gradually, the panic eased, the air was clear again, and there was . . . nothing.

"Well?" he asked after a moment.

"It's gone." I opened my eyes. "Whatever it was, it's gone."

"'Twas a dream then," he said, but there was worry in his voice. Still, he wrapped me in his arms, and I fell asleep again, listening to his breathing.

I didn't dream, but my mind felt wide-open, and I heard my brother's voice, as clearly as if he stood beside me: *You've done it, Grace.*

When I woke the next morning, those words lingered, along with a sense that something else had changed, something more than just the shift I sensed in myself. When Diarmid stirred, I said, "I had the strangest dream."

"You mean what woke you last night? Or something else?"

"Something else."

"No longer thinking we should go back?"

"I don't feel that anymore, but . . . things have changed."

"What things?"

"I don't know."

"Well, then, there's nothing to do but keep going until you have a better sense of it. I've thought of a way to get into Fort Jay, but it won't be easy."

"Fort Jay?"

He swept his hand through his hair. "To find your clue to the archdruid. Don't tell me you've forgotten already. I knew I was good, but—"

I hit him lightly. "No, I haven't forgotten. But we don't need to keep looking. I've already found what I was sent here for—it was you."

"Me? But I've been with you this whole time."

"Yes, but—" I struggled to explain. "I told you, I feel stronger since we . . . since yesterday. The power of the *veleda.* I think it was you that I needed."

"That's what Aidan said the night of the raid on the tenement. He said you needed me."

"How did he know that?"

Diarmid shrugged. "How does he know anything? He's playing with lightning—I'm thinking 'tis best not to question him."

"Last night, it was as if—"

"Sssh." Diarmid put up his hand.

I heard the sound almost the same moment. The scrape of stone against a hull. Close, on the beach just below.

Diarmid grabbed his trousers and his daggers from the floor and went to the door, cracking it open, wincing as it creaked. Now I heard voices—loud enough to be heard on the sea air, not loud enough to understand.

Diarmid pulled on his trousers and shoved his feet into his boots. He mouthed, *Stay here*, and I nodded, but my panic from last night returned.

He was already out the door. I grabbed my chemise, sliding it over my head. I looked about for a weapon of my own, and saw the broken oars. I grabbed one and stood near the door, prepared to whack anyone who came through. I felt I waited there forever, my heart pounding, until I heard a scuffle, a loud squeak. "I mean no harm! I'm just lookin' around!"

I recognized the voice. Miles.

But my dread didn't ease. Diarmid said, "I thought I taught you better than that. I shouldn't have been able to sneak up on you."

"I didn't think to be attacked on a beach!"

Their voices lowered so I couldn't hear the rest. I relaxed my hold on the oar. Diarmid called, "Grace, it's only Miles," and soon after, they came inside.

Miles smiled at me. "Hey, Gracie. 'Tis good to see you."

I was so uneasy that it wasn't until Diarmid raised his brow that I realized I was still only wearing my chemise, and Miles was staring at me with unabashed admiration.

"Turn around, lad," Diarmid said, cuffing him good-naturedly before he grabbed my gown from where we'd hung it to dry.

Miles grinned sheepishly and turned his back to me. Diarmid gave me my corset and petticoats, too, taking the oar from my hands. "Good thinking," he said, but even that didn't warm me.

"So what brings you here, lad?" Diarmid asked. I heard the edge in his voice.

The laces of my corset were still too damp for me to tighten well; I had to turn to Diarmid to do it. I wished only to be rid of it, but the dress wouldn't fit otherwise.

Miles said, "We've word from Finn. Things're bad in the city. The police are comin' down hard. The protest over on Bleecker Street yesterday got . . . out of hand. We think the police knew of it ahead of time."

I pulled on my dress.

"And?" Diarmid asked.

"'Twas bad. A thunderstorm in the middle of it, and lightning killed a couple of people. Finn called for retreat, but . . ."

"But what?"

"They caught Oscar."

This was it, then, the urgency I'd felt, the panic. Oscar, captured by the police. Diarmid looked as if his world had just crumpled before his eyes.

"Oscar? But when? How?"

"They got him during the fight. Took a whole slew of 'em to get him into the Black Maria."

The Black Maria. Even I knew the slang term for the police carriage used to transport prisoners.

"Yesterday," Diarmid said. "Then we haven't much time. Let me get my things—"

"You're not to come back," Miles said. "Finn just wanted you to know. Hugh will tell you—he's waitin' in the boat below. He's the one who got the message. He says Finn wants you to stay out of it and keep her safe."

"But they'll need me for this. Oscar's the best of us. Without him, they're crippled."

"You can't," I said. "Finn doesn't want you there."

"It won't take long. A few days only. Hugh can take me to the city, and Miles will stay here with you until I get back."

"Finn said to stay out of it."

His eyes flashed. "I can't let them do this alone. This is *Oscar*, Grace."

"You'll only make things worse," I insisted. I was afraid for him. He had no concern for his own safety. He would plunge into peril without a second thought. He might be a Fianna warrior, but he wasn't invincible. I'd seen those fights. And my dreams—were they premonitions or memories? I'd

seen bruises and sweat, screaming and blood, panic and terror.
"They'll have made plans without you. No one's going to let
him just languish in jail—"

"He won't be in jail. *They've* got him. Your precious
Patrick and the Brotherhood."

"Then he's safe enough. Patrick won't hurt him."

"Patrick won't, no. But the others . . ." Diarmid gave me a
warning glance. Miles knew nothing of the Fomori.

I remembered the dinner I'd attended. Lot's kindness,
and Miogach's. The way they'd promised to save me. Patrick's
assurances that they were reasonable, that they could be controlled. That they meant to *help*. This was not the ancient
world of legend. There were laws and juries and judges. They
couldn't just throw a man into prison and torture him, could
they? No, they wouldn't. "They *won't* hurt him. Finn told you
to stay with me. He told you to *stay.*"

"Grace, Oscar is . . . He's the closest thing to family I've
got. 'Twill take only a few days."

"Then take me with you. If you mean to go, take me too."

"You heard what Miles said. The police aren't on our side.
I won't lead you into danger, especially one I don't know. You'll
be safe here."

Even though Miles stood watching, I reached for Diarmid,
thinking that I could convince him to stay if I could only find
the right words, the right touch. But the moment I touched
him, I heard music. One chord, complex and soaring, a sound
made of other sounds. It held, lingering, a forever kind of
chord, and then it split into its separate notes, unwinding like

a thread spun of many finer threads, and each formed a path and a music of its own.

And suddenly I knew: He had to go. This fight was where he belonged. It was not mine.

I let go of Diarmid's arm; the music stopped. I looked up at him.

"Grace?" he asked. "What is it?"

"You have to go."

He said fervently, "Sweet Danu, but I love you. I'll be back, I promise. I want you to wait for me here." He took my face between his hands, his gaze searing into mine. "Wait for me."

"Yes," I said.

He kissed me. Hard at first, and then it gentled into a good-bye, one he didn't want to make. But his fate already pulled him onward, pulling him away from me.

"Wait for me," he whispered again. "I love you."

"I love you too," I said. Then I let him go.

TWENTY-EIGHT

July 27
Diarmid

Diarmid's guilt weighed on him as he walked down to the beach, where Hugh and another of the Dun Rats waited with the tiny sloop that had brought Miles. His best intentions had been pummeled into dust since Grace had seen the *ball seirce*. It was bad enough that he'd given in to his desire; what was worse was the way he'd used her love to make her stay.

As bad as he felt, though, there was a part of him that was glad for the spell, because he knew she would wait for him as she'd promised, and he couldn't be worrying about her now. He had to concentrate on not panicking as he boarded that tiny sloop, its mast creaking and groaning in the heavy chop. The short trip to the docks of Manhattan seemed the longest, most perilous distance he'd ever crossed.

When they reached a landing spot on the river, past the docks of the big steamers and ships on the Hudson side, he scrambled out of the boat so quickly that Hugh laughed at him. Hugh wouldn't be laughing if he'd seen the things

Diarmid had. A sea monster could swallow a boat like that in a single mouthful. Cliodna's deadly wave would have drowned it without the slightest effort.

Diarmid asked again, "Finn didn't tell you lads where they were?"

Hugh shrugged. "They're keeping it tight, ya know? But ask around—there'll be word, at least for when the next fight is, and they'll be there."

Diarmid nodded his thanks and walked down the tilting wharf to the street. Men were looking for him. 'Wanted' posters were everywhere. So he took the back way to the burned tenement, even though he knew the others were no longer there. It was a place to start. He dodged into alleys, snaking along saloon walls, keeping his head down, meeting no one's eye. The bustle of the working waterfront meant no one was looking to get into anyone's way. Curiosity here sometimes meant a knife in your throat. There were so many people about—sailors, drovers, dockworkers—that he went unnoticed. He saw no police; there were a few gang boys hanging about, but no one he knew, and he wasn't asking, not when the Fomori were busy recruiting gangs to their side.

When he got to Houston Street, things began to look familiar, the saloons and the tenements—but he grew warier. Now there were police. It was stupid to come here, where he was known, but he hadn't any other choice.

There were more police about than he'd ever seen. Things had changed in the time he'd been gone. He felt resentment and anger in the air like a fog. There had always been resentment, but now there was violence, too, barely held in check, ready to explode at the smallest provocation.

Diarmid had no wish to be that provocation. He dodged through a hole in the wall that led to another makeshift doorway, and ended up in the hallway of a tenement where a man was selling broken crockery. Beyond was a wall made of tacked-together cardboard, and a woman sitting with a pile of goods—broken-heeled shoes and ragged bits of lace and ribbon, no doubt all scavenged from ash cans. A group of young men lounged idly on the stairs.

He went past them, pausing at the door, looking for police or Fomorians. No one. He was just stepping onto the walk when he heard:

"Derry! That you? Whatcha doin' back 'ere? Ya know they're lookin' for ya."

Diarmid tensed, his hand creeping to his dagger. One of the young men was emerging from the darkness of the stairs. Billy, the leader of Billy's Boys. They were allied with Finn— or they had been. He didn't know if they still were. Especially since he'd saved Grace from them not so long ago. He wondered if Billy held grudges.

Cautiously, he said, "Good to see you, Billy."

Billy was tall and lanky, with stringy light-brown hair, a big nose, and clever eyes. "Yer takin' yer life in yer hands, lad, comin' round here."

"Because of the police, or because of you?"

"Hey, don't I always got your back?"

"Usually," Diarmid agreed. "But I've been gone awhile. Things look to have changed."

"Aye." Billy gestured for Diarmid to follow him. They went past the makeshift hallway shops to a confusion of rooms blocked out by more cardboard. There were other boys there. Billy said, "Private chat, boys. Only be a moment."

The boys scurried out like cockroaches. When they were alone, Billy said, "You here 'cause you're mad?"

"Not me."

"Good." Billy looked relieved. "I saw the posters, ya know. It was that same girl, weren't it? The one they're lookin' for?"

Diarmid's gut tightened. "Aye."

"Run off with her, did ya? Hell, I didn't know she was no rich girl. Figures you'd end up with one o' them."

"I'm looking for Finn."

"Ya heard they got Oscar?"

"'Tis why I'm back."

"No one knows where their panny is. But there's a new protest set for three days from now. At Tompkins Square. Finn's sent the word to gather. The Warriors'll be there."

Three days. Too long. "I need to find them before that."

Billy lowered his voice. "You remember Justin?"

Justin was the newsboy who had rushed into their room the day they'd awakened, warning them about the Whyos and preventing a surprise massacre. Diarmid nodded.

"'E's got a post on Printing House Square. Tell 'im you need Finn, and 'e'll find a way. But be careful, lad. Your face is plastered everywhere, and there're some people—I ain't sayin' who—wouldn't mind the little extra muck for turnin' ya in, eh? Times is hard."

"I understand. Thanks. I appreciate it."

"Just tell Finn, will ya? Let 'im know I helped ya out."

Printing House Square. Getting there without being spotted wouldn't be easy. The New York Times Building, and buildings that housed several other newspapers, were on that block, and all kinds of people would be about. It was also directly across the street from city hall—another example of Finn's cleverness. No one would suspect a newsboy selling papers there to be the Warriors' courier.

Diarmid was sweating by the time he reached that part of the city. He held back in the shadows between buildings, watching for Justin and avoiding police—and there were many. He was there for an hour, growing more impatient and anxious by the moment, when the newsboy appeared.

Diarmid tagged a passing sweep girl. "See that boy over there?" He pulled a penny from his pocket. "Tell him Derry wants to see him."

She snagged the penny and crossed the street. Diarmid watched as she approached Justin. He saw the way Justin stiffened, his quick glance to the spot where Diarmid hid. The newsboy nodded.

A police officer meandered by. When the officer turned the corner, Justin crossed the street, approaching the shadows cautiously.

"Derry?" he asked. "Damn me. There's coppers every-where. It ain't safe for ya to be 'ere. Everyone's lookin' for ya and that lass."

"I need to get to Finn. Can you take me to him?"

"I don't know where 'e is," Justin said. "No one does. I can get 'im word, though, but sometimes it takes a bit."

"Then tell him I'm here. Tell him I'm waiting at"—Diarmid paused, trying to think—"Washington Square."

"It might be a couple o' days."

"Just tell him to hurry."

"All right then. But Derry, ya got to watch out. Things're"—Justin threw a quick and wary look over his shoulder—"things're bad."

The boy dashed away, and Diarmid hurried toward Washington Square, impatience growing with every step. Every moment Oscar was in Fomori hands . . . every moment he was away from Grace . . .

But impatience would cost him. It might already have been a bad decision to come here. He didn't want to make it worse. Settle in. Wait. Three days at the most, because he could always catch up with them at Tompkins Square.

The park was busy today. It was bordered by row houses belonging to those who were respectable, if not rich, and the park was filled with women, children, and a few idle men. Diarmid wandered about, trying to look like a boy who had been granted a free afternoon on a hot summer day, waiting.

And waiting.

The afternoon turned to evening. Promenaders wandered away; nursemaids with small children departed. Businessmen hurried through on their way home. When the sun set and night came on, Diarmid hid near a tree to avoid any policemen looking to roust a vagrant. The lamplighters came around with their long-poled flames. Then it became quiet. The moon climbed past the tall buildings, peeking through the leaves of the tree. Diarmid was just thinking he should find a safer place to sleep when he heard footsteps.

His every sense went on alert. Then he heard whistling, low and familiar. It was a song he knew—one of his favorites from feast days. He'd always requested it of Garrick, the bard he liked best, because the man had a soft and wistful way of singing it. *"Fair lass of Kincora, let down your dark hair . . ."*

And then . . . an odd minor note. Familiar again. Conan had always teased him with the song, changing the melody so it was a little off-key, adding a bawdiness to it that made Diarmid laugh.

Conan. It had to be.

Diarmid stepped out from the tree's cover. There, near the fountain: the faint shine of gaslight on a bald head. The whistling grew louder. There was no one else around, only a horse and carriage parked on the street. As silently as he could, Diarmid moved toward the man. When the whiff of stinking sheep filled his nose, he let out a sigh of relief.

Without turning around, Conan said, "You were loud as a charging boar, lad."

"I've got sharp tusks too," Diarmid said, brandishing his dagger so the blade caught the light. "And I might have to gore you if you keep mangling my favorite song."

Diarmid embraced his fellow warrior. Conan slapped him on the back. "'Tis good to see you, my brother." Conan's smile died. "But you should not have come."

"I couldn't stay away. Not when I heard—"

"Finn's not happy." Conan motioned for Diarmid to walk with him through the park, past the row houses, into the alley. "You didn't follow orders."

"I thought you needed my help."

"You were supposed to stay with the girl. She's the most important thing."

"Grace is safe."

Conan grunted. "She'd be safer if you were with her."

Diarmid couldn't deny it. "I've heard how things are. No one's done anything but warn me of it. You need me. You know you do. I've been away too long—"

"There are posters of you all over the city. How're you to help rescue Oscar when everyone knows exactly what you look like?"

"I'm not leaving until he's back. D'you know yet where they're keeping him?"

"Aye, there are plans. You'll hear them from Finn, I'm guessing. Before he sends you back to your little love nest. Fine duty, isn't it? Spending your days lolling in the sun and kissing while the rest of us are training militia and getting our heads bashed in."

"I've been training the Dun Rats," Diarmid protested.

Again, Conan grunted. They went down one alley and then another, and the smell of that fleece made Diarmid feel sick. He had lost track of where they were—somewhere around Bleecker, he guessed, but heading toward the Hudson. Conan kept to the alleys and the shadows. "We don't need any-one recognizing either of us. You endangered us all, coming here, you know."

"Then why did Finn send *you*? Your bald head and that sheepskin mark you a mile away."

"Everyone else was busy."

"Why not send a lad then?"

Conan snapped, "We're under *siege*, Derry. The only rea-son we've survived is because Finn trusts no one. The Fomori have spies everywhere—we couldn't take the chance that we'd unwittingly send one after you."

Conan was right; Diarmid had endangered them by coming here. He was too visible. He should have stayed with Grace. Those had been his orders, and he should never have disobeyed them. He should have trusted that Finn and the others had things well in hand.

Conan turned down a slender corridor. Another maze of doors and alcoves, the smell of sewage and garbage. Diarmid followed Conan through the puzzle—obscuring their trail for anyone who might be following. They reached a decrepit three-story mansion that Diarmid remembered passing twenty minutes ago. The streetlamp in front had been knocked out, glass shards crunching beneath his boots. Oil lamps cast light from some windows, while others were boarded over. Piles of garbage loomed in the yard behind cast-iron railings. People slept on the porch.

Conan took him around the side, into a space so tight they had to flatten themselves against the wall to get through. It opened onto a backyard with privies leaning drunkenly against each other and a cesspool that glimmered in the moonlight.

Conan dodged the cesspool, leading Diarmid to a crooked back door. "Home sweet home." He pushed past the door and into the darkened hall of an old kitchen, which was now crowded with pallets of straw and snoring men. Conan turned abruptly to the left, rapping on another door—the code. Conan jerked the door open. Dank air rushed out.

"Careful of the stairs," he whispered. They went into a basement that stank of mildew, sweat, and cooking onions. A dim light barely illuminated slatted steps bordered by seeping stone walls. Diarmid heard nothing from below. No talk. No laughter. Not even snoring. He knew that silence, and he knew what he would see when they reached the bottom.

A tribunal. Cannel leaned against a wall, watching, but the rest of the Fianna were lined up, one beside another, arms crossed over their chests, icy stares. And in the middle, his hair gleaming golden red in the light from an oil lamp, stood Finn.

Conan joined them. Diarmid was left to face his brothers alone. He cursed himself again. He'd been impatient and stupid. Finn rarely failed to punish disobedience—severely.

Diarmid looked at his fellows, missing Oscar acutely in that moment. Oscar would have at least winked. All the faces looking at him now were stern and forbidding.

Finn stepped forward. "Why are you here, Diarmid?"

"I thought you would need my help."

"I see. Second-guessing me, were you?"

Diarmid went silent.

"Where's the *veleda*? Don't tell me you brought her into the city."

"No. She's safe. And guarded."

Finn stepped closer, his power radiating, his blue eyes no longer cold but flashing hot. "Let me see if I have this right. All the Fianna are standing right here, which means you've left our *veleda* in the hands of someone who cannot possibly be as competent as you are—though I'm having doubts as to that just now. By morning every spy in the city will know you're back and will be doubling their efforts to find you. You've forced us into a position where we must protect you, and at the same time, you've endangered us when the Fomori and their cohorts are tightening the noose by the hour. Do I have it right? Or is there something else I'm forgetting?"

"I think that's all," Diarmid said hoarsely.

"Ah. There's something to be thanking the gods for."

"I can only say that I thought to help. When I heard about Oscar, I thought you might have need of me. I'd ask you to remember that when Miogach attacked us in Ireland, 'twas only by following my instincts that I saved you from the House of Death."

"Another lifetime ago," Finn said dismissively.

"Aye, but I had reason to think this might be the same. The Fomori found Grace and me in Brooklyn, and we had to run; I didn't know if they'd found you too. I didn't know if you even knew where we were."

"I told you to stay with the *veleda*."

"I was also told you were under attack," Diarmid said. "And I saw Aidan's lightning. I couldn't just ignore that."

"The *veleda* is what matters just now, and you left her for a *battle*. Could you really think that a fight was so important? We need her to win the war."

Diarmid swallowed, but he didn't back away. "But if you lose this battle, there may be no war."

"Where is she?"

"On Governors Island."

"Whose watch?"

"One of the Dun Rats—"

"You left her with a half-trained gang boy?"

"He'll protect her. And it's not as if she's defenseless."

"What if she tries to escape him?"

"She won't. She's promised to wait for me."

Finn stilled. "You used the *ball seirce*?"

Diarmid nodded.

It was the first moment since he'd stepped into the room that Finn didn't look angry. "That's the best news I've heard in some time."

Diarmid didn't trust himself to say anything.

"And . . . is she swayed?"

"You'd have to ask her, but I don't think she wants me to die."

"Then, I suppose execution for disobedience is off the table, eh, lads?"

There were grins. One or two laughed. But Diarmid was unsettled by Finn's measuring gaze.

Finn went on, "Don't think I've forgotten your punishment, but as the *veleda* apparently likes you"—more laughter—"and we need her, it will hold. As long as you're here, we might be able to use you. We mean to rescue Oscar tomorrow night. Once he's safe, you'll go back to her. And there you'll stay until *I* tell you to come home, whatever else you hear or see. We can't protect her well enough here, and 'tis no place for a lady." Finn's eyes glittered. "Disobey me again, and you'll be sorry you're alive. Do you understand me?"

"Aye," Diarmid said.

Finn turned away. The others came forward now, welcoming him. Diarmid felt Finn watching as Keenan slapped his shoulder and Goll and Ossian made jokes about his current duty.

Diarmid saw the worry for his son in Ossian's eyes. "Oscar would be relieved to know you're with us on this. As am I."

"Where is he?" Diarmid asked.

"A dungeon cell in the Tombs," Ossian said.

The Tombs was the nickname for the city's House of Detention—an Egyptian-style monstrosity with a pillared entrance and marble stairs where the courts were, and the jail behind. "How d'you think we'll get in there?"

Before the others could answer, Diarmid felt a presence behind him. A pull, like the threads of a web tightening within him. He thought, *Grace,* in the split second before he realized who it must be.

"You were supposed to protect her! Why did you leave her?"

Aidan.

The same day
Patrick

P atrick stood outside the cell, watching as one of Balor's policemen bent over the young man slumped in the chair, white-blond hair matted with blood.

"We'll try it again, then," the policeman snarled, raising the leather bag filled with shot. "Where are your fellows?"

Oscar raised his head. One eye was swollen shut. His nose was broken and bloody and his cheek bruised black, but he did what he had done every single time the question was asked. He grinned.

The policeman cracked the bag across Oscar's head. The Fianna warrior groaned, his chin falling again to his chest.

Patrick didn't even wince. This was the cost of war, and he'd seen it too often in Ireland to feel discomfort. Oscar knew to expect it—he was trained for it—and Patrick couldn't afford to show regret or compassion, especially now. Since he'd saved Aidan's life, he'd felt the eyes of the Fomori upon him and the questioning of his loyalty even by the Brotherhood. Jonathan

Olwen had said, "We know he was once your friend," and Patrick had understood: *Don't do it again.*

The Fianna had asked for this war by refusing to fight beside him. They deserved what they got. Patrick had been running his father's business since he was eighteen, and the rebellion he'd helped organize in Ireland had taught him that sometimes you must sleep with the devil to get what you want. Freeing Ireland was the important thing. The Fomori were still the best way to accomplish it, but beyond that . . . Patrick could not dismiss his worry over how Grace's power might tempt the Fomori. Until they found the archdruid, he trusted only Aidan and himself to keep Grace safe. If nothing else, the Fianna were keeping her out of the city—and she needed to stay away. It was why he was here today, to deliver a message.

So he watched as the policeman tortured Oscar. Another question, another strike. He waited through two more rounds before he said, "Let me talk to him."

"What makes you think you'll get anything from him?" Balor grumbled.

"You haven't asked the questions I'm interested in," Patrick said.

Balor did not look happy—not that he ever did, really, unless he was in the middle of a battle—but he stood aside as Patrick went to Oscar. The torturer *thunk*ed the shot-filled bag in his palm as if he could hardly wait to use it again.

Patrick looked down at the warrior, whose breathing had become short and ragged with pain. Patrick squatted until he was even with Oscar's face.

"I want to know about Grace," he said.

Oscar said nothing.

"I care only for her happiness. I know she must be afraid. She wants to come home. I'll do whatever I must to bring her back. Tell me where she is."

Again, nothing.

"She doesn't belong to the Fianna. Where are you keeping her?"

Silence.

"Tell me. She's only a girl. She can mean nothing to you."

Oscar laughed, and the sound was gruesome, rattling with blood. His mouth and cheek were so swollen that Patrick had to strain to understand him. "Nothing? Do you think me a fool? She's the *veleda*."

"She's my fiancée. She loves me. Do you really think she'll choose the Fianna when she has a life with me waiting?"

"Does she still love you?" Oscar mocked. "D'you think he waited to show her the *ball seirce*? He had her within the hour."

Patrick struggled to keep his feelings in check. He reminded himself of his greater purpose, and glanced over his shoulder at a restless Balor. He didn't have much more time. "Tell me where she is, and it will go much easier for you."

Oscar snorted. "You think *this* is hard?"

"Enough, Devlin. Let us beat it out of him," Balor snarled.

Patrick grabbed Oscar's hair, yanking him forward, looking the Fianna warrior in the eyes. "Do you think we won't kill you? How will the Fianna win without their best warrior?

Do you think we would hesitate to cripple them?" He leaned closer threateningly, close enough to whisper, "Keep her out of the city."

If he hadn't been so close, he wouldn't have seen the flicker of surprise in Oscar's eyes. The warrior's gaze met his with understanding before he said exactly what Balor would expect: "Go ahead—kill me if you want. It won't matter. You'll never find her. She's in love with him. She'll choose us."

Patrick let him go. The torturer struck Oscar on the back of the head. The Fianna warrior slumped forward, passing out.

Patrick said, "You'll get nothing out of him if he's unconscious, you fool. Next time use a little care."

He left the basement cell with its one flickering oil lamp and went up the stairs to the main floor of the jail, gloomy and dim, the air in the enclosed, windowless space heavy with the noxious scent of gas. The cells stretched the long halls, rising four tiers, with iron bridges crossing from one side to the other above.

He passed quickly outside, feeling a strange mix of exhilaration and despair. He'd given Oscar the message, but he knew the Fianna warrior had not lied about the lovespot. Patrick hadn't really expected otherwise, but still . . . The Fomori had said the spell would fade with time, and that was what Patrick clung to. How much time was there now, though? Not much. *Just keep her safe, Diarmid,* he prayed. *Until I know what to do.*

First, he had to figure out how to help Oscar escape so he could get Patrick's message to Aidan.

Patrick was so lost in thought he was startled to find he was at his front door. Lucy stood in the hallway, waiting for him. She held a letter out to him with a trembling hand. Her mouth was set tight; her eyes blazing.

"It just came for you," she said. "I mistook the writing. I thought it was for me."

The wax seal had been broken. Patrick glanced down at the writing—feminine and clearly addressed to him. He looked back at his sister. "You mistook it?"

"All right, no, I didn't. I thought it was from Grace, but it's from that friend of yours who was at dinner. Lot—what kind of a name is that?"

"Short for Charlotte," Patrick lied, distracted.

His sister seemed barely to hear him, rushing on with, "Derry's back! 'The one we've been searching for has returned, but without his captive.' That's what she says. She means Derry, doesn't she?"

Patrick scanned the contents. It was as Lucy had said. Diarmid had been spotted in the city. Without Grace.

Lucy said, "I want to see him. You must find him for me. Bring him here."

Patrick stared at the letter, thinking of Oscar sagging in the chair, only his bonds keeping him upright. Diarmid would not have left her unless the Fianna meant to rescue Oscar. If Diarmid was here without Grace, it must be happening soon.

Patrick should warn the Fomori but . . . *Grace. Keep her safe.* This was what he'd been hoping for, a chance for Oscar to escape. Now all that remained was making sure of it.

Patrick crumpled the note in his hand, throwing it to the floor. He spun on his heel, back to the door.

"Patrick, tell me what's happening! Where is he?" Lucy asked shrilly. "Where are you going?"

"I have an appointment at the Tombs," he said.

Late that afternoon
Diarmid

D iarmid had forgotten how much Aidan looked like his
sister, but now the likeness seemed more pronounced
than ever. The only difference was the eyes, Aidan's piercing
blue stare.

"Where is she?" Aidan asked.

"She's well protected."

"But not by you. You made me a promise."

"Grace needs you," Aidan had said the night of the raid.
"Protect her. That's all I'm asking of you." Diarmid told Aidan,
"I'm going back as soon as we rescue Oscar."

"Too late. It's too late." Aidan turned away.

Diarmid grabbed his shoulder. "What does that mean?"

"Do you have any idea what you've done?"

Diarmid was aware of the others watching—of Finn. "I
don't know what you're talking about."

"You've released her power and left her alone."

"She's not alone! And—"

"Stop," Finn ordered. He turned to Aidan. "You said he released her power. What do you mean?"

"It was blocked but now, thanks to him"—Aidan jerked his chin at Diarmid—"she can use it. He's a fool who has no idea what he's done."

Diarmid's stomach knotted. He recalled the things Grace had said, things he'd only partially understood, about feeling stronger since they'd lain together, about music. Slowly, he said, "When you told me she needed me, this is what you meant. She *is* stronger. She wasn't just saying it."

"Yes, she's stronger," Aidan snapped. "Even I can feel it, and I'm across the water from her. You were right there. You were *with* her. You should have known. God save me from warriors. You've spent a lifetime with Druids—don't tell me you don't recognize power when you see it."

"So it's released," Finn said. "'Tis good for us, isn't it?"

"You don't understand. It's even more dangerous for her now. She'll be as drawn to the archdruid as the *sidhe* are," Aidan said. "She'll try to find him, with or without Derry."

Finn said, "But she's promised to wait for Diarmid's return. And the *ball seirce* has bound her. Which will rule her more, do you think? Love or power?"

Aidan looked at Diarmid, and Diarmid felt that web of connection tightening again, as if Aidan could somehow see inside him, as if he somehow knew everything Diarmid felt and wanted, and Diarmid saw that Aidan *did* know what had happened between him and Grace. Impossible, but . . .

Aidan said, "All I can tell you is that at one time she would have done anything for Patrick."

Jealousy struck Diarmid, mixed with shame. He hated both feelings.

Finn asked Diarmid, "You bound her, you're sure of it? You wrought a promise?"

"Aye. She'll wait for me. But there's something else, Finn. What Aidan says, about the archdruid—Grace and I found an old Druid at Coney Island. The *sidhe* sucked all his power long ago, but he had this ogham stick with a prophecy. It made no sense to me, but Grace said her grandmother told her some of the same words. The old man said it needed a key. We never did figure out what that meant. Of course, we didn't look at it again after—" He bit off the words, ignoring their knowing glances, not wanting to share the most intimate and powerful moment of his life. He reached into his pocket, but he knew already the ogham stick wasn't there. He'd been looking at it when Grace had seen the lovespot, and after that he hadn't thought of it again. It was on the floor in the storehouse somewhere. "Grace was certain the prophecy had something to do with the archdruid. And . . . there's one other thing."

"There's more?" Finn said. "Ah, I can hardly wait to hear it."

"Grace and I ran into a gang of river pirates."

"We've attempted to ally with some of them, but they prefer to do things on their own."

"Then you never got a message from them about our escape?"

Finn shook his head. "We knew you'd been pursued. The Rats said they knew where you were."

"These river pirates weren't just a gang," Diarmid said. "They're *sidhe*."

Finn looked surprised; Aidan did not. If Aidan had known this already, why not tell Finn?

Diarmid went on, "They're led by one of the most powerful *sidhe* queens I've seen since we woke to this time: Battle Annie. I thought she might know where the archdruid was. She didn't, but she promised to help look."

"Why?" Finn asked suspiciously. "What did you bargain?"

"I didn't bargain anything. 'Twas Grace who made the deal. I don't know what she offered. They had an . . . agreement."

"You let the *veleda* make a bargain with the *sidhe*?"

"I had no choice. I was in the ship's hold at the time. And Grace is convinced she didn't make a bad bargain."

Finn let out his breath. "I'll decide what to do about this later. For now, 'tis time we focused on our plans."

Diarmid was glad to turn to that, to concentrate on something he could do, something he was good at—though he would've said he was good with girls, too, and look what that had got him. As they gathered to go over the plan, Aidan sent electricity arcing from hand to hand, his gaze set on Diarmid as if he were imagining incinerating him. It raised the hair on the back of Diarmid's neck. He wished Grace's brother would go to sleep and leave him alone.

Cannel sat on a pile of bedding, laying out cards, doing his divination and Finn's pale eyes gleamed with an almost evil satisfaction as he spoke. "Aidan will come along—hopefully we won't need a storm, but better to be prepared. Diarmid and Ossian will get arrested for drunkenness. They'll be taken to the Bummers' Cell."

"Me?" Diarmid asked. "You don't think they'll spot who I am? You'll recall I'm wanted for kidnapping, and theft too. Probably breaking and entering. Or maybe trespassing—I'm not sure. There are so many *laws*. I don't know how people in this time keep them straight."

"Mostly by not breaking them," Aidan said sourly.

Ossian grinned, and Keenan let out a bark of a laugh, but Finn ignored them all. "Once the two of you are there, you will create a distraction. I don't care how you do it. Diarmid, use your notoriety to serve us if you must. Buy enough time for Ossian to sneak away. He'll get us inside. I expect we'll see our old friends at some point. The Fomori are all through the police force, and the word will be out already that Diarmid's back. They'll know that means we plan a rescue, and they'll be expecting us. Once the alarm is sounded, we'll have little time. We get Oscar and fight our way out again."

"When Ossian sneaks away, what should I do then?" Diarmid asked.

"Find a way to join us for the fight or get out—but do one or the other. I don't want to have to risk another rescue attempt."

"You're so much trouble, we might decide to leave you," Conan joked.

Finn cuffed Conan. "You wanted to help, Diarmid. This is what we need. Am I understood?"

"Aye." Diarmid understood all too well. He was on his own, and he supposed he deserved it. He wondered if Finn would be all that unhappy if Diarmid failed the attempt and got shot by some guard.

"I guess you wish you were back kissing the lass, eh?" Keenan teased.

Aidan glared at him.

Finn said to Cannel, "What about you, *cainte*? What do your cards say?"

The Seer looked up. "Adding Diarmid changes things. Only a little, but it adds a new obstacle."

Finn's gaze sharpened. "Obstacle? What kind of obstacle?"

Aidan said quietly, "Fate is ever-changing."

Diarmid felt a shiver of dread.

They spent the day preparing. Ossian covered his white-blond hair with an old scarf and pulled a hat down on top of it. Diarmid required no such disguise—his coloring was no different than half the Irish in the city—but he dirtied his face until he looked as filthy and anonymous as any of the men who worked the docks.

Then Conan doused him and Ossian with whiskey. "Seems a waste."

"Broadway or Fifth Avenue," Finn directed. "Madison Square Park. Go where the wealthy are. They won't tolerate drunken fools in those places."

Diarmid didn't want to go anywhere near Madison Square, where Patrick Devlin lived, but he didn't say it. He tried not to see the brooding way that Grace's brother watched him—just as he had been since Diarmid's return.

"Here we go," Ossian said with a tight smile.

Diarmid followed Ossian through the pathways out of the neighborhood. This time he forced himself to pay attention. He had no doubt he'd have to find his own way back. The evening seemed full of shadows and sounds, children crying and playing, the *clank* of a bottle hitting the cobblestones, a man screaming at his wife. The smell of the whiskey polluting his clothes was nauseatingly strong.

"We'll go to upper Broadway first," Ossian said. "Theaters will just be filling." Ossian dodged into a saloon and bought a bottle. They each took a swallow—cheap whiskey, wretched stuff—and then Ossian emptied most of it on the ground. The buildings began to change to respectable businesses, the walks filling with theatergoers and promenaders, women in rich silks and shawls and beribboned hats decorated with flowers and birds, men with shimmering top hats and well-shined boots, all eyeing him and Ossian with worried disgust as the night came on and the streetlamps were lit. Carriages lined the walk before Wallack's Theatre, their drivers tensing the moment Ossian and Diarmid approached. Near the door of Wallack's, Ossian nodded at Diarmid, and Diarmid gave a short nod back.

It was time.

Ossian fell against a wall and lifted the bottle to the sky. He shouted, "'Ere's to the rich! May they always be so while the rest of us rot away!" He tilted the bottle to his mouth, letting the whiskey run freely down his chin.

Diarmid staggered toward him. "Let me 'ave some!"

Ossian jerked the bottle away. "Get yer own."

"You said we'd share!"

"I changed m'mind." Ossian set the bottle to his mouth again.

Diarmid snatched the bottle. Ossian shouted, "'ey!"

One of the drivers approached.

"Here, boys," the man said. "Move along, will you?"

"Why? So the rich don't 'ave to look at us?" Ossian lurched toward the driver, half falling on the man.

Diarmid sneered. "It'll spoil their appetites to see us, will it? Well, I got an appetite too—an nothin' to fill a 'ungry belly."

"Just go or I'll call the police." The driver extricated himself from Ossian's grasping arms. Ossian stumbled and fell.

Diarmid burst into drunken laughter.

Ossian glared up at him. He tried to get to his feet, falling flat on his face. "Give me that!"

Diarmid put the bottle behind his back. "Come 'n get it."

A crowd gathered. Horrified men and women, but no police, not yet, and there needed to be.

Diarmid reached to help Ossian stand. Ossian grabbed his hand and pulled hard, and Diarmid sprawled on top of him. "Fight me," Ossian whispered.

Diarmid obliged. When Ossian grabbed for the bottle, Diarmid hit him, easing off just before his fist connected—the blow looked and sounded worse than it was, and Ossian flopped like the best actor on any stage, flinging his head back.

He lunged for Diarmid, grappling, pushing him into the crowd. Diarmid deliberately fell into a woman, wrapping his arms around her. "Oh, ain't you lovely," he said, kissing her on the lips before he pushed away.

She screamed, looking ready to swoon. "Let go of me, you brute! Someone get the police!"

Ossian grabbed his shoulder, and Diarmid twisted around, tripping Ossian so they fell. He heard the sound of running footsteps. Voices saying, "Move aside, ladies and gentlemen."

"Thank God—the police!" someone said, and Diarmid's anxiety over being recognized rushed back. An officer wrenched him off Ossian. He kept his head down and reeled. Another policeman grabbed Ossian.

"They stink of whiskey," the officer who held Ossian said.

"Jus' lookin' t'see what the rich do while the city falls 'round 'em," Ossian slurred. "No 'arm, gentleme'."

"You'll be spending the night in the Bummers' Cell, I'm afraid."

The other policeman hadn't let go of Diarmid's arm. "Come along, lads. We got a nice place for you to sleep it off in."

The officers led them to a waiting wagon. So far, so good. He and Ossian stumbled into it. No one had recognized him yet, and no one had searched them for weapons either—whether out of incompetence or because they seemed too drunk to be a danger, Diarmid didn't know and didn't care. As the wagon set off, bouncing over the paved street, Diarmid's tension rose. Getting in was the simple part of the plan.

The police picked up two others on the way, men who were truly glassy-eyed drunk, then drove the short blocks to the Tombs.

"'Ere we are, boys," one of the officers said.

The Bummers' Cell was large and open, separated from the main hall by an iron railing. There were benches, but nothing else, and some were already filled with drunks.

"It's not full enough yet," Ossian whispered to Diarmid as the policemen shuffled them inside.

There were perhaps half a dozen men in the cell now, and there needed to be more to create a real distraction, one that would keep the police too busy to notice Ossian slipping away. Diarmid eyed the railing—easy enough to leap if one wasn't drunk—and then the hall leading to the cells.

He sat against the wall, and Ossian did the same, and then there was nothing to do but wait and pretend to be sleeping like the others.

As the night went on, the room began to fill with men so drunk they couldn't see straight—some of them no better dressed than he and Ossian, but others who were clearly better off and having a night on the town. They reminded Diarmid of Aidan, that night in the gambling hell, and the way Aidan had stood out among the derelicts there, and then he pushed Aidan from his mind. He couldn't think about him or Grace right now.

The place was growing crowded. Two policemen stood against the rails, watching. It would be no effort to overcome them. No doubt they thought drunken men light duty, but

Diarmid guessed they wouldn't think so when they had to control a swarming mass of them.

"See that drunkard over there? The one in the striped vest?" he asked Ossian. "I'm going to start a fight with him. His friend will join in. When he does, get to the railing."

Ossian nodded. "Don't wait too long to run for it yourself."

"Believe me, I've no wish to hang."

"Whatever Finn says, you know he won't let that happen."

"Aye. He'll fight the whole Fomori army for me, I'm guessing," Diarmid said sarcastically.

"If he won't, we will."

Diarmid took a deep breath. "I don't want to cause another rift. Do what he wants. I'll be fine."

"Sometimes Finn has to be told what to think."

"I'm telling you now: *don't*. It cost too much last time. Do me a favor—just get yourselves and Oscar out. Don't worry about me. Don't come back for me. Promise me you won't."

"Very well," Ossian agreed slowly. "Just be careful."

Diarmid forced a smile. "See you back home."

Diarmid stood, adopting a drunken walk, staggering across to where the dandy and his friend were laughing uproariously at something. He walked up behind the one in the striped vest and shoved him. The man fell into his friend.

"What the 'ell?" The dandy turned to glare at Diarmid. "I'll 'ave an apology, m'friend."

"No you won't," Diarmid said. "I don't like the way you look."

The man stared at him as if he didn't understand.

Diarmid jabbed his finger into the man's chest, and then up, flipping the man's pointed chin. "Who d'ya think ya are, comin' in 'ere like this?"

The man looked back at his friend. "D'you 'ear that, Ainsley? Who is this young pup?"

The friend laughed. "'Ey now, boy. Go on."

"I don' think so." Once again, Diarmid pushed the man.

This time, the striped vest came up fighting. He swung a fist at Diarmid, missed, and Diarmid swung back, pulling his punch at the last moment, a graze to the stomach. *Keep the man on his feet*—too hard a punch and he'd be passed out and no use to them. The dandy was clearly too drunk to fight effectively, and Diarmid fought as if he were the same. He shoved the man back again and leveled another punch, this time into the friend's shoulder.

The friend let out a bellow of rage and set upon him. Two of them now, which wasn't a problem, especially given how drunk they were. But Diarmid yelled, "Get 'em off me! Get 'em off me! Rich sons of bitches!"

Ossian shouted, "'Ey there! They're beatin' on 'im! Just 'cause they got money don' mean they can do that!"

The whole place erupted in a melee. There were men trying to come to Diarmid's aid and others keeping them off, a swirling, shoving, twisting mass of fight. The police climbed the railing into the crowd, shouting and raising clubs. Diarmid ducked, letting two others take his place with the dandy and his friend, shoving his way backward through the fight, coming up for air just in time to see Ossian break through. While the police were consumed with keeping order, Ossian just climbed over the rail. No one even saw him. The plan was working beautifully, and Diarmid hadn't needed to reveal who he was.

But now . . . to get out.

It took him some time to get to the railing without looking like he was trying to do so. The door to the street was blocked by a police officer, which meant Diarmid had to go over the rail himself and search for another door. The fight had become a riot. The police were shouting for help—Diarmid had no idea if anyone could hear them or if anyone would come. He got to the rail, pulled himself over, and then he was in the hall, which stretched long and empty. He ran in the direction that Ossian had gone, hearing the shouts and cries of the fight behind him.

He expected no guard at the door to the cells—Ossian would have taken care of him already—and there wasn't. Diarmid slid through a set of doors and into a hall lined on either side with darkened cells. With the door shut behind him, the roar from the Bummers' Cell was only a dull buzz. There was the guard—unconscious on the floor before him, a lump of shadow. From overhead came the sound of guards' footsteps as they crossed the bridges from one side to the other, but Ossian had been silent and quick in dispatching those on this floor—no others had been alerted. Yet.

Diarmid hustled down the hall, keeping to the shadows, brushing against the iron-barred cell doors as he passed, hoping those inside would stay silent. No one said a word but for a man who whispered, "Hey! Take me with you!" None of these prisoners would alert the guards to him, he knew. The Tombs was well-known for its escape attempts; they all hoped for a chance themselves.

Footsteps rattled on the bridge above. Diarmid stilled until they passed. The basement stairs were just ahead, the door wedged open for easy escape, which meant Ossian had already got the others in through a ground floor window and they'd gone down to the cell where their spies had said Oscar was being kept. They would be there now. *"Join us or get out,"* Finn had said, and as long as he was here . . .

Diarmid hurried toward the stairs, nearly tripping over another unconscious guard—a deeper lump of shadow within shadows. Then he heard a noise from the end of the hall, and what he saw coming toward him made his heart stop.

Balor, Daire Donn, Bres, and a dozen Fomori warriors.

His brothers were below, in the basement with only one way out—this door.

THIRTY-TWO

The next moment
Diarmid

Diarmid's only thought was to get the Fomori away from the basement door. He stepped fully into the hallway.

"Well, well." He let his voice ring out, strong and loud. He was already caught; all he wanted was to warn the others. "Balor—what brings you here? Bres. Well met. Where's Tethra? Still chasing fairy ships?"

Balor raised a hand to halt the warriors streaming in behind him. His long-bladed knife winked in the light.

Bres stepped forward, smiling, and in that smile Diarmid saw the charm that had led to the near destruction of the Irish. "Diarmid. Should I be assuming from your presence that the rest of the Fianna are here?"

"Here and gone," Diarmid lied, smiling back. "You've just missed them. What a pity. I'm the rear guard. Looks like you'll only have me to deal with."

"He's lying," Daire Donn said.

"Am I? Hear the ruckus down the hall? What a mess we leave in our wake, eh?"

"Guards!" Bres shouted. "Prisoner escaping!"

Diarmid turned and ran, looking over his shoulder to be sure that Balor and some of the warriors were following. Even if only half of them came after him, it gave his friends an advantage. The basement door crashed open. He glanced back. The rest of the Fianna surged from the basement.

Bres commanded, "After him!"

Guards rushed to the lower levels. Diarmid was fast—he had always been the swiftest of the Fianna. He was pushing through the door back to the Bummers' Cell, hoping the chaos there would aid his escape, but the warriors were gaining, Balor's steps shaking the floor as he shouted, "It's Diarmid, you fools! Stop him!"

The railing had broken in the drunken melee. Men staggered and stumbled, punching and grappling, and more police had joined the fray. Diarmid dove into the crowd. Balor plunged after him. If Diarmid could just get to the door—

The door from outside burst open. Men rushed in.

One of them was Patrick Devlin. Behind him came Miogach and another man who Diarmid didn't know.

Balor, who towered above everyone, called out, "Diarmid is here!"

Diarmid saw Patrick searching the crowd for him. Diarmid felt a rush of rage; he had to restrain the urge to confront Patrick now. *No. Get out.* He couldn't help anyone from a cell.

He tried to lose himself in the crowd, moving toward the door. He was almost there. Once he was past that policeman . . . As Diarmid pushed, the officer in front of him looked up.

Diarmid saw recognition dawn in the man's eyes. "I have him!" he cried. "He's here!" He grabbed Diarmid with a twisted hand, but his grip was strong.

"Hold him!" Balor called.

Then a whistle became a howl as a sudden, fierce wind swirled around Diarmid, whipping his hair, screaming and rushing, blowing papers and men's hats so the air was full of flying things. Aidan.

The Fomori police officer struggled to keep his footing and his hold. It was Diarmid's chance—he grabbed the dagger he'd hidden in his boot and stabbed it into the man's hand. The officer screamed, releasing him. Diarmid raced for the door, fighting the wind. He was there—only one person blocked it. Patrick Devlin.

Diarmid flashed his dagger. "Don't make me kill you, Patrick. I don't want to upset Grace, but I will if I have to."

He expected Patrick to fight him, but he only said, "Hit me. And make it look good."

Diarmid stared at him, then he did what Patrick wanted: he slugged him in the gut. Grace's fiancé doubled over, gasping as he did so, "Go! And for God's sake, keep her away."

Diarmid wrenched open the door, throwing himself outside. There was no time to wonder what Patrick Devlin had just done or why. Police on their way inside started at the sight of him—one shouted, "Hey there! You, lad! Get back in there!"

He looked behind only once, to see that Balor was right there. Of course—the poisonous god was so large the wind hadn't rocked him. After that, Diarmid didn't pause. Balor pounded behind him; the shouts of the Fomori warriors filled his ears. The Tombs fronted Five Points, the Fianna's old haunt. He could lose the Fomori there, if he could just get a little farther, just a few more blocks.

"Fifty dollars to the man who stops him!" Balor shouted.

Fifty dollars. A fortune. Three men tried to catch him; a group of boys joined the chase. He could practically feel Balor's hot breath on the back of his neck.

At the last minute, he turned to go down one alley, but his pursuers weren't fooled. He dove through an alcove. Balor hardly slowed.

Diarmid dodged and raced, at one point sliding sideways to brush through a passageway. But when Diarmid burst onto the street again, the Fomori giant was only steps behind him.

"Grab him!" Balor ordered. "He raped my sister!"

Another clever call—five gang boys stepped in front of Diarmid. One grabbed his arm, another his shoulder. There was no choice but to fight. Desperately, Diarmid whipped around.

One of the gang boys said, "Derry?"

Another of Billy's Boys. No one he called a friend. He focused on Balor, who wasn't even breathing hard.

"Well met again, lad," the giant said, advancing. His knife glimmered.

Diarmid wielded his dagger. "Going to lift that patch and kill me with your poison eye, Balor? Or is it to be a fair fight?"

"Where's the *veleda*?"

"Out of your grasp."

Balor's smile was ugly. "We'll see about that, won't we?" His hand went to his eye patch.

As Diarmid prepared to die, all he could think was: *Grace*.

"No!" said the boy that Diarmid had recognized. He and the four with him surged between Diarmid and Balor.

"Run, Derry!" the boy shouted, and Diarmid didn't think twice. He turned and ran. Behind him, Balor howled with rage—those boys were dead, there was no doubt, but there was no time for regret. He heard the warriors tearing after him again, but he had the advantage of surprise. He was halfway down a shadowed passageway when he heard them race right by.

He kept running, clinging to shadows, maneuvering through corridors and in and out of stale beer dives and two-cent lodging houses. He'd lost them, but still, he didn't stop running, not until he'd cleared Five Points and reached the seawall at Battery Park. He sagged against the wall, resting his head on his folded arms, trying to catch his breath.

He was alive. Alive and free, and he had Patrick Devlin to thank for it. Patrick Devlin, who had faked a fight and helped him escape.

Why?

"Keep her away."

Bleakly, Diarmid raised his head. The lights of steamers and ferries sparkled on the black water. Beyond them was the looming shadow of Castle Garden, then the darkness of Staten Island and Governors Island beyond. He heard the faint pulse of the ocean, the soft slap of waves against the wall. For a moment, he fancied that the water lapping onto this beach was the same that had washed the rocks at Governors Island. Water that had somehow touched her.

She was waiting for him. He wondered if she could feel him standing here, the way he thought he could feel her, as if his soul were stretching to touch hers. Ah, but no. She didn't really love him, not the same way. She thought she did, but the spell felt like real love. Or at least, that's what he'd been told by other girls. He didn't know—was there some way to tell the difference? Like all fairy spells, was the compulsion only a glamour that felt real until you realized something was just *off*, a detail that wasn't right because the *sidhe* didn't feel what humans felt, because their stock-in-trade was illusion, not truth?

He'd never thought to wonder before now. It had never mattered so much to him.

He tried to pierce the darkness between here and the island. To imagine her staring across the water toward Manhattan, thinking of him. To feel that connection between them, that tenuous thread. Her *veleda* to his Fianna. And, according to Aidan, even more than that.

Again, Diarmid felt dread. He closed his eyes. *Grace,* he thought. *Grace, I'm coming.*

He had to go back to the basement flat and his brothers. He had to see that Oscar and everyone else was safe. But tomorrow morning, he would be on his way to her.

Tomorrow.

THIRTY-THREE

The same day
Grace

I felt lonely the moment he left. Even with Miles there, the day and night without Diarmid passed slowly. The next morning, I was bored and listless. I sat staring at the sun slanting over the floor and scratched patterns in the scrim of dirt and sand with my fingers. I brushed against something hot, burning. A snippet of song leaped into my head. I pulled my hand away before I realized it was the ogham stick.

I'd forgotten all about it. The bit of melody reminded me of when Finn had handed me the ogham stick that called the Fomori. How the words he'd quoted had sounded wrong, the way I'd known instinctively how the spell must be said, the singsong cant.

I pushed at this stick with the very tips of my fingers. Again, I heard that smattering of song. I hadn't heard it before, not when I'd touched it at Lewis Corley's.

Then the stick began to glow.

It was the sunlight, I thought; but no, the ogham stick was in shadow. The light burned from within it. *As if it were the sun.*

The way Diarmid and the Fianna had glowed.

The stick hadn't done this before. Neither the glow nor the music. I tried to touch it again—but I couldn't. It burned too badly. Battle Annie had told me to listen, so I did.

The sea is the knife. Great stones crack and split. Storms will tell and the world is changed. The rivers guard treasures with no worth. To harm and to protect become as one, and all things will only be known in pieces.

The words played in my head like a song. Chaotic but so . . . *present.* Each line of the prophecy had its own melody; like the woven strands of a spiderweb, all led back to the center, but also radiated in distinct and opposite directions. I could follow one, or another, but some of them were confusing; some needed time and thought. Two things were startlingly clear:

Diarmid *was* the key I'd needed.

And I knew where the archdruid was.

He was supposed to stay with you.

My brother's voice whispered in my ear as if he stood beside me. The air felt full as if his presence surrounded me, and with him was something else. *Someone* else. The same presence I'd felt in my dreams. Watching, waiting, silent. Aidan said, *Without him you'll need to be very careful. We need you.*

I didn't understand why I could suddenly hear him so clearly, or why my connection to him felt so strong. But it wasn't a dream, and it felt right, as if this was how it should be, as if the darkness closing between us had been the wrong thing. I knew then what I had to do.

I had promised to wait, but I could not keep that promise. I had to go on alone. I had a different task, a different fate. I had a choice to make, a choice that would change the world, and I could not let my love for Diarmid influence me—because in the end, love was only love. It wasn't right or wrong; it wasn't worthy or unworthy. It just *was*.

If his side was in the wrong, I had to let him go. I had to let him die.

I was the descendant of Neasa, of generations of *veleda*s whose purpose had been set two thousand years ago. I could not ignore it or make it less. The fate of the Irish—my own people—depended on me. I could not be frightened or love-struck or paralyzed by what I felt. I was the *veleda*. I had to be strong enough to choose what was right, whatever the consequences for me.

And that meant I had to find my own way.

That evening, I played cards with Miles and bided my time. I heard my brother's music singing, *We need you. Be careful.*

By the time it was dusk, my nerves were strung tight. Miles sat whittling while I sent my thoughts toward the water. *Listen.* I closed my eyes to hear the sounds of fishermen haul-ing in nets and the creaking wash of paddle wheels, people talking on the ferries and the lap of wakes against the hulls of schooners. A part of me didn't believe I could do this—I had never been able to do anything like it before. I couldn't really hear sailors call to one another or the cawing of seagulls as they swept the Brooklyn beach looking for food.

It had to be my imagination. But it felt real when I heard Battle Annie's song, when I *knew* it was hers, and that she was listening too.

Night came on, and Miles curled up and said, "Good night, Gracie. See you in the morning."

I said, "Good night," and pretended to sleep, but when the moon came up, broad and full and blinding, I felt the call of it as I always had. *Come with me. Let me show you.*

Miles was deeply asleep. He was no Fianna warrior, and he didn't rouse when I crept to the door. I left the ogham stick behind—its burn made it too hard to carry, and I had no more need of it. The prophecy and its songs were in my head. I cracked the door, which creaked and squealed, and I froze, waiting for Miles to wake, ready to run, but he only rolled over. I squeezed through the opening. Spots of white moonlight tangled with the shadows of the trees. The clay scarp was steep; I mostly slid down. I stumbled the last few feet, half falling to the beach.

The water lapped at the toes of my boots. The lights from Brooklyn shone in the near distance, the passing lanterns of ferries and ships. The moon cast a river of sparkling white onto the water, a river leading right to me, as if it offered me a path.

The soft splash of an oar, and a shadow emerged from nowhere, a small rowboat, and a person within who glowed silver. One of Battle Annie's *sidhe.*

I was relieved. It hadn't been my imagination.

The hull scraped against the rocky shore. Then a whisper. "Milady?"

"Yes," I answered. He held the boat steady as I climbed inside. The fairy boy rowed us toward the sloop that I now saw anchored a short ways out, camouflaged by a wisping fog.

He rowed swiftly and well. Soon we arrived at the ship, and someone was lowering a rope ladder. When I stepped onto the deck, Battle Annie waited, her hands on her hips, her glow more intense than the others'.

"Learned to listen, did you?"

"I need you to take me up the East River. To the wharf at Cherry Street."

"Corlears Hook," she said. "Not a good part of town for a lass alone."

"The archdruid is there."

"Very well, *veleda.* As you command."

She turned to give orders to her sailors, and I went to the bow, leaning over the rail. The sails filled with cold moonlight, the water slipped by, rippling as the sloop moved toward Manhattan and Battery Park.

And I heard him.

Diarmid.

I felt the tug of him like a kite feels the tug of its string, anchoring me, calling me. The melody of him, a song of despair and longing and something else. Fear? Or love?

Or perhaps they were the same thing. I was beginning to think that they were. I wanted only to love him, but I knew that this web binding us was bigger than we were, and it required courage and sacrifice. Before I could commit to it, there was more I had to learn, and answers I had to find.

Who I was. Who I was meant to be. And I could not make the right choice—between Diarmid and Patrick, the Fianna and the Fomori—until I understood what was true.

I looked up at the moon, then down at the silvery-white path it laid before me, leading me right back to Manhattan, to whatever future waited.

Come, the moonlight said. *I've something for you. Follow me.*

I lifted my face to the night air, to the smell of salt and river and smoke. The future that belonged to me was calling.

"I'm coming," I told the moon.

ACKNOWLEDGMENTS

The Fianna Trilogy has truly been a labor of love, and I've been privileged to have some excellent people working on it with me. Many, many thanks to my wonderful editor, Robin Benjamin, for her discerning pen and sharp eyes—the books became stronger and better in her hands. Also, thanks must go to Courtney Miller, for being such an enthusiastic champion, and to Miriam Juskowicz, Timoney Korbar, Erick Pullen, and the team at Amazon/Skyscape for their remarkable support. I am proud to be one of your authors. I cannot thank enough art director Katrina Damkoehler, cover designer Regina Flath, and artist Don Sipley for the stunning covers that brought Grace and her world to life in such a richly beautiful way. Thanks also must go to Kim Witherspoon and Allison Hunter at Inkwell Management, who achieve great things on my behalf. As always, I owe Kristin Hannah more than I can say— her enthusiasm for the project kept me going—and thank you to Elizabeth DeMatteo, Jena MacPherson, Melinda McRae, Liz Osborne, and Sharon Thomas, for reading early versions of the manuscripts and taking the story to their hearts. Thanks to my artist sister, Robyn Chance, for her encouragement and exquisite vision. And lastly, I am so grateful to Kany, Maggie, and Cleo for their inspiration, support, and love.

ABOUT THE AUTHOR

© 2012 C.M.C. Levine

Megan Chance is the award-winning author of several adult novels, including *Bone River* and *Inamorata*. A former television news photographer with a BA from Western Washington University, Megan lives in the Pacific Northwest with her husband and two daughters. Visit her at www.meganchance.com.